the Keeper's Calling

HOPE YOU ENJOY!

Kelly

♡

THE KEEPER'S SAGA: BOOK ONE

the Keeper's Calling

Kelly Nelson

WALNUT SPRINGS PRESS

For Dad, who instilled in me the belief that I could do
anything I put my mind to, and
Mom, my cheerleader, my first fan, and my friend.

Walnut Springs Press, LLC
110 South 800 West
Brigham City, Utah 84302
http://walnutspringspress.blogspot.com

ISBN: 978-1-59992-844-9

Acknowledgements

A special thanks to Linda and the staff at Walnut Springs Press for transforming my dream into a reality. Thanks to my husband and my children, who patiently endured the countless hours I spent on my computer, lost in Chase Harper's world. Thank you to my family and friends who critiqued the first draft of my manuscript and offered an endless supply of encouragement, especially my sister, Laura, who shares my love of creative writing. Thanks to Charity and Nancy at The Mighty Pen, LLC, for their wise grammatical counsel. Most importantly, I am grateful for a loving Heavenly Father who hears and answers every prayer.

According to Greek mythology, the Fates have the power to decide man's destiny. They may bless him with good fortune, or subject him to evil. They spin the thread of life and sever it at will. Yet, through it all, man has agency—the power to act.

ONE
The Cave

I would look back on that summer as the defining moment of my earthly existence. Everything prior fell within the realm of normal. Everything to follow didn't, leaving me at the mercy of the Fates' every whim.

I folded the map and tossed it on the picnic table. Zion National Park—the final stop on our camping trip the week before the start of my senior year. After driving for hours, we had checked into the Watchman Campground and pitched our tents. I wanted to explore the park before dinner. Sitting around the campground all afternoon would bore me to tears. But Dad and Uncle Steve collapsed once their air mattresses hit the floor of their tents. Both men now slept. My cousin Amanda and my sister Jessica sat in camp chairs under a large tree, absorbed in reading their books.

I threw my bag into the tent I shared with my cousin. "Hey, Adam, I'm bored. You up for a bike ride before dinner?"

Adam eyed the grassy shade where the girls were reading. "Chase, you're crazy. It's way too hot."

I pulled my baseball cap onto my head. "Well, if my dad wakes up, tell him I'll be back before dinner. After sitting in the car all day, I've got to do something."

Adam walked toward the shade. "Have fun, dude."

I grabbed my backpack and threw in three water bottles and a handful of granola bars, then shot Adam a confident smile. "Always do."

I loved my family, but after a week of camping with them 24/7, I needed some alone time. I unclipped my mountain bike from the rack and pedaled into the park. The lecture I'd endured the day before still burned my ears. Dad was on a roll. I swear I've heard the same thing a hundred times since freshman year, and yesterday was no exception. "With school starting next week, this is game time. High school is when it really counts. If you don't get the grades now, you won't get into the college you want."

The college I want? Who knows what college I want? I think it's the football thing again. That's what put a bur under his saddle. Both my dad and Uncle Steve played high school football. Yesterday morning they started talking about Adam's chances at playing college ball. Adam is the star wide receiver for our high school team, and I know my dad wishes I'd gone out for football as well. He hates it when I remind him I do play football—soccer. I may be athletic, but I'm not the superstar I know my dad dreams of. He didn't think I'd ever really applied myself. He was probably right. I didn't stick with youth football. Bailed out of that after four years and switched to soccer. He thinks I could have been good if I would have worked at it. As a senior at Hillsboro High School in Oregon, I approached school the same way I did sports: my goal was to have fun. Next to my straight-A-earning, swim-team-captain, and ultra-competitive twin sister, I didn't measure up. But it didn't bother me. I had my own agenda.

The magnificent scenery brought me back to the present. As a native Oregonian, my eyes were used to seeing towering

Douglas firs and beds of ferns, not colorful, jagged cliffs and scrawny, water-deprived juniper trees. I coasted to a stop, and as usual, I veered off the beaten path. After climbing down a red-rock hillside, I ditched my bike and helmet and hiked through a sagebrush flat. Before long it narrowed into an old wash. Thousands of flash floods had worn a gap in the rocky hillsides. The orange rock walls rose twenty-five feet or more on both sides. At times, shade completely immersed me. Clumps of hardy desert weeds dotted the sandy floor, and lizards zipped away in front of me.

The wash widened, and I spied a hole in the rock wall. The crevice opened five feet above the ground. I got a foothold on the sandstone face and climbed in. I had seen several of these cave openings, but usually they were shallow indentations. This one, however, carved its way deep into the hillside. Crawling on my hands and knees, I edged my way into the darkness.

As an almost-Eagle Scout, with only the paperwork holding me up, I carried a mini Maglite in my backpack along with my compass. I dug out the light and looked around. The cave opened into a larger space with boulders and rocks piled near one wall. The ceilings were tall enough that I could stand. Graffiti decorated the walls, and cigarette butts and trash littered the sandy floor. Obviously, I hadn't discovered a hidden, natural wonder of the world.

I checked my cell phone. No coverage in here, but I'd been gone an hour. It was cool in the cave, much cooler than outside, and the air had an earthy smell. I climbed onto a flat boulder and sat down, then grabbed a water bottle from my pack and took a long swallow. With a sigh, I wiped the water off of my chin. As I replaced the lid, the flashlight slipped out of my hand and fell between the rocks.

"Dang it," I muttered.

I considered leaving the light, but my dad had given it to me on my twelfth birthday when I started Scouts. It had been with me on more camping trips than I could count. That flashlight was like an old friend. I set the water bottle on the ground. In the remaining sliver of light, I began clearing boulders out of my way. Finally, I wedged my arm between the rocks and reached for the flashlight, succeeding only in knocking it to the floor of the cave. I moved more rocks, and a pile stacked up behind me before I could grab my flashlight. Gently, I retracted my hand, squeezing the light between my fingertips. I maneuvered it to a foot above the ground, where I could almost grab it with the other hand, when it slipped out of my grasp.

The flashlight clanged, sounding like it hit something hollow and metallic. I reached down again, and my fingertips brushed across metal. I turned the light toward the ground. After brushing away the dirt, I saw something.

Curious, I moved more rocks. Fifteen rocks and two boulders later, I brushed away the dirt from a metal surface. Using a stick, I dug out a small, metal box. It looked ancient and pocked with rust. There wasn't a lock, but corrosion had sealed the lid. I banged the box against the wall, at first only loosening the dirt and chipping off pieces of rusted metal, but the box finally opened. Decaying wood lined the inside, and a soiled piece of leather lay at the bottom. Years of hiding underground had left the leather dark and stiff. Prying it open sent a tarnished gold object tumbling into my hand.

I turned it over. It reminded me of a pocket watch, only a little larger and oval-shaped. The object had a small hook on the top. Strange symbols were engraved into the metal casing, making the thing look like an ancient artifact. In the glow of my flashlight I made out the shape of a shield etched in the center. I felt a latch on the side. The top flipped open when I pressed it.

The thing opened so fast, it must have been spring-loaded. An eerie light with a bluish tint emanated from within. I focused my eyes on a miniature glass globe, colored in a perfect replica of the earth. I saw the outline of North America, and noticed that the light inside the globe focused into a pinpoint on the lower Rocky Mountains.

There were three buttons and an odometer-looking thing, with dials, located below the globe. Each button had a foreign symbol or some kind of pictograph on it—like the hieroglyphics on an Egyptian cartouche. When I slid my thumb across the first button on the left, it clicked under the pressure. A wave of nausea hit me, and my vision blurred. Lowering my head, I rested my hand on my knee. I felt dizzy. *What's wrong with me?* I thought. *Must have a touch of heatstroke or something.*

The wave of nausea left as quickly as it had come. I closed the lid on the gold device, deciding to look at it later. My stomach rumbled. Time to head back to camp. Maybe after a good meal, I'd feel better.

With the device stored in the pocket of my shorts, I crawled to the opening and jumped onto the desert floor. I glanced up and down the wash. Something seemed different, but I couldn't put my finger on it. I shrugged it off and started back the way I'd come. Nothing was how I remembered. The wash wasn't as deep as I'd thought, and more lizards were out now. High above me, a hawk screamed, talons extended, as it dived for its prey. When I reached the sagebrush flat, I looked at the sky. I could have sworn the sun had switched sides of the horizon. I pulled off my cap and scratched my head.

I dug my compass out of my backpack and ate a granola bar. Lining up the compass arrow with the "N," I turned my body to face north. The sun beat down on the right side of my face. I'd left camp at three o'clock, so by now the sun should be getting ready to set. It should have been in the west, to my left. *Did my compass break, or is there some magnetic field messing it up?* I wondered. I shook it and tried again, but it still offered me the same confusing result.

I finished the granola bar and reached for my water bottle. It wasn't there, and I realized I'd left it in the cave. It was too far to go back for it, so I got out a fresh one. Regardless of what my compass said, I knew the direction I'd come from. I started across the flat, discovering desert wildflowers I didn't remember seeing before. A coyote mother and her pups chased jackrabbits in the distance. I definitely hadn't noticed any coyotes before. They scurried off once they spotted me. Ground squirrels chattered everywhere. Three hawks circled the cloudless blue sky, taking turns screeching at each other. The scene in front of me teemed with wildlife, and I shook my head in awe.

A half hour later, I searched for my bike. It was gone. I found the same kind of bushes I'd hidden the bike under, but they were in different sizes and different places than I remembered. Yet I knew I was in the right location because of the distinctive color swirls on the solid rock hillside. I climbed up it, expecting to see the road, cars, and other bikers. This place had been crawling with people an hour ago. All I saw where the road should have been was a game trail. Not even a well-worn, heavily used game trail. In my imagination, I saw where the road should have been.

Completely baffled, I kept walking. Was I going crazy? Where was the road? If it wasn't where I expected, it had to be close. I kicked a rock off the path, confident that at any moment I'd hear the hum of a car's engine in the distance or at least encounter another hiker. But for the next mile, as far as the eye could see, nothing appeared except rocky cliffs and sagebrush.

Ahead of me, four turkey vultures circled a stand of junipers. One by one, they landed. As I drew closer, my curiosity got the better of me. I pushed through the trees. The flock of vultures took to the air as I rustled the branches.

I expected a dead rabbit or ground squirrel. Instead, my eyes widened at the sight of human legs sticking out from under a pile of sticks. Panic seized me like a coastal sneaker wave. Unable to move, I listened. The thundering of my beating heart seemed loud in the sudden stillness, and I wondered if I was truly alone.

Although sickened by the sight, I edged closer, powerless to turn away. The scene sent a shudder down my spine. The vultures had pecked open the man's pant legs and begun to rip into the flesh of his thighs. Any hope I had that he might be alive vanished. I pulled the branches off him, shooting nervous glances over my shoulder.

He was a large man who looked like he had hit the weights at the gym. His wavy white hair and gray beard were matted with dried blood. His skin was weather beaten and tanned, like he had worked road construction or something. Death rendered his eyes a dull brown. I had expected a younger-looking face to go with the muscular build. His chest was bare, and he lay on his side. His pants were covered with blood. Removing the last branch revealed a mutilated right hand. His fingers were gone. I brought my fist to my mouth, cringing. One glance at his shoulders left me fighting the urge to throw up. If missing fingers weren't enough, massive cuts crisscrossed his back, leaving it looking like rotten hamburger. Had he been whipped? I didn't think that stuff happened anymore.

Horrified, I scrambled away. Someone had tortured this man to death! My hand shook as I dug my cell phone from my pocket. Nervously, I scanned the horizon for anything unusual, but only natural sights and sounds surrounded me. The hum of black flies and yellow jackets filled the air as they competed for a piece of flesh. And the vultures still circled above me, occasionally landing to eye me with obvious distaste as I monopolized their find. The only disturbances to nature seemed to be me and the corpse.

I slid my cell phone open and dialed 911. I held the phone to my ear, waiting—nothing. A loud beep drew my attention to the display. "No network coverage." I tried again. Still nothing. Next, I typed a text message to 911. After I pushed "Send," the phone display read, "Message saved for sending." Hopefully it would go through.

While texting, I had involuntarily moved farther away from the hideous sight. The vultures got braver. They strutted back and forth, moving closer to the body with each pass. They alternated with the ones in the air, each taking a turn circling the carcass. The smell of blood baking in the sun had emboldened them, I decided, and suddenly I didn't want to be alone anymore. I sent text messages to Adam and Jessica. Then I dialed my dad's number. A blaring beep answered my plea. No network coverage.

No sooner had I turned my back than the vultures began consuming the bloody flesh again. I'd seen my share of TV shows and knew not to mess with a crime scene, but soon there wouldn't be a body left to investigate if the vultures had their way. Although I had no desire to get involved, my conscience was pricked, and I knew I should try to preserve the body. The pile of sticks hadn't kept the scavengers away, so there was no use replacing them. Numerous rocks littered the landscape. I gathered what I needed and covered the man with stones.

For all the torture he went through before he died, he looked peaceful as the final rock slid into place. The relentless sun beat down as I stood to survey my work. "Hmm." My mound of stones resembled a burial job in a Western movie. Bizarre. This whole thing was surreal.

I left the stand of juniper trees, more anxious than ever to find someone—anyone I could tell about the body. In my forced solitude, I began to wonder about the man and why he had been tortured. Most likely the answers were buried with him.

I wiped the back of my hand across my forehead. I was a mess. Dust clung to every bead of sweat, and orange dirt stains covered my shirt and shorts. I downed the rest of the water bottle as I hiked away from the circling vultures. Only two birds were left—the others must have given up. My filthy hands tempted me to open the last bottle of water. Thankfully, I didn't.

TWO
Lost

The farther I walked, the more it felt like I had entered the Twilight Zone. Where was everybody? In a national park, within a two-hour walk of a major campground, I should have seen somebody by now. Had I gone the wrong way? With a disgusted grunt, I turned around. I'd go back to the cave and start over. Plus, I wanted my other water bottle after all.

Retracing my steps, I passed the stand of juniper trees. It looked like the vultures had abandoned their efforts to get to the body. I entered the wash and located the cave. Although I was certain I'd found the right cave, I easily jumped onto the ledge. Wasn't this a five-foot climb last time, not a three-foot hop? I shook my head at my mixed-up memories, then crawled through the tunnel and into the cavern. The beam of my flashlight panned the room. There was no water bottle, and the pile of boulders lay eerily untouched. Something else looked different, too. It took a minute to recognize it: the cave was clean. No trash littered the floor. No graffiti colored the walls. My heart rate skyrocketed as I blinked my eyes. Scrambling backward, I left the cave.

Had I found the wrong cave? Once outside, I spun in a circle, looking at my surroundings. It had to be the same cave.

There wasn't another one in site. I thought I had gone the right direction in the first place, but it had gotten me nowhere. In utter confusion, I turned in the opposite direction.

I wandered through a canyon cut into the sandstone hills and entered a forest. After seeking the shade of a pine tree, I tried to study my compass. The sweat pouring down my face dripped onto the plastic, leaving it a blur. Using a relatively clean spot on my shirt, I wiped off the face of the compass, but I still couldn't make sense of what I saw. Exhausted and famished, I lowered myself to the ground. Even though it felt like bedtime, the sun blazed directly overhead, mocking me.

In the heat of the day, it wouldn't take long to dehydrate. I laughed, and it sounded unnaturally loud in the nothingness around me. Although I'd been sure I knew where I was, it was painfully obvious I was completely lost. There wasn't a soul in sight. I repeatedly tried to phone Adam, my dad, and Jessica. But every time I got the same result: no network coverage. I had sent Adam and Jessica text messages telling them what I'd seen. But since I didn't have coverage, it was no surprise they hadn't replied. Discouraged, I ate another granola bar and drank a third of the water in the last bottle before I closed my eyes.

In the hazy moment when I hovered on the edge of consciousness, something crawled up my leg. I slapped my thigh. Instead of relief, a stinging sensation shot through me. Jolted awake, I jumped to my feet and shook my shorts while stamping my foot. A bee fell onto the top of my hiking boot. I kicked it off and ground it into the dirt. When I rolled my shorts above my knee, I saw a small stinger. "You've got to be kidding me," I muttered. "I hate bees." I scraped out the stinger and watched as the sting swelled.

I looked at the sun, trying to judge how long I'd slept. I guessed not more than three hours had passed. My dad is an avid hunter and outdoorsman, and he'd taken me on more backpacking and hunting trips than I could count. As a result, I knew basic survival skills and my way around the mountains. At sixteen I'd spent a night alone in the Eagle Cap Wilderness when I'd been separated from my dad on a deer hunt. Needless to say it rattled me, and I didn't sleep much. I spent the night leaning against a tree with my rifle across my knees. But consequently, at first light when a four-point buck walked past, I was in position for a perfect shot. My dad found me cleaning my deer an hour later.

I knew the basic layout of this canyon from studying the map. The North Fork of the Virgin River cut through Zion Canyon and Watchman Campground. I didn't know what had happened to me, but I definitely wouldn't survive for long without replenishing my water supply. My tongue already felt swollen in my mouth, and my hands and feet were retaining water. A dull ache filled my head. Sipping from my last water bottle, I set out to find the river.

I walked the rest of the afternoon, finishing off my water and then realizing I should have rationed it. My head throbbed, and my tongue and lips were parched. Strangely, I wasn't perspiring like I had earlier. The effects of heat exhaustion were wreaking havoc on my body. I needed to find the river.

The setting sun bathed the rocky landscape in an orange glow. Bighorn sheep grazed the hillsides, and mule-deer herds came out of the trees for the night. In spite of my discomfort, I was admiring the glory of the sunset and the rugged beauty of Mother Nature when I noticed a trail. A cloud of dust appeared on the horizon. Steadily, the dust moved closer.

My initial excitement at possibly having found someone faded as the image of the tortured man flashed through my mind. Taking a deep breath, I opted for a healthy dose of caution. I checked my backpack for the binoculars. The last time I'd seen them was on the hike through Bryce Canyon. I had used them to glass the mountain for mule deer and remembered storing them in my pack rather than returning them to my dad. I prayed the binoculars were still there.

A sigh of relief escaped my lips when I felt them. I settled myself behind an outcropping of rocks and waited. With the binoculars, I observed three horses with riders. They moved at a slow trot. The two lead riders looked Mexican or Spanish. They were dressed in black sombreros and leather vests, like actors in a Western movie, and dust covered their trail-beaten clothing. Each man sported a six-shooter and a sword strapped to his hip. Gun scabbards adorned their saddles, and bandoliers full of bullets hung across their shoulders.

The lead rider carried what looked like a whiskey flask. He brought it to his lips more than once. He was of medium build, a little thick around the middle. The second rider was younger, maybe late twenties. He was taller with a slighter build, a mustache, and what looked to be a permanent scowl on his face. He held the lead rope attached to the third horse. The third rider instantly caught my full attention. This rider was a girl and she was hot—not the temperature kind of hot. She had curly, honey-colored hair and wore a grim expression. Like the other two, she also wore a costume: a long skirt and a shirt with puffy sleeves. She had eaten the dust of the other two riders, and it showed. Dirt streaked her clothes and face. She tried to wipe her mouth on her shoulder.

"What?" I muttered, shifting the focus of the binoculars. Her hands were tied behind her back. What was going on here?

I ducked behind the rocks when the riders drew closer. As they passed within hearing distance, I interpreted portions of the conversation. My Spanish was mediocre at best after taking two years of it, but I caught the words "river" and "camp."

If I'd stumbled onto the set of a movie, the whole scene would have made perfect sense, but there was nothing in sight except the three horses and their riders. No cameras. No crew. No director. Nothing.

An anxious knot twisted my gut at the thought of that girl taken captive by those two rough-looking cowboys. When they were a good distance ahead of me, I ventured out of hiding and jogged down the trail. Giving up on making sense out of what had happened to me or where I was, I chose to simply roll with it. And at that moment, the pretty girl in the long skirt became the center of my universe.

With the binoculars and the tracks the horses left in the dirt, I easily followed the riders. Sheer exhaustion and the beginnings of heatstroke threatened to overtake me, but the memory of the girl dangled before me like a carrot. A drastic change in the landscape appeared on the horizon. Lush green foliage below me marked the winding path of the Virgin River. When the horses started picking their way down the switchbacks, I caught up to them and hid behind a clump of sagebrush.

The horses neighed, and I figured they could smell the river. I ventured closer to the edge and risked a look at their progress. All three horses stepped onto the canyon floor, their ears pricked forward. They tossed their heads and picked up speed, probably anticipating the grass and water that lay ahead. The cowboys followed the path upriver, while I hustled down the switchbacks. Suddenly, my feet slipped on the loose rocks, and I started to slide. Fearing I would draw their attention, I froze, staring at their backs. But the cowboys and the three horses seemed oblivious to the tumbling rocks at my feet.

When I reached the bottom of the switchbacks, I set aside all thoughts except one: the river and its promise of water. I angled away from the direction the horses had gone, getting myself out of earshot. Spider webs stuck to my face as I shoved my way through the brush lining the water's edge. I glanced up and down the river—no one in sight—and kicked off my hiking boots. Hopping on one foot and then the other, I stripped off my sweaty socks and splashed into the river. The cool water rushed past my tired legs. When I stood knee deep, I dunked my face. Then, gasping from the cold, I shook my head, spraying water everywhere. I scooped handful after handful of water and drank.

After I filled my water bottles, I worked my way over the moss-covered rocks to the riverbank. With my thirst quenched, visions of the captured girl haunted me again. I hadn't heard a sound from the horsemen, and now I was afraid I'd lost them. I hustled to pull my boots on.

The sun dipped behind the mountains, bringing relief from the intense desert heat. I walked upriver while the gray light of evening settled into the canyon. It wouldn't be long before dark, and along with the dark came the mosquitoes. Swarms of them hovered along the riverbank.

My head jerked up at the sound of three gun blasts echoing down the canyon. Sneaking from tree to tree, I worked my way toward the noise. Soon, I passed the three horses, hobbled in a meadow, hungrily devouring the sparse grass. The horses hardly noticed me as I crept by. Not knowing where the men were, I kept to the cover of the trees. Before I saw anyone, I heard them. I slowly moved closer. One of the men laughed. "Rabbit for dinner, eh, senorita?" he asked.

Clearly, the girl was their captive, but why? A trail of smoke reached into the sky. I peered through the bushes at their campsite. Both of the men sat on their haunches, skinning a rabbit. They had tied the girl to a nearby tree. When she shook her head in an effort to escape the attacking mosquitoes, her curly hair bounced over her shoulder, covering half her face.

The younger man leered at his captive. "Miguel, after dinner, how about a little senorita for dessert?"

Miguel took a swig from his flask. He narrowed his eyes and stared at her. "No, Ortiz. How many times do I need to say it? We need her to get us what we're looking for. The old man must have hidden it in the canyon, and if anyone knows where, it's her. But I promise, if she doesn't prove useful, you can do what you want."

My mind churned. The dead man—could he be the old man they talked about?

Ortiz grumbled something under his breath and skewered a piece of rabbit on a stick. He held it over the fire, and soon the savory smell of cooking meat wafted in my direction. My stomach growled in wishful anticipation, and my mouth salivated as I watched Miguel salt the meat with a small packet from his saddlebag. Ortiz sulked by the fire, fixing his gaze on the girl while he turned his portion of the rabbit. She continued tossing her head, apparently trying to fight off the mosquitoes but not even looking at her captors.

I moved away from their camp and ate my last granola bar. No need for a growling stomach to betray my whereabouts. I savored each bite, careful not to lose even a crumb. While I scratched the mosquito bites accumulating on my legs, I formulated a plan.

I couldn't leave the girl to the likes of those two—that was certain. And whatever I did had to be done tonight, because if they had anything to do with the old man's death, I didn't want that girl anywhere near them in the morning. I would wait until they fell asleep, then sneak in and free her. With a little luck, they wouldn't notice anything amiss until we were long gone. Once we got out of there, I'd figure out why everyone was playing dress-up.

While waiting, I watched their horses. I'd been raised with horses, and we boarded them on our property. My mom had insisted both Jessica and I know how to ride. But neither of us had the passion for it like she did. I contemplated stealing one of these horses, shoving my conscience out of the way with the thought that the men deserved it for how they were treating that girl. It would make for a faster escape. But they had all their tack with them and were using their saddles for pillows. Plus, if I attempted to take one horse away, the other two would neigh for it, and that would be too risky. I turned away and resigned myself to more hiking.

I drank another swig of river water and again crept closer to the camp. The girl intrigued me. I guessed she was about my age. She tolerated her deplorable situation with grace, not whining and complaining like I'd expect most girls to do. The constant nagging of my empty stomach made me appreciate the fact that they untied her so she could eat. She took a deep breath and let out a sigh. Then she pulled a strip of meat off the bone and chewed slowly. Miguel sat with his gun aimed at her, still drinking from his flask. Ortiz finished his portion of roasted rabbit and started drinking as well. They both laughed at a joke Miguel told in Spanish.

The moment the girl finished eating, Miguel said, "Ortiz, tie her back up."

Ortiz picked up the rope and knelt beside her. He yanked her wrists behind her back and secured them around the base of the tree. I held my breath when he leaned next to her face and kissed her cheek.

She jerked her head to the side. "Stop it!"

Miguel leaned back and adjusted his sombrero over his eyes. "Ortiz, let's get some shuteye." He laid his pistol next to his side and folded his hands over his belly.

Gritting my teeth, I watched Ortiz trail his fingers across her cheek and down her throat, before whispering something in her ear. She didn't like what he said, because she turned her face away from him. Chuckling, he sauntered to his saddle and lay down. The glow of the dying fire revealed the darting glances Ortiz sent the girl and Miguel. Apparently exhausted, she leaned her head against the tree and closed her eyes. In the quiet darkness, I fought to stay awake. This was the day that would never end.

I heard the loud, even breathing of Miguel turn to a steady snore that sounded like the buzz of a chainsaw. Finally, Ortiz closed his eyes. My legs began cramping from holding a crouching position for so long, and as I started to rise, Ortiz got up. Instantly alert, I watched the camp. Keeping his eye on Miguel, Ortiz slinked toward the girl. He yanked the bandana off his neck and rolled it into a gag.

The girl must have dozed off, because she didn't appear to notice him coming toward her. He pushed the bandana into her mouth and tied it behind her head, choking off her scream. I broke out in a nervous sweat. "Dang it!" I mouthed silently. This wasn't going like I'd planned.

When she struggled, he pulled a large knife from his belt and pressed it to her throat. I shifted my weight to the balls of my feet and leaned closer, my mind racing. Whatever he said quieted her. A surge of anger rushed through me, and I felt an overwhelming urge to protect this girl I had never met before.

Using his knife, he cut the ropes securing her ankles and then stuck the blade in the dirt behind him.

Not wanting to witness what he intended to do next, I slid off my backpack. It was now or never. I picked up a rock and ran toward him. He glanced back in time to see me drive the rock into the side of his head. I tackled him onto the rocky ground. Wincing from the impact, I dropped my meager weapon and clamped my hand over his mouth. He drove his elbow into my stomach and head-butted me. My lip split, and I tasted blood. His fists flailed in every direction as I held him from behind, choking off his air supply. He landed a punch on my face before I wrapped him in a wrestling hold. When I flipped him over, his head bashed into a boulder. I felt his body go limp at the same time Miguel grumbled, "Ortiz, I said get to sleep."

After dropping Ortiz, I scrambled to my feet, anticipating a fight with Miguel, but he simply shifted positions and resumed snoring again. I gasped for air. The adrenalin rush left my heart pounding wildly in my chest. *That went better than I thought. I'm still alive.* Breathing heavily, I turned to Ortiz, who lay unmoving at my feet. My brow furrowed and a stab of fear twisted my gut as I realized I might have killed him. I hadn't intended to—I'd just wanted to get him away from the girl. What would I tell the police? I didn't even know these people. Stunned, I stood there staring at his body.

Wiping the blood from my mouth with the back of my hand, I glanced at the girl. She looked at me and then at her attacker. The sick feeling I had at the thought I'd killed a man disappeared the moment I heard him moan behind me. Spurred into action, I went to her, then dropped to my knees and picked up his discarded knife. For the first time, I got a close look at her face. She gave me a funny expression as I reached behind her neck, untied the dirty bandana, and slid it out of her mouth.

The skin on my fingers felt rough as they brushed across her porcelain-smooth skin. Looking into her face left me speechless as my eyes absorbed every detail. Luminous eyes. Delicate nose. Perfect lips.

"Thank you," she whispered.

Mesmerized by the sweet tone of her voice, I continued to stare. The full moon had risen over the mountains, bathing the land in light. Her face showed a range of emotions—relief mixed with bafflement and maybe a touch of fear.

Realizing I held Ortiz's knife mere inches from her, I cleared my throat and found my voice. "Don't worry. I won't hurt you."

Glancing at her captors, she whispered, "My hands?"

I shook my head in embarrassment. "Sorry." What kind of rescuer forgets to free the prisoner?

I moved behind her and untied the ropes securing her hands. Ortiz groaned, and the girl looked at him.

"You should tie him up," she whispered.

"Yeah, sure." I hurried to where he lay in the rocks, then used the rope I took off her to tie his hands and feet. I rolled the bandana and gagged him like he'd done to the girl. Hopefully that would hold him for a while. I stood and turned, expecting her to be behind me, but she had already walked away. I retrieved my backpack and left. Once I was clear of the camp, I jogged after her.

Every one of my muscles cried in protest as we climbed the switchback trail. The parts of my body that weren't sore from hiking all day were now bruised from my fight with Ortiz. I followed her in silence for more than a mile. My only thought: put as much distance as possible between them and us before they wake up.

She never once turned around. Never said a thing. I grew tired of hiking after her with no plan. "Where are we going?" I finally asked.

She pointed up the canyon, and in a businesslike tone said, "I'm not sure where you're headed, but I'm going this way." Then she continued hiking.

Pretty, but rude. I shook my head and moved forward, keeping myself one step behind her. "Why are you going this way? There's nothing up ahead but a bunch of rocks and sagebrush. I spent all day coming down the canyon." She kept walking and didn't answer me. Frustrated and tired, I grabbed her arm. "Hey, we need to talk—"

Wheeling around, she slapped me across the face. My jaw went slack, and I loosened my hold. She yanked her arm out of my hand and pulled a pistol from her skirt pocket. I stared open-mouthed down the barrel aimed at my chest. She took a step back. "Mister, I reckon I owe you a debt of gratitude for helping me back there. But there's something important I need to do, and I'll thank you to let me be about my business alone. I do appreciate your kindness, but if you don't mind, pull foot and find your own trail. I don't care where you go, but don't follow me. Or—or I'll have to shoot you."

Shocked by the sudden turn of events, I stared at her. Her shoulders sagged, her hands trembled, and she looked exhausted. Actually, she looked near to tears. I rubbed the sting off my cheek, locking my eyes on hers.

In a leap of faith, I called her bluff. "Ha ha. Very funny. You're the first person I've talked to all day. I have two water bottles and no food. So, sorry, but I'm not letting you out of my sight. Who were those guys, anyway? And do you know how to get to the Watchman Campground from here?"

"I'll not have you prying into my affairs. Now leave me be, or I will shoot you."

With the quiver in her voice, I doubted the seriousness of her threat. But to be safe, I took a step back and raised my hands.

Either way I wanted to get her talking. "Come on, what's going on here? Where did you get the gun?"

"I stole it from their camp after you untied me."

I folded my arms and continued looking past the pistol at her face. "Did you take any bullets?"

Apparently thinking about what I'd asked, she said, "No."

Eyeing the antique pistol in her hand, I tried to reason with her. "So, if you're lucky and that thing is loaded and fires, you have six shots, right? I don't think you'll want to waste any bullets on me when you have those two cowboys after you."

She hesitated. Shaking her head at me, she huffed and spun around. "Suit yourself, but I'm warning you, don't get in my way. And I'll thank you not to be making conversation, either." Her skirt swirled around her legs as she marched angrily up the trail.

"Hmph." Rolling my eyes at the bizarre girl in front of me, I twirled my finger in a circle by my ear—crazy, that's what she was. Although she didn't look dangerous, I hung back and kept my distance all the same. Now more than ever, I was curious where she was headed. While the moon made its steady trek across the night sky, we hiked. Coyote calls echoed through the hills, and a chorus of chirping crickets kept us company. Wherever she was going, she knew the way, and we covered a lot of ground.

In the middle of the night, she stumbled. If she felt anything like I did, no doubt she was dead tired. I caught up to her.

"You're exhausted," I said. "Let's rest."

She didn't respond, just kept going. She tripped again a few minutes later. This time she went down on her hands and knees. I offered her my hand, and she accepted with a look of reluctance. As I pulled her to her feet, I noticed a tear escaping the corner of her eye, glistening in the light of the full moon. She wiped her cheek and averted her gaze.

Even covered in dust, she was the best-looking girl I'd ever seen, and I couldn't resist the urge to comfort her. "It's okay. I think we're well ahead of them. You should sit down and rest for a few minutes." At that moment, an eerie howl filled the night sky, and then another echoed from farther up the canyon. "That's no coyote," I said.

She looked toward the sound and sighed. "Wolves. Perchance we should rest a bit and let them move on."

"I didn't think there were any wolves here."

"They've been here as long as I can remember. They usually keep to themselves, though. There's enough wild game in these parts that they rarely bother the settlers' animals."

I shrugged my shoulders and didn't say anything. She was obviously overtired, maybe delirious from the traumatic experience. Looking around, I pointed to an outcropping of rock that would make a good backrest. She watched me as I shed my pack and sat down. A groan escaped my chapped lips as I leaned back, putting pressure on one of my many bruises.

I half smiled and patted the ground next to me. "Come here. Sit down."

She clenched her fist around the fabric of her skirt while she glanced over her shoulder. After hesitating a moment, she sat by me and laid the pistol on the ground, resting her hand on top of it. I watched her lean against the rock, shifting her head from side to side as she tried to get comfortable. The howling of the wolves moved farther up the canyon.

"You can lean your head against me, if you want," I offered.

She glanced at my face. "Considering the rules of propriety, I should decline, but under the circumstances—" She shrugged her shoulders and looked at the moonlit peaks. Then without another word she rested her head on my shoulder. I closed my eyes, enjoying the feel of her next to me. A moment later, she said softly, "Thank you."

I grinned. "It's my pleasure."

Sleep overcame her, and I gently leaned my head against the top of hers. Her soft curls brushed my face, and the evenness of her breathing lulled me to sleep.

THREE
The Counter

An awful kink in my neck awakened me. *Where am I? And why on earth am I not in my tent?* I strained to open my eyes, my heavy lids resisting. Once I looked around, it all came back to me: the fight, the girl, getting lost, and the never-ending hiking. I glanced at her head resting peacefully on my shoulder and smiled. She was so pleasant when she was sleeping.

I eyed the gun and contemplated taking it from her. Slowly, I moved my hand through the air until my fingertips nearly hovered above the pistol. But to grab it, I'd have to lean forward, moving the shoulder where her head lay. I looked at her hand resting on the ground next to the gun. If I wanted it, I would have to move quickly or her fingers would beat mine to the pistol. In that moment of hesitation, I changed my mind and pulled my hand back. After what she'd been through yesterday, I wouldn't take her only sense of security.

I turned to wake her up. That was when I realized I didn't even know her name. "Hey, wake up. We better get moving."

She stretched her arms above her head and yawned. After rubbing her eyes, she picked up the pistol and put it in her pocket. The stiffness I'd endured the night before was nothing compared to how I felt when I woke up. Like a sixty-year-old man I pushed myself to my feet, groaning from the effort. The girl stood and massaged her lower back before brushing the dirt off her skirt and starting to hike up the trail. No "Good morning," nothing. After visiting a bush to take care of morning business, I caught up with her.

Surprisingly, the soreness I'd felt at waking rapidly disappeared. Within no time at all, I felt refreshed, even strong. The grogginess of sleep deprivation slipped away, leaving my mind alert.

Her determination intrigued me. "You know, we never really introduced ourselves last night. I'm Chase Harper."

She turned, extended her hand, and took a deep breath. "It's nice to make your acquaintance, Mr. Harper. I'm Ellen Elizabeth Williams, but all my friends call me Ellie."

I shook her hand, smiling at the formal introduction. "Then I hope it's all right if I say, Ellie, it's nice to meet you."

"Of course. What kind of name is Chase, anyway? Do you get *chased* often?"

Holding a straight face, I met her gaze. "Very funny. Actually, the chasing began as soon as I met you. Before that it was never a problem."

She let out a delicate laugh, and I saw her smile for the first time. I couldn't help but smile back. We continued up the trail, and she fell in step next to me.

"What's the deal with the costume?" I asked.

She looked as if she didn't understand. "What?"

I waved my hand at her dress. "The old-fashioned, Western get-up you're wearing?"

Ellie looked me up and down, from my baseball cap to my hiking boots. "Old-fashioned? Pardon me, but considering your choice of breeches, who are you to comment on women's fashion? Of all the confounded things—leaving half of one's legs exposed to the elements. Don't you know there are rattlers around here?"

Her sharp reprimand left me backpedaling to get my foot out of my mouth. "Don't get me wrong. It's not that I don't like it. In fact the dress looks nice on you. It's just that . . . never mind." I looked away and rolled my eyes, vowing to ask a safer question. "So what's your story? Where do you live?"

Ellie raised her skirt as we climbed a steep part of the trail. "The short version is my mother died of pneumonia when I was an infant. My father raised me on his own until he got sick with typhoid fever. He passed away when I was eight. After that my grandfather came and got me. He brought me out West, and I lived with him until I went back East to school at age fourteen. I've been there for the past four years, attending the Girl's High School in Boston and living with Aunt Lydia—my grandfather's sister. When I arrived in St. George two days ago, my grandfather didn't meet the stagecoach in town like I expected. Fortunately, our neighbor, Mr. Johnson, came along and gave me a ride in his buckboard. But when I got to my grandfather's cabin, he was gone. Later that night, those two vaqueros showed up."

I raised my eyebrows, but held my disbelieving comments in reserve. She was really taking the dress-up thing seriously. I failed to make any sense of her crazy story and the strange events of the past twenty-four hours. "Huh," was all I said, wondering if her kidnappers had hit her over the head. Since meeting Ellie, I had simply lived in the moment. There hadn't been time to contemplate the missing campground or why everybody dressed funny.

When she didn't offer to say any more, I asked, "Did you know those guys who kidnapped you?"

"No, but they're fixing to steal something that belongs to my grandfather—a family heirloom. I must get it before they do. I fear they've either captured or killed him. If they didn't already have my grandfather, they wouldn't be bothering with me."

"Hmm." An image of the dead man's face flashed before my eyes. I didn't think it was a coincidence. Should I tell this girl I thought I buried her grandfather yesterday?

"What did your grandfather look like?" I finally asked.

She put her hand on my arm and stopped me. "Why? Have you seen him? Tell me what you know."

I took my hat off and faced her. "Well, yesterday afternoon, or morning—I don't know, it was a weird day—I found a man. Dead. He was old with shoulder-length white hair and a beard. He was a big man, not fat, just tall and buff." Catching sight of the tears welling in Ellie's eyes, I shut my mouth.

She slowly nodded her head as tears escaped her eyes. "Can you take me to him?"

"I tried to call 911, but I couldn't get—"

She looked at me like I was crazy. "You did what?" she interrupted. "Oh, never mind. Please, can you show me? I need to see for myself."

I saw an opportunity to bargain for what I wanted. "All right, I'll take you to where I found him, but only if you promise to help me find some food and civilization."

She squared up her shoulders and lifted her chin. "I'll help you, but only after I get what I came for. It's too valuable to leave the canyon without it."

I ran my fingers through my dirty hair and pulled on my ball cap. "What are you looking for, anyway?"

Her eyes still brimmed with tears as she wiped her fingertips across her cheek. "I can't tell you. I'm sworn to secrecy." As if that was the end of the discussion, she turned and extended her arm toward the trail. "After you, Mr. Harper."

I took the lead, wondering what her big secret could be. Studying the lay of the land, I found the trail I'd been on the day before and retraced my steps. Like an alarm clock, the sun rose over the jagged cliffs, waking the desert. The jackrabbits, ground squirrels, and hawks all came out to greet the day. Groups of lazy lizards sunned themselves on the rocks.

We walked in silence until I spotted the stand of trees where the makeshift grave was. Ellie seemed absorbed with her grief and didn't notice my occasional staring. "That way—in the trees," I said, pointing at the junipers. At a complete loss as to what else I should say, I closed my mouth.

The sky was empty. Fortunately, the vultures hadn't returned, and I hoped no predators had broken through my fortifications overnight. I didn't relish the thought of Ellie seeing her grandfather's mangled corpse. I pushed through the trees surrounding the gravesite and nodded at the pile of rocks. "I covered him to protect his body from predators," I said.

"Thank you." A new round of tears trickled down her cheeks as she looked at the grave. Suddenly, she raised her beautiful eyes to meet mine. "What if it's not my grandfather? Perhaps we're mistaken."

"Do you want me to uncover his face?"

She nodded. "Please."

I bent down and rolled away several rocks. Once Ellie caught a glimpse of the man, she turned away. "It's him," she said, her voice breaking with emotion.

I replaced the stones, while she picked a handful of desert flowers. They were small and insignificant, but the gesture seemed monumental. The tenderness with which she placed them on the rocky grave showed the depth of their relationship.

She had obviously loved her grandfather. Wanting to allow her time to grieve, I stepped away and sat on a boulder.

Alone for a moment, I scanned the horizon and then dropped my head into my hands. To say something wasn't right was an understatement. Since seeing the horsemen yesterday afternoon, I'd been in a whirlwind of hiding and running. It felt like a bad dream. A wave of longing came over me. Oh, to be back home again, to tease Jessica, or have my dad tell me to take the trash out. What would he think if I never came back? He didn't like us going off by ourselves, so he'd definitely be mad. But looking on the bright side, if I never got home, I would never get in trouble.

But that was ridiculous. People didn't just disappear. I'd help this girl find what she was looking for and then I'd get out of this canyon, making a stop at the first fast-food joint I found. A hot, juicy burger and a reliable phone sounded awfully good.

I raised my eyes. In the distance, a horse and rider crested the hill. I slipped back into the cover of the trees. Could the Mexican cowboys have circled around in front of us? I pulled off my backpack and got the binoculars. I gasped at what they magnified—a Native American dressed in traditional Indian costume! I watched while five more followed the first over the hill, all on horseback. They leisurely zigzagged down the rocky hillside. "This has got to be the wildest dream I have ever had. When am I ever going to wake up?"

Ellie moved to my side. "I beg your pardon?"

I handed her the binoculars. "Please tell me I'm hallucinating and those aren't Indians. Here, look."

She raised her eyebrows and gave the binoculars a quizzical look. She lifted them to her eyes, looking randomly over the hillside. "Incredible. Look at that rabbit. It looks so close. I've never seen such fine field glasses before—the clarity and magnification. Wherever did you get them?"

Impatiently, I pointed at the six horses. "A sporting goods store, but do you see the Indians?"

"Oh, let me see. Hmm. That's not good, not good at all."

"What? What's not good?"

"Those Indians are dressed in war paint. Probably Paiutes. Yes, from the looks of it, it's a Paiute raiding party. We haven't much time. I've got to get to the cave before they get any closer." She started to move.

I put my hand on her arm. "Would you tell me what you're looking for? This is crazy."

Scrutinizing my face, she paused, appearing to consider what she would say. "What I'm looking for resembles a pocket watch." She looked me in the eyes. "You must understand, it's very valuable—it's more important than me or you. My grandfather died to protect it. It is his legacy. I have to find it. I owe him that much."

My jaw dropped. I slid my hand to the button-down pocket of my cargo shorts. The cave I'd found was probably a twenty-minute walk from here. The gold device pressing against my leg fit her description. I undid the button.

"You said this pocket watch was hidden in a cave, right?"

"Yes, it is, or at least that was the plan. The cave is close to here." She pointed in the direction I'd come from yesterday. "It's down that way, up a wash. If we hurry we can cross this open stretch and drop behind those rocks before the Indians see us. Grandfather stashed a metal box in the cave. He planned to hide it, in the event things became dire."

She turned and started walking while I pulled out the gold device. A slight dent marred the back cover, probably from my fall during the fight. Sadly, I knew what needed to be done. Apparently this was what she wanted. If it belonged to her grandfather, she deserved to have it. I smiled to myself.

So much for making a fortune on my first archaeological dig.

I ran to catch her and held the gold device in front of me. "Wait. Is this what you're looking for?"

Ellie spun around. A look of distrust clouded her face at the sight of what I held. She tilted her head to the side. "Where did you get that?"

"Yesterday, I dug up a metal box buried in a cave not too far from here. This was in the box, wrapped in an old piece of leather."

She held her breath, as if I was a child holding an expensive piece of china. Slowly, she extended her hand. "May I have it, please?"

I set it in her outstretched palm. "Sure, it sounds like it belongs to you. Look, I'm real sorry about your grandfather."

She clutched it to her chest and closed her eyes, mouthing words of thanks. She opened her eyes and smiled before studying it. "It's a little dirtier than I remember. I'm surprised he let it get so tarnished."

Fondly, she caressed the gold cover. She slid her thumb over the latch, and it clicked open. A frown replaced her smile. Quickly she closed the device and then reopened it. A flash of anger darkened her beautiful face. Hadn't I given her what she wanted?

We both looked through the brush, monitoring the Indians' progress down the hill. In an effort to be less conspicuous, I pulled her down to a crouch. "What's wrong?"

"Did you use it?" she whispered.

It angered me she hadn't even said thank you. "What? No! I don't know. Look, I don't even know what it is. I opened it up, saw a weird light, and touched it. After that, I put it in my pocket, that's all."

She opened the device and held it toward me. "Did you touch a button? How could you? Which one did you push?"

The light was gone now—it probably broke when I fell on it. I pointed to the button I touched in the cave. Scowling, she yanked the gold device away from me. Her right hand moved to her pocket, the pocket with the gun. I began to think I should have snagged it when I had the chance.

"Ellie, what's wrong? Why are you mad? Talk to me."

She shook her head in disgust. "I can't believe you used the counter. My grandfather's been gone one day, and I'm already too late. It's maddening."

"I'm sorry. I had no idea. But in my defense, the box I took out of the ground had been there a long time. It was rusted shut."

A puzzled look crossed her face. "You said it was yesterday? When did you open the box? What was the date?"

I stared back at her. My mind churned. Why was she asking about the date? Her clothes. The way she talked. The vaqueros, as she called them. The lack of people around. The only answer I came up with seemed too unrealistic. Surely my imagination had run wild. Or maybe I still suffered from the effects of heatstroke. I quickly dismissed the idea. "It was yesterday—August 24, 2011."

Although still far away, the Indians were making slow but steady progress toward us. I watched her, waiting for her response. She dejectedly sat down and pulled out the pistol. Her elbows rested on her knees. She leaned forward. "Give me your hand."

I held my hand out. She touched the gold device to my finger, and immediately the light turned on inside. "So you're it, then," she said. "The new Keeper. It was supposed to be me, you know. Grandfather talked for years about giving it to me. The counter will only light up for its true Keeper."

Closing it, I pushed the gold device toward her, then pulled my hand away. "Well, I'm giving it to you, so don't feel bad. It's yours now."

She shook her head and pointed the gun at me. "It's not that easy, Mr. Harper. You can't give it away. Once you've used it, you're the Keeper of the counter. Until you're dead, that is. It won't work for anyone else. I'd have to kill you if I wanted to use it."

I eyed the gun barrel waving in front of my face. "Great," I muttered. Stepping away from her, I pulled my baseball cap off and gave my sweaty head a good scratch. Maybe she was crazy. It couldn't be a good sign that she openly talked about killing me. I would have to take the gun from her. I imagined I could easily overpower her and get it, but my timing would need to be impeccable. A split second was all she needed to pull the trigger.

I approached her from the side and used my softest voice. "Ellie, look, I'm sorry."

Luckily, she hadn't repositioned the pistol between us. I darted forward and grabbed her wrist, twisting her arm above her head. She fell backward, and I straddled her. Forcing her wrist onto the ground, I wrenched the gun from her.

Ellie pounded the fist of her free hand into my face, my chest, my arm—anyplace she could reach. And she still held the counter, as she'd called it, so it smacked my jaw. "Mr. Harper, get off me this instant!" she yelled.

The guttural voice of an Indian mixed with the sounds of Ellie's struggle. I stuck the gun in my back waistband and clamped my hand over her mouth. I didn't know what to expect from a bunch of guys dressed like Piute Indians, but I'd rather not find out first hand. "Shh! What are you trying to do? Get us killed?"

She peeled my hand away from her mouth. Her eyes flashed with anger. "Get off me."

I raised my finger to my lips and shushed her again. Through a gap in the branches, I watched the Indians. They motioned to each other and began to fan out. Within minutes they would surround us. But to leave the cover of the juniper trees would put us in plain sight. Slowly, I loosened my hold on Ellie's wrist and hopped off her. I moved away and pulled the pistol out, studying it. I figured I could fire the thing. It didn't look too complicated.

I glanced at her. She sat up and brushed the dirt from her shirt. I realized that even though I'd known her only a short time, I was willing to die for her. If necessary, I'd fight these Indians, without a second thought. I'd face the Mexican vaqueros and fight to the death before I'd let them touch her again. Her beautiful face. Her deep eyes, full of expression. Her soft, sweet voice and captivating laugh. They were irresistible. But right now, it didn't look like she reciprocated my feelings. Was she so calloused that she would've pulled the trigger and ended my life to have that counter light up for her?

I heard the hooves of the Indians' horses shuffling down the rocky trail. We were running out of time. Whether she liked me or not, we had to deal with these guys. "Ellie, what are we doing? What's a Keeper anyway?"

She sighed. "You're the Keeper, and this is yours. Here." She handed me the gold counter. Her face paled, and she pulled her hand up to her mouth as a look of alarm filled her eyes.

Concerned, I bent down next to her. "What's the matter? Ellie, did I hurt you?"

She shrugged away from me. "No. But you could have asked for the gun and I would have given it to you. No need to get your dander up and shove me in the dirt."

"How was I supposed to know that? You said you had to kill me."

"I said if I wanted to use the counter, I had to kill you. But I couldn't have pulled the trigger. In truth you saved my life. I surely would have died last night without your assistance."

She sounded sincere. At least I wouldn't always need to watch my back around her. In a lame attempt to comfort her, I said, "Well, I don't know that I saved your life. You probably would have lived through it."

Ellie shook her head and raised her eyes to meet mine. "No. I died. If I had lived, I would have come for the counter. The fact you found it in 2011 means I died. Do you not realize it is 1863? What you're telling me is the counter lay hidden in the cave for well over a hundred years. That means I never lived long enough to collect it from my grandfather's hiding place."

She paused, allowing me time to digest what she'd said. If what she told me was true, she had confirmed my wildest suspicions. Stunned, I shook my head at her, unwilling to accept her explanation. It seemed too unlikely—too impossible. She couldn't be serious. She had to be crazy.

But no matter how hard I thought, no plausible explanation for what I'd experienced came to mind. Unless she was crazy. Unless I was crazy. I had traveled back in time!

She interrupted my wild train of thought. "You're obviously not a man of evil intentions, but I must press upon you the importance of protecting the counter and keeping its existence secret. If I find you are ever a threat to the safety of the counter or its secret, I will kill you or die trying."

When I didn't immediately answer, she urgently spoke again. "Do you understand what I'm saying, Mr. Harper? You must keep the counter safe."

Her intensity surprised me. "Okay, I'll do my best." I raised the left side of my mouth into a half smile, chuckling softly. "I wouldn't want you hunting me down."

Ellie scowled at me. "This is no laughing matter."

I lowered my voice to a whisper. "Okay. But do you seriously think it's 1863? You're not playing some sick joke on me, are you?"

"No, this is not a joke. Today is June 4, 1863."

I listened to the Indians' horses closing the distance between us. "So you're telling me this is a time-travel device?"

"Yes, among other things."

"How do you use it? Have you used it before?"

"No, but I've had it explained to me."

"I want you to show me. But first, we've got to deal with those Indians." The thought that I was in 1863 in the near vicinity of real Indians in war paint made our situation all the more daunting. My heart thudded ominously in my chest. A pistol and the Mexican's knife were no match for the six Indian braves approaching our hiding place.

A sneaky smile turned her mouth. "Don't worry about the Indians, Mr. Harper. We'll be long gone by the time they arrive. Open the counter, and I'll show you."

FOUR
Shuffle

Willing to try anything, I clicked open the counter. Again the eerie bluish light illuminated the globe. I returned the gun to my waistband and gave Ellie my full attention.

She pointed to the button on the far left. "I suppose you pushed this one time, correct?"

I thought back to what transpired in the dark cave when I'd held the counter for the first time. "I think so."

I glanced up. The Indians were close now. Only two were visible through the branches. I didn't know where the others were, and that bothered me. Soon they would reach our hiding place.

Bright stripes of war paint covered their faces and chests. The lead horse had yellow handprints on his shoulder and rump, and bold eagle feathers were braided into the rider's black hair. The Indian brave had a regal set to his jaw. He sat tall and proud on the smooth back of his horse. In his right hand, he held a spear with an arrowhead tip chiseled to a sharp point. The end of the spear rested on the top of his foot. He had a quiver and bow strapped to his back, and a large, bone-handled knife at his waist. His eyes scanned the trees where we hid.

Ellie pointed to the buttons on the counter. "This time, press the middle button, Shuffle, followed by the left one, Return." After picking up my backpack from the dirt, she grabbed my wrist.

The sparse brush wouldn't conceal us much longer, so I hoped whatever I was about to do worked. The middle button and then the left one clicked under the pressure of my thumb. Instantly the nausea returned, and a blurry shimmer moved in front of my eyes. With the Indians approaching, I hated being unable to see.

I blinked. Tall grass now surrounded us, and our bodies were in the same position as when we left the juniper trees. Ellie sat cross-legged, while I crouched next to her. Her fingers held tightly to my wrist, above where the counter rested in the palm of my hand. Green grass swayed in the breeze, and even with the sun high in the sky, the grass was moist. Ellie jumped to her feet. Still holding my arm and my backpack, she moved through the waist-high grass, pulling me behind her.

A smile spread across my face. Reaching to take the backpack, I said, "Here, I can hold that. This is awesome. Where are we?"

Ellie's face mirrored my feeling of awe. "Look at the globe. Where is the light? The date is displayed on the dials, but I don't remember how to read the symbols."

I studied the pinpoint of light on the small globe. "I'd guess the Midwest, maybe Kansas or Nebraska."

"This is quite astonishing. My grandfather explained it to me years ago, but he never allowed me to accompany him. I expect we'll soon be going somewhere else."

I glanced at her hand on my wrist. "Why are you holding onto me? I mean I don't mind or anything. I'm just wondering."

She looked up at me. "As I've been told, whatever you're touching when you press the button goes with you. I don't fancy the idea of being lost in time, so I intend on keeping a tight hold."

My head reeled as I scrambled to comprehend this new reality. The shimmer and the nausea revisited me. I stopped and bent over, worried I would throw up. The hum of airplanes overhead became deafening, so I looked skyward, then did a 360-degree turnaround. I knew exactly where we were now.

White planes with bright red circles swarmed the sky. We stood on a beach. Palm trees swayed in the breeze, and frothy waves lapped at the sand. Behind me, lush green mountains pierced the skyline. Hawaii, December 1941. The attack on Pearl Harbor was imminent. Ellie stood rooted in place, staring at the sight overhead. I laced my fingers through hers and pulled her toward the cover of the trees. Gauging where the planes were headed, I angled in the opposite direction. As I wondered if there was anything I should do—anything I *could* do—it began. One after another, explosions bombarded my senses, and then the shimmer returned.

We reappeared somewhere in the dark—darkness so thick with fog I could almost taste the moisture. It was bitter cold. Through Ellie's hand, I felt her shivering. Goosebumps rose on my arms and legs. I wanted to walk around to generate some heat, but it felt like we stood on the side of a steep mountain. Not wanting to step off a cliff, I opted to stand still. A shiver shot its way up my spine. Flipping the counter open, I saw we were in Scotland.

"What were those big, noisy, flying things?" asked Ellie. "You looked horrified."

"Oh, those were airplanes," I said.

"I take it they're dangerous, then?"

"Those were, but airplanes in general aren't dangerous. It depends who is flying them. That had to have been Pearl

Harbor, December 7, 1941, a Sunday. The Japanese launched a surprise attack on the United States navy early that morning. I think a couple thousand American soldiers died. After that, the U.S. entered World War II. My great-grandpa fought in the war. He was one of the lucky ones who came home."

For the first time I considered how overwhelming everything would seem to Ellie if we actually appeared in 2011. How would someone from 1863 survive our highly technological world? Another round of nausea and shimmering interrupted my thoughts.

A blast of heat hit us. The nausea passed, but the shimmering lingered. A mirage. Our feet sank in deep orange sand. As far as the eye could see, wind-swept sand dunes surrounded us. The intensity of the heat was stifling, like standing too close to a blazing bonfire. I'd never felt anything like it before.

"I'll bet we're in the Sahara Desert." I looked down to check the counter. "Yup, that's what it looks like."

Ellie's eyes widened as she scanned the horizon. "Land sakes, look at all that sand. Not even a cactus in sight."

I'd seen the Sahara on TV, but for her, everything was new. We walked down the sand dune. With each step, sand poured over the top of my hiking boots. I stopped and smiled at Ellie. "All right, I'm ready to move on now."

She laughed softly, shielding her eyes from the sun. "Yes, I am too. I imagine the devil's backyard would feel something like this."

I chuckled. "Yeah, I can't imagine any place hotter." Again the nausea and shimmering started. Before it passed and I could see clearly, the concussion of an explosion assaulted my eardrums. Instinctively, I crouched, pulling Ellie down next to me. Bullets ricocheted off the buildings. The dimness of twilight filled the narrow alley we found ourselves in. Two soldiers caught my attention. One threw something before they both ducked for cover. Seconds later, an explosion sounded in the street. In the chaos they advanced, leaving us alone. I looked at the counter as I pulled Ellie deeper into the shadows. She covered her mouth and nose. The stench of rotten garbage mixed with sewage made it difficult to breathe.

"We're somewhere in Eastern Europe, I think. I need to brush up on my world geography," I muttered.

"Perhaps the devil's backyard wasn't so bad."

I stopped next to the wall and looked over my shoulder. We were at a dead end. "Yeah, at least we could breathe and we weren't in imminent danger of dying from a stray hand-grenade."

After another wave of nausea and more shimmering, we stood in quiet darkness. Not too cool, but not too hot. I took a deep breath.

"If I counted right we completed five shuffles," Ellie said. "We should have returned to the last place the counter was used. I wish we had a candle to see by. I reckon we're in the cave. That is where you first used it, right?"

I slid my backpack off my shoulder and pulled out the Maglite. Shining it around the cave's interior, I saw the graffiti. I chuckled to myself. I never thought I'd welcome the sight of graffiti, but at that moment, I appreciated it as much as an art connoisseur seeing the *Mona Lisa* for the first time.

The rocks I'd moved lay right where I'd put them. Flooded with relief, I said, "Yup, this is where I found it."

Ellie touched the Maglite in my hand. "What is that?"

I handed it to her. "Flashlight. Pretty cool, huh?"

"Cool? It doesn't feel cold."

"It's an expression. Cool means you like it. Or it's good."

Ellie shined the light in my face. "Yes, light is good."

I blinked and put my hand over the light. "Whoa, not in the eyes, though."

She turned the light onto the pile of boulders. The rusty, old box sat where I'd left it, next to the hole in the ground. Ellie walked over and picked up the hardened piece of leather. She ran her fingers over the metal box. My discarded water bottle sat on the ground. I bent down and picked it up, expecting it to be warm. It was cold, cold enough that it still held the layer of condensation that had formed during my bike ride. Thirstily, I guzzled half the bottle before remembering my manners. "Do you want a drink?" I offered her the bottle.

She shined the light on it. "What is it?"

"Water. It's cold, too."

She took the bottle and read the label. "Water in a bottle? The glass is soft."

"It isn't glass—it's plastic."

"Hmm." She raised it to her lips and took a sip. "Now what?"

"I'm starving. Are you hungry?"

"Yes, I'm famished."

"Then let's go get some food."

I located the exit, and we crawled into the sunshine. After jumping down, I turned to offer Ellie a hand.

"This is a bigger drop than what I remember," she said as I helped her down.

"Yeah, I noticed that too. It's what years of erosion will do."

"Oh, I see." Ellie raised her hand to shield her eyes from the sun. "Looks like things haven't changed too much."

Chuckling, I took a step. "Come on. Maybe not here, but you just wait. Things have definitely changed."

I led the way to where I'd stashed my bike, carefully stowing the counter in my pocket. This time my bike was where

I expected it. My cell phone buzzed. Sliding my phone open, I saw "911: Error. Invalid number. Please resend using a valid 10-digit mobile number or valid short code."

"Oh crap! I sent a message to 911, trying to report your grandfather's death to the police. But good, it looks like the message didn't send."

She propped her hands on her hips. "What in Sam Hill are you trying to tell me, Mr. Harper?"

I tried not to laugh. "This is a cell phone. You use it to talk to people all over the country or to send text messages." The phone vibrated again. My messages had finally sent, now that I'd returned to civilization. This time, "2 new messages received" appeared on the display. The first was from my girlfriend, Kim. It said, "Miss u. Can't wait til Sat. Got my hair done 2day. Luv u." With Ellie watching me, I didn't feel like replying to that right now.

I opened the next message. It was from Adam, "Where r u? What do u mean u found a dead body? R u kidding? How can u b lost? The dads r awake asking abt u. Do u need me 2 come get u?"

I selected "Reply" and typed, "Never mind, I'm not lost anymore. Sorry. J/k abt the body . . . lol. On way back now." Pausing, I looked from Ellie to the bike then back again. She still had a what-the-heck-are-you-doing? look on her face, but she waited patiently for me to finish. I continued typing, "Flat tire on bike, walking back, not far so don't come pick me up."

My phone vibrated again, and there was Jessica's reply to my text for help. I opened the message and read, "R u serious? Did u call police? How can u b lost? Should I tell Dad?" I hit "Reply" and sent my thumbs into a flurry of typing. "No, I'm on way back. Got turned around 4 a min & thot I saw a body. False alarm, lol. Flat tire on my bike, walking back. Tell Dad I'll b there soon." I hit "Send."

I returned my phone to my pocket and looked at Ellie. "That was my cousin Adam and my sister Jessica. They're wondering where I am. What should I say about all this?"

"If you feel you must tell them about the counter, I'll allow that it is your decision. However, I wouldn't recommend it. You're apt to cause a stir. You'd be better off keeping it a secret. It's a difficult concept for most. My grandfather warned me people would exploit it if they knew what was possible. The fewer people who know, the better. And the safer it will be for you and the counter."

While I pushed my bike up the hill, I pondered what she'd said. I didn't understand this counter thing, but I knew it was powerful. And she was right. If what I'd seen became common knowledge, people would try to use it for their own gain. And I had no doubt there would be some willing to kill for it. Time travel. The possibilities were endless.

Questions raced through my mind, bouncing off the dull pain throbbing in my head. The lack of food and water had taken its toll. While the realization I'd traveled through time was awe-inspiring, the image of the old man's mangled body flashed before my eyes. They killed him because of the small gold device now buttoned into the pocket of my shorts. Yes, it was clear I needed to be cautious. By the time I reached the road, I had the makings of a loose plan in mind.

Ellie walked ahead of me and scraped her boot along the blacktop. "What is this hard black surface?" She stepped farther into the road, studying the yellow lines sparkling in the sunlight.

The familiar sound of an approaching vehicle spurred me to action. I grabbed her arm and pulled her to my side. "Whoa there, you gotta stay on the edge."

A moment later one of the Zion shuttle buses zoomed past. Startled, she jumped back. "What was that?"

At the look on her face, I started laughing. I couldn't help it.

She scowled at me. "A loud, big . . . big box contraption nearly runs us over, and you're laughing at me?"

I tried to keep a straight face and failed. "That was a bus. It takes people places. If we stay on the outside of this white line here, we'll be safe. The cars and buses use the lanes in the middle, the area between the white and yellow lines."

A truck and trailer, followed by three other cars, came up the road. Cautiously moving farther away, Ellie observed the procession with wide eyes.

A smile spread across my face as I watched her. How would it be to see a motorized vehicle for the first time, after growing up with horses and wagons? After they passed, Ellie's face lit up, and she turned to me.

"So like a stagecoach or omnibus, only without the horses?"

I nodded and pushed my bike down the road. "Yeah, that sounds about right." I looked over my shoulder. Ellie stood staring after the cars. "Come on," I yelled. When she caught up I continued. "I'm camping with my dad, my sister, my cousins, and my uncle. We've got three tents set up on the North Fork of the Virgin River. We can get something to eat there. My mom, Jennifer, is a nurse at a hospital in Oregon. She wasn't too excited about spending a week of vacation sleeping on the ground, so she stayed home. Same with my aunt. My dad is Joe. He's a professor of accounting and information systems at Portland State University. Jessica is my twin sister. My cousin Adam is my best friend. His little sister Amanda is a sophomore this year. And my uncle Steve is a big shot at a high-tech company. You'll get to meet them all in a few minutes."

Ellie listened intently while I rambled on about my family and filled her in on my plan, which included confiding in my sister. Ellie seemed a little overwhelmed by everything I told her.

But all things considered, I thought she took it quite well. I had simply assumed she would come with me, but I realized I never asked her. Concerned, I stopped walking and faced her. "What do you want to do, though? Do you want to go back where you came from? We could take you back with the counter, right?"

Ellie folded her arms and raised her chin. "My grandfather meant for the counter to be my responsibility, so I intend to keep an eye on it and ensure you're doing your job properly. But, yes, we could go back. However, I confess, I am curious to see what the future looks like now that I'm here. One more word of caution, Mr. Harper. According to my grandfather, a Keeper is forbidden to take anyone with them when they use the counter."

I shrugged my shoulders. "Well, what about you? You came with me. I didn't see any problem."

She smiled. "I did, didn't I? I apologize for that. But I couldn't resist the temptation. I've waited a long time to see how the counter works, and I'll admit I was disappointed you beat me to it."

I smiled back. "No need to be sorry. I don't mind." I couldn't define my feelings for her, but I wouldn't have wanted to leave her behind.

FIVE
The Family

As we neared the campground, I phoned Jessica. I glanced at Ellie when my sister answered her phone. "Jess, will you bring an extra pair of clothes and meet me at the bathrooms? The one that's closest to the entrance. No, not clothes for me. Girl clothes. Bring an extra pair of your clothes, and don't say anything to Dad, okay? Jess, I'll explain later—please just bring the clothes. Thanks, Sis. I knew I could count on you. Bye."

We got some strange looks as we entered the campground. "Between your old-fashioned dress and my filthy clothes, I guess we make an interesting-looking pair," I said to Ellie.

Her wide-eyed expression drew a chuckle from me. "Well, all of these people most certainly look interesting to me," she said.

I pointed to the girl with shoulder-length brown hair, standing in front of the bathroom. "That's Jessica."

"She doesn't look like your twin," Ellie said.

"She takes after my dad. I got my mom's blond hair and blue eyes."

"Oh, I see."

When we were close enough that Jessica noticed our deplorable condition, she ran forward. My vivacious, outgoing sister looked Ellie over and then settled her eyes on me. Jessica scrunched her eyebrows and touched my cheek. "What happened to you? Are you hurt? Chase, you are hurt. You've got a cut lip, and bruises on your face. You're a mess! What happened? Did you get in a fight? Did you crash your bike? Your bike looks okay. I thought you had a flat tire. And what was all that nonsense about a dead body? You know you shouldn't joke about stuff like that."

I rolled my eyes and sighed. "Jess, if you'll let me get a word in, I'll explain."

"Sorry. Okay, explain."

"Yes." I paused, teasing her.

After a moment of silence, she affectionately punched me on the arm. "Oh you. Tell me, now!"

"Ouch!" I rubbed my shoulder. "First of all, Jessica, this is Ellen Elizabeth Williams, but she goes by Ellie. Ellie, this is my twin sister Jessica. I was trying to say, yes, I'm hurt. Yes, I got in a fight. Yes, I know my lip is cut. I haven't looked in a mirror, but my face hurts, and now, thanks to you, there's one more bruise on my arm that wasn't there before."

Jessica frowned. "Sorry. I didn't think about that before I hit you."

I looked at her and chuckled. "No worries. It didn't really hurt."

"Oh, Chase, be serious. What's going on?"

I yawned. "Can we find someplace to sit down first?"

We walked to a grassy spot under some trees, and I sank to the ground in exhaustion. I told Jessica about finding the counter, the time travel, Ellie's grandfather, and the Mexicans who hunted for her and the counter. Jessica didn't interrupt as Ellie explained my obligation as the new Keeper.

When Ellie finished, Jessica looked at both of us and shook her head in dismay. She leaned closer and whispered in my ear,

"Chase, just because she's wearing a long dress doesn't mean you were in 1863. Can I talk with you alone for a minute?"

I rolled my eyes. I was tired, hungry, and in no mood for Jessica's skepticism. I sighed. "All right." I smiled at Ellie and muttered, "I'll be right back." I pushed myself to my feet and followed Jessica across the grass.

"Chase, are you crazy? I know you have a soft spot for cute girls, but this is ludicrous. Are you sure you didn't hit your head? You can't actually be thinking about believing her. Time travel is impossible. The past is in the past. You can't have gone there."

I buried my hands in my pockets and shrugged my shoulders. "Yesterday I would have agreed with you, but now I'm not so sure. I know what I saw. I can't explain it, but I can't deny it either. Look, I'm tired, I'm starving, and I don't have a better explanation. Ellie is convinced what she's saying is true. Not to mention, I saw her tortured grandfather with my own eyes. Jessica, I buried him. I fought her captor with my own hands, and I have the bruises to show for it. And I did time-travel. I don't know how, but I was there. I saw things—things from the past. Right now I can't explain it any better than that. I know it sounds ridiculous, but until I can figure this out, will you believe me? Can you take a chance and go with it? That's all I'm doing here. I need your help, please."

"Where is this counter thing she's talking about?" Jessica asked.

I reached in my pocket and pulled it out. "Right here." She extended her hand, and I turned it over to her. In the glow of the sunset, she examined it.

"Interesting. Is it real gold?"

I quickly grew impatient. "Probably."

"Does it open?"

I reached over and pushed the clasp, springing the top. "Yeah, this clasp here opens it." The eerie blue light emanated from the interior of the counter until I pulled my hand away.

"Wow," Jessica said. "Why did the light go off?"

I reached over and touched the counter again, and the faint blue light radiated from inside. I chuckled, experimenting with Ellie's explanation as the words rolled off my tongue. "Because you aren't the Keeper, and I am."

"If you're the Keeper, show me how it works."

"Later, Jess. Can't you take a leap of faith and help me? It's going to be dark soon. Dad's probably already mad at me."

Jessica handed back the counter. "Okay, Chase, I'll go along with your little game for now."

I sighed with relief. "Thanks, Sis."

The two of us walked back to where Ellie waited.

Jessica looked from Ellie back to me. "So, what are you going to do now?"

"Somehow we've got to take Ellie with us when we leave tomorrow," I said.

Ellie looked worried, and her mouth turned down in a frown. "I wouldn't want to impose on you and your family. Maybe I shouldn't have come."

Jessica smiled, but it didn't look genuine. "Don't worry, you're not imposing. I'm grateful you brought my brother back. It sounds like he would have been lost if it wasn't for you."

I lifted my bike and helmet off the grass. "As I was saying, we need an excuse to take Ellie with us. I thought if you two pretended to be friends from school or something, we could tell Dad her grandfather passed away in Oregon and she needs a ride back for the funeral. You could play up the fact she's an orphan and there isn't any other family around. What do you think, Jess?"

"All right," she grumbled. "I can work with that. But how are you going to explain your face?"

"I'll tell him I crashed my bike."

Jessica raised her eyebrows. "Well, you told Adam and me you had a flat tire, but that's obviously not true. If you're going to pull off a bike-crash story, you'd better get your bike looking like it crashed." She turned to Ellie. "Come on, Ellie, we've got girl stuff to do."

I offered Ellie my hand and pulled her to her feet. She glanced back at me once before following Jessica into the bathroom.

I started toward the campsite. Better face my dad and get it over with. I stopped near a vacant site to let the air out of the front tire. Then I picked up a softball-sized rock. It was painful, but I smashed one side of the front brakes, scuffed the paint on the side of the frame, and then tipped the bike on its side, rubbing the seat in the dirt. There, that should pass for a bike crash.

I froze when a siren blared in the distance. The sound drew closer. I grabbed my phone. Did the 911 text message go through after all? I thought it failed to send. Clicking through my outbox, I found the message still said, "911: Error. Invalid number." Attempting to erase the evidence, I deleted all of my messages. Had they tracked the signal sent by my phone using a GPS? I had heard they could do that. With my heart racing, I lowered my head and kept walking.

They silenced the siren, and a police car pulled into the campground. It headed my direction. I was two camp sites away from ours when the car parked behind me. I stopped. How would I explain falsely calling 911? Maybe I could plead heatstroke or say I hit my head in the bike crash. I looked the part. Taking a deep breath, I turned to face the policemen. They got out of their car, and one of the officers barked orders as he ran. "Son, move out of the way. We've got an ambulance coming."

I let out a sigh of relief and kept walking, looking over my shoulder to see what was happening. A group stood huddled near the river.

My dad left our campsite and walked toward me. "Chase, what on earth happened to you?"

"It's good to see you too, Dad."

He stared me down, waiting for the answer.

"Bike crash. It's no big deal though. I'm sure it looks worse than it is. What happened over there?" I asked, nodding toward the people huddled together.

"A little girl nearly drowned in the river, but it looks like they were able to revive her."

The ambulance pulled in, and two EMTs ran over with a gurney. A few minutes later, they loaded a small girl into the ambulance. The clearly distraught mother climbed in behind her, and they drove away. The father, along with three older boys, got into a van and followed.

My dad and I watched the crowd disperse. "That's good. I'm glad she'll be all right," I said. "A death would really ruin a family vacation."

"Yes, it would," he said, still standing in front of me. "I wasn't happy you left without telling me where you were going. It's not smart."

"I know, Dad. I'm sorry."

"All right, but be more careful next time. And take someone with you. Where were you riding, anyway?"

"I went up the road before going cross-country. I was going too fast when I hit the brakes, and my tires slid in the gravel."

"Were you wearing your helmet?"

I groaned. I wanted to get out of interrogation, so I needed to change the subject. I lifted the helmet. "Yeah, Dad, I was. But I'm starving. When are we going to eat?"

"Steve's cooking spaghetti tonight. Next time, slow down and be more careful. You're lucky you didn't break your arm. You get an injury like that, and it'll ruin your soccer season—"

"I know, Dad," I interrupted him. The last thing I wanted to hear right now was a lecture. "I know."

He smiled and slapped me on the shoulder. "Okay, go get cleaned up. Dinner's about ready."

I clenched my teeth to keep from grunting at the blow to my bruised back. "Hey, Dad," I said when he turned to leave. "We might have company tonight. Jessica ran into a friend from school. I got the feeling she was inviting her to dinner."

He nodded indifferently as he walked toward the bathrooms. At least I had planted the idea of company. The rest would be up to Jessica. Hopefully she could pull it off.

I parked my bike and climbed in my tent. I dug out clean clothes, a towel, and some soap. There were no shower facilities at the Watchman Campground, but I was in dire need. I changed into my swim trunks and flip-flops.

When I stepped out of the tent, Jessica nearly ran me over. Her arms were loaded with shampoo and conditioner bottles, a hairbrush, a washrag, and a razor.

"What are you doing now?" I asked her.

She seemed to be in a better mood. "Going back to the bathroom. None of your business—girl stuff."

I meandered down to the river. Trying to clean up in a bathroom sink might work for Jessica and Ellie, but it didn't appeal to me. I wasn't sure if they allowed bathing in the river, but I planned to be in and out before anyone noticed. I dropped my towel on a rock and waded out with my soap and shampoo. I dropped to my knees and immersed myself in the cool current, gasping for air until my body adjusted to the temperature. I soaped and scrubbed in record time. After rinsing, I stuffed the shampoo bottle and soap in my pocket and waded back to shore. *Great,* I thought, *I left the counter in my dirty shorts.* If I wasn't careful, I'd wind up losing it. Then I'd never hear the end of it from Ellie. I hustled back to my tent and put on clean clothes. I moved the counter and my cell phone from my dirty shorts to the clean ones and went to check on dinner.

"I'm starving," I said to Uncle Steve. "Is there anything I can do to help?"

"We're about ready. Why don't you slice the bread for us?"

I grabbed the knife and sliced the French bread. The first two slices went in my mouth, but the rest made it to the picnic table. Adam stirred the sauce on the Coleman stove while Uncle Steve drained the noodles. Dad pulled out the drinks from the cooler, plus a bag of lettuce and some ranch dressing.

My head shot up as Jessica and Ellie made their way through the campsite. Jessica steered Ellie toward her tent. They dumped off a garbage sack and an armful of bath supplies. From my perch on the corner of the picnic table, I watched Ellie. She wore Jessica's white Portland State University hooded sweatshirt and a pair of tan Bermuda shorts. She walked funny. Looking down at her feet, the reason became obvious. She wore Jessica's green flip-flops. No wonder. I'd bet her feet had never seen flip-flops before. Jessica led Ellie in the direction of the picnic table, and I dropped my gaze.

"Dad, I want you to meet a friend of mine," my sister said. "This is Ellie. Can she stay with us for a little while? She came down here with friends, but they aren't leaving for another week. Ellie got a call this afternoon from her neighbor, saying that her grandfather, who she lives with, passed away suddenly. Can you believe it, Dad? Isn't that sad? Anyway, she needs to get back to Oregon. Since we're leaving tomorrow, I told her she could hitch a ride with us. I hope that's okay."

Everybody stared at Jessica.

Way to lay it all out on the line, Jess. Breaking the silence, I said, "I'm sorry to hear about your grandfather, Ellie."

She played along with the charade. "Thank you."

Jessica introduced everyone to Ellie, and they offered their condolences.

"Jessica, we'll talk about it after dinner," my dad said.

When my sister walked by me to dish up a plate of food, I whispered in her ear, "Thanks. Hopefully he agrees."

"No problem, Bro. I'll convince him. But you'll owe me one." If anyone could persuade Dad, it was Jessica. She always managed to get her way.

I walked to where Ellie stood and handed her a paper plate. She discreetly turned her back to everyone else. "I don't think your sister likes me much."

I glanced over Ellie's head at my sister. "Jessica? I'm sure she likes you. She just needs a little time to warm up to the idea."

Ellie took a deep breath. "I hope so. Everything is so strange here that I hardly know how to act. I feel utterly out of place. Jessica introduced me to the toilets—like self-cleaning chamber pots—how heavenly that must be. My aunt Lydia would have loved that. But these clothes I'm wearing! Why ever would you insist I wear such uncomely clothing? I'll warrant I've never shown this much leg in my entire life. Why, I'm half naked."

The intensity of her accusation caught me off guard. "What do you mean? I didn't insist on anything."

"Jessica claimed you insisted she dress me in this clothing."

I scratched my chin and tried to look at it from her perspective. Yeah, it was a big leap in fashion. But whether she liked it or not, she had to conform. "Well, I'm sorry about that. I guess I did tell her to get you some of her clothes to wear. But I don't think any of us brought anything except shorts. Ellie, look around you. This is what everybody else is wearing. Plus it is really hot, so you should give them a try. You just might like 'em.'"

She looked at Adam and Amanda, and then at the girls in the neighboring campsite. She kept a straight face. "I highly doubt I'll like them. I look dreadful."

Amused, I stepped back to give her a thorough look up and down. She squirmed under my scrutiny. I leaned forward and smiled. "Don't worry. You look anything but dreadful. Now come on. Let's eat."

After thinking I'd never see my family again, I felt extra charitable and volunteered to do the dishes. That drew a surprised look from both my dad and Uncle Steve. Ellie followed me to the water spigot, where I started scrubbing the pans.

"Would you like some help?" she asked.

"Yeah, that would be great. Do you want to rinse and dry?"

She picked up the towel from the camp chair and tossed it over her shoulder. "Certainly."

I scrubbed a pan then handed it to Ellie. She twirled it under the water and then whipped the towel off her shoulder for a quick dry before waiting for me to finish the next one.

Noticing the ease with which she handled the dishrag, I said, "I'll bet you've hand-washed a lot of dishes in your day."

"Well, of course. How else would a person wash their dishes—with their feet?"

"I was comparing it with using a dishwasher, actually."

"Well, it seems to me if you had a dishwasher, they would still need to use their hands."

I started smiling. Then I started chuckling.

Ellie glared at me. "Perchance you'll tell me what you find so funny?"

I forced myself to stop laughing. "There's so much I want to show you. We have automated dishwashers now. It's a big box you stack your dishes in. You put the soap in and press the 'Start' button—then voila! When you come back an hour later, your dishes are clean and dry."

She let out a deep sigh, worry clouding her expression. "Hmm . . . I reckon I have a lot to learn before I'm going to blend in here."

I offered my most encouraging smile. "You'll do great. Stick close to me and Jessica, and we'll help you out."

Movement caught my eye and I glanced up. Adam walked over and rested his hand on the water spigot. "Ellie, what year are you?"

I answered for her. "She's a senior, like us."

"I don't remember seeing you around last year," he said.

"I attended a different school last year," Ellie said politely.

"Really, which one was that?" Adam asked.

Ellie cast a questioning glance in my direction, and I jumped in to help her. "She was at Glencoe."

Thankfully, Jessica saved us from further scrutiny. She bounced over and grabbed his arm. "We're starting a game of cards. We need you, Adam."

When we were alone again, Ellie said, "That was frightening. I had no idea what to say to him."

I rinsed the dishrag and wrung it out. "We need to get our story straight. Between you, me, and Jessica, we should at least be telling the same lies. Otherwise, we're going to be in a world of trouble."

Ellie finished drying the last pan. "Yes, we are."

"Tomorrow morning we're hiking the Gateway to the Narrows. Do you want to come with us?"

"I don't want to intrude on your family time, and I am feeling fatigued after the last two nights. Perchance I could stay here?"

"Yeah, that's no problem. Hey, sometime I want to hear the long version of how those guys captured you in the first place."

She tilted her head and smiled up at me. Her smile was warm and inviting, like one shared between friends, and I wondered when we'd moved our relationship from forced acquaintance to actual friendship. "Certainly, Mr. Harper, and there is something else I would like to tell you about the counter as well, but now is probably not the time. Maybe we can talk soon."

"Sure, but you've got to call me Chase. No more Mr. Harper. That's my dad's name, not mine."

She nodded. "I'll try to remember."

"Good. Did Jessica find you a pillow and show you where to sleep?"

"Yes, she did. Good night."

I watched Ellie walk to the girls' tent. I couldn't help but smile at the way she lifted her knees with each step to keep the flip-flops on her feet. My mouth opened wide as a giant yawn escaped. I packed the pans in the Rubbermaid camp box, said my good nights to the card players, and hit the sack.

SIX
Talking

The sun wasn't up yet, but the warbling of birds roused me from a solid night's sleep. I hadn't heard Adam come to bed, but he now slept next to me with his head buried in his sleeping bag. Come to think of it, I'd been so tired last night I hadn't even brushed my teeth. I slid my tongue around my mouth. *Disgusting. I've been to 1863, hiked more miles than I can count, and visited Pearl Harbor, the Sahara Desert, Scotland, Eastern Europe, and the Great Plains, all without brushing my teeth. Yuck!* That settled it. I threw off my sleeping bag and rummaged through my stuff. With toothbrush and toothpaste in hand, I unzipped the tent.

I relished the cool, morning air, knowing it would soon give way to the scorching desert heat. The first stirrings of life had begun around the campground. While I stood by the spigot brushing my teeth, my dad came out of his tent and stretched his arms over his head. "Morning, Chase. That's a nasty bruise on your face. Does it hurt?"

I spit and got a drink. "Good morning to you too, Dad." I fingered my split lip and bruised cheek. "Actually, it's not too bad."

"That's good. What do you know about this girl, Ellie? I'm a little concerned about picking up a stranger. Is she a good girl?"

"Yeah, Dad, she's a good girl. You could say she was brought up with good, old-fashioned values. And she's not a stranger to me and Jessica. We know her. Ellie's an orphan. She was raised by her grandfather since she was eight. Now that he's gone, she's got nobody. Have you thought about what Jessica said last night?"

"About giving Ellie a ride home?" he asked.

"Yeah, I think we should. It doesn't seem right to say no when we're going home anyway and there's room for her in Uncle Steve's Suburban."

"I talked with Steve last night, and he doesn't object to giving her a ride back. I suppose it's all right with me too. But who is she here with? I'd feel a lot better if I talked with the adult who brought her."

Thinking fast, I improvised. "Well, I think she's here with friends—college-aged friends, so not much older than us. I don't think there are any older adults, Dad."

"Hmm," my dad muttered. Obviously he was still a little skeptical.

"Dad, I know Ellie. You don't need to worry about her."

"Okay. I just want to make sure we're doing the right thing."

I tried not to sound too excited. Truthfully, I hadn't come up with a back-up plan if he said no. "So we're giving her a ride home, right?"

"I guess there's no reason why we can't."

With the first obstacle in my plan successfully navigated, I smiled in relief. "Hey, when are we leaving for the Narrows?"

"We'll go as soon as everyone wakes up."

I poured Cheerios into a plastic bowl and sat in a camp chair to eat. Jessica, Amanda, and Ellie emerged from their tent and headed straight for the bathrooms. I felt the counter through my pocket. I had questions I wanted to ask Ellie, but I needed to get her alone. And after a good night's sleep, I was curious what she wanted to talk to me about. Maybe she'd changed her mind and wanted to go home, to the past.

My dad pulled me out of my daydreaming. "Chase, let's go. You ready?"

"Yeah, let me get my boots."

I hurried to the tent and pulled on clean socks and my dirty hiking boots. I dumped out my backpack and discarded the empty water bottles. Spying the pistol and the large knife I'd taken from the Mexican, I hid them in my duffle bag. I went to the picnic table and opened the cooler. Fresh water bottles, a handful of granola bars, the extra French bread from last night's dinner, and two oranges were loaded into my backpack before I felt someone watching me and looked up. Jessica stood next to Adam with her hands on her hips.

Adam broke into a chuckle. "Dude, did you pack enough? This isn't an overnighter."

Jessica piped in with her know-it-all tone of voice. "Dad already has sandwiches and snacks for everyone in the Suburban."

I looked down and zipped my backpack closed. "Well, you never know what might happen."

Appropriately named, the Narrows was so narrow in places that you could extend your arms and touch both sides of the canyon at the same time. Magnificent, sheer walls of colorful sandstone and granite reached into the sky. At times the hike could almost be called a swim. But the cool water felt refreshing after days of desert hiking, and my dirty boots got a good washing. The strength of the Virgin River's current threatened to knock our feet out from under us while we threaded our way through the mass of hikers.

As the morning sun climbed toward its apex, I found myself thinking about Ellie. Was she safe? What was she doing? I hoped nobody bothered her. There was too much she didn't know yet. Maybe she should have come with us. I started to wonder why I had left her by herself. On the other hand, what was wrong with me that I couldn't stop thinking about her? I'd known her for one day, and she'd worked herself so thoroughly into my life that I barely thought of anything else.

Lost in thought, I didn't notice how far ahead I'd gotten until I heard Jessica splashing behind me. "Chase, wait up," she called.

I turned and waited for her. Adam and Amanda were a ways behind Jessica. Dad and Uncle Steve were even farther behind. "What's up?" I asked.

"Why are you in such a hurry?"

"I didn't realize you guys were so far behind."

"You're hiking really fast. You should slow down."

"Sorry, but maybe you should speed up. Do you think Ellie's doing okay?"

"Yes, of course she's okay," Jessica said.

"Did she say what she was going to do while we were gone?"

My sister stopped and grabbed my arm. "No, but why are you so worried?" She looked me straight in the eye. "You like her, don't you?"

I yanked my arm away. "No . . . I don't know. I hardly even know her."

Jessica laughed. "Well, time can take care of that."

"Knock it off, Jess. I feel responsible, that's all, because it's my fault she's here. And there's so much she doesn't know about. I just don't want her getting hurt."

"We'll help her figure it out. Ellie's not stupid. She'll be fine."

After our lunch break, I stood waiting, anxious to get moving up the canyon again. Once we hit the trail, it felt like everybody moved at a snail's pace. I couldn't figure it out. At least Adam should have kept up with me.

"Hey, slowpoke, you hikin' with the girls today?" I taunted him.

That got him riled. I heard the water splash as he ran up behind me. I took off running, hoping to avoid getting tackled from behind. He never caught me. As a wide receiver, Adam was fast, and normally he could have outpaced me. Thirty yards later, I slowed up to look over my shoulder. Adam went back to walking, and I stopped to wait for him.

"Dude, you're fast." He seemed a little surprised. "I thought I was going to twist an ankle on these rocks."

"I thought you were coming to tackle me."

Adam laughed, grabbing me around the shoulders and playfully shoving me. "I was trying to. What about Kim?"

I hadn't thought about my girlfriend since her text the day before, the one I still hadn't answered. "What about her?"

"Are you going to break up with her, now that Ellie's on the scene?"

I playfully shoved him back, nearly toppling him into the river. "What's this? Are you and Jessica ganging up on me now?"

"I saw the way you looked at her last night."

"What are you talking about? I didn't look at her."

"Yeah, you did. You gave her *the look.*"

I shook my head. "I don't know what you're talking about. You're seeing things."

Adam shrugged his shoulders. "Whatever. You can deny it, but I know what I saw. Just tell me if you're dumping Kim."

"No, I'm not breaking up with Kim. I hardly even know Ellie."

Adam raised his eyebrow. "Then do you think I should ask her out?"

"Ellie? No," I said too quickly.

Smiling knowingly, Adam laughed. "I figured the answer would be no."

We filled the rest of the hike with casual conversation and a joking banter back and forth. But my anxiousness over Ellie never left. The shuttle ride back to the trailhead and the drive to camp felt like being stuck on the bench during a big game. Finally, the Watchman Campground came into view. I bolted out of the Suburban door before Uncle Steve had it in park.

"Ellie?" I called, walking toward the girls' tent. No one answered. I looked at the river and down the campground loop, but didn't see her. Jessica walked up behind me and looked in their tent.

"She's not here," my sister said.

I strained to keep my voice low. "Where could she have gone?"

"Maybe she's in the bathroom or on a walk. Relax, or Dad's going to think something's up."

I took a deep breath and nodded. I walked to the picnic table and unloaded my over-prepared backpack. We set our wet hiking boots out to dry in the sun and began packing the tents and sleeping bags. Every few minutes, I looked for Ellie.

"Where's that friend of yours, Jessica? We need to get going in the next hour," Dad grumbled.

Calm as usual, Jessica replied, "She's probably at her friend's campsite. I'll go look for her after I'm packed."

The intense worry I felt at not knowing Ellie's whereabouts was maddening. I looked up the road over and over again. I couldn't help myself. When I finally saw her walking toward me, I let out a sigh of relief. I closed the sack that held my sleeping bag and tossed it on the pile accumulating behind the Suburban. I slipped away to walk up the road and meet her. "Are you okay?"

"Fine, thank you. And you?" she said politely.

"I'm good. Where were you?"

She flashed me a smile. "Oh, I walked into town for a bit. I never would have dreamed there could be so many people out here on the frontier. The buildings—my goodness, they're large. I found a place called the gift shop. It was like a mercantile, but everything was so impractical and expensive. How does anyone afford a thing around here? I read a book in the gift shop about the history of Zion Canyon. That interested me. My grandfather would roll over in his grave if he knew how his canyon has changed.

"But earlier, when I was walking into town, a man in one of those big moving boxes, a little like that one over there—" she pointed at an old blue and white van "—he offered me a ride, but of course I declined. I'm not sure I'm ready to get in one of those contraptions. It became rather annoying when he didn't want to accept my refusal. But after his rudeness, what lady would ever accept?"

A sick feeling hit the pit of my stomach, and I stopped walking. Putting both my hands on Ellie's shoulders, I turned her to face me, then looked deep into her eyes. "Ellie, promise me you won't ever get into a car with anyone you don't know. Which I guess would be everybody except me. Okay? Please, promise me. There are a lot of weirdos in 2011. You can't trust anybody these days."

She cocked her head back at the intensity of my plea. "All right, I won't."

I lowered my arms and relaxed my stance. "Good." I stepped back, readjusting my baseball cap and wiping the sweat from my forehead. I turned to walk toward the campsite. "We're packing up now. We should be ready to leave in the next hour." I glanced down at Ellie's feet. She wore her 1860s button-up leather boots with the shorts and T-shirt she got from Jessica. "Hey, I like your boots," I said with a chuckle.

"Well, I wasn't about to walk to town in those floppy shoes Jessica had me wearing last night."

I nodded. "Yeah, flip-flops can be a pain to walk in."

Later that afternoon I sat in the middle of the Suburban, literally, in the middle seat of the middle row. I had Adam on my right side, asleep with his iPod plugged into his ears. Jessica and Amanda both slept in the backseat. Uncle Steve and Dad were talking politics and the economy in the front. Ellie sat to my left, keeping a constant watch out the window. Every few minutes, she leaned over and whispered something about the passing scenery. Everything fascinated her—the cars, campers, horse trailers, and buildings. It was all new. Her excitement over the wonders of the modern world was contagious. Telephone poles, irrigation sprinklers, stores, gas stations—she had questions about all of them. I found new appreciation for all these modern conveniences after seeing them through her eyes.

That evening we pulled into a dude ranch in Antimony, Utah. The town of Antimony consisted of a handful of buildings along a mile-long section of highway, including a post office, a church, and a couple of small shops. Aunt Marianne had asked Uncle Steve to check out the ranch for her, as she was considering using the location for the next family reunion. We arrived in time for a buffet-style dinner. The food tasted incredible, especially after a week of camp meals. Following dinner and a shower, I left our room to explore the ranch. Dad and Uncle Steve were busy getting the information Aunt Marianne wanted from the ranch manager.

In the center of the lodge was a vaulted sitting area and a huge stone fireplace. Ellie came down the stairs as I sat admiring the antler chandelier hanging from the ceiling.

She sat next to me. "I don't know if I'll ever become accustomed to such large buildings."

I looked at her. "Yeah, they're pretty big, but you haven't even seen the skyscrapers yet. They're huge. Just wait. You'll see some of those tomorrow. Hey, do you want to go for a walk outside?"

She flashed her brilliant smile at me. "Yes, I'd like that." I stood, and she slid her hand under my elbow. I raised my eyebrows and smiled back at her. I guess it shouldn't have surprised me that her actions and mannerisms were like something out of an old Western movie. Luckily, Dad and Uncle Steve had their backs to the door as we walked by. I didn't need my dad getting the wrong idea about Ellie and me.

Outside, the sun hovered on the horizon. A breeze stirred the leaves, making the temperature pleasant. Gravel crunched underfoot as we walked toward the pond. After feeding the animals in the barn, the wranglers turned a group of horses loose on the grassy field surrounding the pond. Ellie and I meandered between them as they grazed.

"What did you want to talk to me about?" I asked.

"We need to go back."

Disappointment hit me like a slug in the gut. "Back where? You want to go back home now?"

Ellie looked up at me. "Not to stay, but we need to get something from the cabin. My grandfather kept a journal. I don't know what's in the journal, but it's important. He kept it buried under the hearthstones of his fireplace. If anything ever happened to him, I was to collect the counter from the cave and the journal from the cabin. He said everything I needed to know would be in the journal."

"So you think he knew how to read the symbols on the counter?"

"Oh yes, I'm certain he did. He had the counter since he was a young boy. My grandfather had years to figure it out, and he used it often. He visited me nearly every week while I lived in Boston, and he also visited my pa when I was a small child."

As much as I wanted to see that journal, I had my concerns. "What about those Mexican cowboys?"

Ellie leaned toward me and raised her voice in excitement. "I think we can manage it so we go back to the same time we left, only we will go to the cabin. Those no-account vaqueros should be following our trail up the canyon. It won't take more than a few minutes to dig up the journal, and then we'll be gone."

The bruise on my cheek had turned a garish mixture of purple and yellow. The thought of revisiting the 1860s didn't exactly thrill me. "Let's wait a few days. With the counter, we can go back to whatever point in time we want, right? So it won't matter if we wait a week."

Ellie let out a sigh. "Yes, that's right. But I'm anxious for you to read the journal. The sooner you know how to use the counter, the better off you'll be. Grandfather warned me to study the journal before I used the counter. He said a person could get lost in time if they weren't careful."

I ran my tongue across the scab on my cut lip. "Well, I won't use it till then. I'm still recovering from last time."

She frowned and squeezed my arm. "I'm sorry you got hurt when I dragged you into that awful fix I was in."

"It's okay. It wasn't your fault."

She furrowed her brow. "I don't know about that."

I shook my head. She didn't need to take the blame on herself. Things happen. "I don't remember being dragged into anything. Didn't I barge in, uninvited, on your little party with that cowboy?" She didn't answer right away, so I pushed the issue. "Ellie, you can't blame yourself. If I didn't want to be involved, I would have walked on by."

Ellie turned away and lowered her gaze. "I suppose you're right." She must have sensed my desire to move on to another topic, because she said, "I worry about you not having the journal. What if you have to use the counter and you don't know how?"

I shrugged my shoulders. "Ellie, don't worry. I'll be fine. Nothing's going to happen."

"I hope you're right. Do you feel any different now that you're a Keeper?"

"What do you mean?"

"I'm not sure exactly, but I recall my grandfather saying something about the magic of the counter transferring to its Keeper. He said it changed him."

"Huh, that's interesting," I said, trying to remember back to how I'd felt the last couple of days, and thinking about how I felt now. I felt great, actually—I felt normal. Could that be the difference? Considering how far I'd hiked and how beat up the Mexican left me, I shouldn't be feeling normal. I should be exhausted. I shouldn't have been able to outrun Adam in the Narrows. And I should be aching all over from the punches I'd taken during that fight, but I wasn't. In fact my bruises seemed to be healing really fast.

"I guess I feel stronger . . . healthier."

Ellie nodded her head, smiling. "That's good." We continued walking in silence, her arm still resting lightly on mine. "Do you think we can go out on the water?" She pointed to a green canoe on the grass by the pond.

"Sure, I don't see why not." I collected the paddle that lay on the bank and slid the canoe to the water's edge. I smiled at her. "Hop in and I'll take you for a ride."

Ellie climbed in, and I used my foot to push the canoe off the bank into the water. The little boat rocked back and forth, adjusting to our weight. I dipped the paddle into the green water, propelling us forward.

The solitude of the pond seemed to relax Ellie, and she started talking about her grandfather, about growing up in Utah Territory, about him teaching her to ride and shoot. She talked about being sent to live with her great-aunt when she was fourteen so she could learn to be a lady and get her education. She talked, and I listened. The differences in our worlds left me speechless. We talked until the mosquitoes zeroed in on our location.

Ellie swatted a mosquito on her calf and waved others away from her face. "I suppose that's enough canoeing for me."

The pesky insects bit my legs as I paddled toward the closest shore. Once we hit land, I jumped out and pulled the canoe, with Ellie sitting in it, out of the water onto the grass. She laughed.

I offered my hand and helped her out of the canoe. "What's so funny?"

Giggling, she pointed at the canoe pulled well out of the water. "This. My, aren't you strong," she teased.

I smiled. "Oh yeah, that's what all the girls say." Her melodic laugh mixed with my own. Still holding my hand, she ran toward the lodge, away from the swarm of mosquitoes hovering over the pond.

SEVEN
Preparations

I yawned and rolled onto my stomach. My own bed had never felt better. We'd driven all day Friday, getting home late. We hadn't done much once we got home except unpack and go to bed, and I'd looked forward to sleeping in. I didn't have anything until 4:30 PM. My date with Kim—horseback riding at my place, and then dinner with her family to celebrate her grandmother's birthday. Kim was a cheerleader for Hilhi. I wouldn't have thought myself the type to date a cheerleader, but we'd had two classes together during our junior year, and the relationship evolved over the summer.

To put it plainly, Kim's parents were rich. Her dad owned two car dealerships in the Portland area. They lived in a mansion in the country, but nothing about their lifestyle said country.

The enchanting strains of a melody brought my attention back to the present. Maybe my mom was playing one of her CDs. But it couldn't be. Jessica had a swim meet today, and she and my mom should've been long gone. Dad planned to go to the university to check his mail and get caught up on things in his office. Certainly he would have left by now as well, and this wasn't his type of music anyway.

I threw off the covers and sat on the edge of the bed, listening. It was piano music. I got up, opened my door, and left my room. The music grew louder as I walked down the stairs. Someone was playing our piano. I hadn't heard that piano in years. I paused at the entrance to the living room. Ellie sat at the piano, her hair piled on top of her head. Blond tendrils brushed her neck and cheek. Her fingers seemed to caress each ivory key as she played.

It had been no small feat getting my dad to agree to bring her here. At the ranch in Antimony, Jessica worked him over for a good hour before he consented. She appealed to his compassionate side, which was small in comparison to my mom's. Jessica asked how he could reasonably expect Ellie to go home to an empty house by herself when her grandfather had passed away. He finally softened and let Jessica invite Ellie to stay with us for a few days. I still faced the daunting challenge of either getting my parents to agree to a more permanent living arrangement or finding someplace else she could stay.

I stood quietly in the doorway and listened to the music crescendo. Ellie finished the song and looked over her shoulder at me, her eyes twinkling with amusement. "Good morning. I hope I didn't wake you."

It was then I realized I stood before her in my basketball shorts, no shirt, bare feet, and messy morning hair. I turned around. "No, I was awake. I'll be right back."

Once I left, she began to play again. I hurried up to my room, but I soon gave up trying to tame my hair and pulled on a baseball cap. With a clean T-shirt on, I went back downstairs. "Are you hungry?"

She got off the piano bench to follow me into the kitchen. "Yes. Your home is beautiful. It's so big."

"Believe me, it's not that big." I noticed she was wearing the same sweatshirt and shorts Jessica had loaned her two days ago. "We need to go shopping and get you some of your own clothes," I said, pulling a couple of bowls out of the cupboard.

"I'm sorry. I feel as if I didn't think this through. My being here is likely a terrible inconvenience."

I pulled the milk from the fridge and set it on the counter. "It doesn't inconvenience me."

"Well, I do appreciate your hospitality," Ellie said. "But speaking of clothes, I think we should find you something suitable to wear when we go back to the cabin. If we run into anyone on the way, I'll not have you sticking out like a sore thumb. We wouldn't want to attract undo attention to ourselves with those vaqueros lurking about."

I opened the pantry. "Okay, we'll go shopping for both of us after we eat. What kind of cereal do you want? Corn Flakes, Honey Nut Cheerios, Raisin Bran, or Lucky Charms?"

Ellie looked at me with wide eyes. "Chase, I simply have no idea. I've not heard of any of that before."

It captivated me—the melodic way my name rolled off her tongue. Smiling, I grabbed a box. "Well, how about Cheerios? They're my favorite."

She smiled back at me. "That sounds fine." Halfway through her bowl of cereal, she looked up. "This is delicious."

"Good, I'm glad you like it."

When we finished breakfast, she said, "I'd like to wash my dress before we go back to the cabin. Where do you wash your clothes around here?"

I put our bowls in the sink. "Get your dress. I'll show you."

Soon, I led her to the laundry room, where she leaned over my arm and eyed the inside of the washer with skepticism. I stuffed her long skirt and blouse into it and dumped a generous scoop of detergent on top. I pushed in the knob and turned it to the normal wash cycle.

"Oh!" she gasped when water sprayed onto the clothes. "Now what do we do?"

I closed the lid. "Nothing. Now we go shopping."

With two fingers, she gingerly lifted the lid and peered inside.

"Don't worry," I said. "When we get back it'll be done."

"Really? Just like that? Without any scrubbing?"

I walked out of the laundry room. "Yup, just like that, without any scrubbing."

Before we left the house, I grabbed my wallet, the counter I was now responsible for, and the keys to the truck, then stuffed them in my pockets. "I've got to feed the horses. Do you want a tour of the place before we leave?"

We lived in the country on an eighteen-acre horse property. The house was an older farmhouse—nothing to get excited about by today's standards.

"That would be lovely," Ellie replied.

"My mom has this horse-boarding business, but somehow I got roped into the feeding and the stall-cleaning. She pays me, though, so it's not too bad."

I showed Ellie the two barns. The older one had stalls and hay storage. The other was an indoor riding arena with more stalls and a large tack room. "This is amazing. I love horses. I missed riding when I lived in Boston," she said.

The feeding took half the time, with Ellie eager to help. Half an hour later I opened the door to Washington Square Mall. I tried to remember what I'd seen my girlfriend Kim wear. She had impeccable style. Ellie wandered through the mall in a state of awe. Here and there, we walked into stores. Sometimes we tried on clothes, and sometimes I took her into a store simply to show her the marvels of the modern world. Soon I carried bags of clothes and shoes in both hands.

I'd spent the summer working construction for a contractor. When I got my first paycheck, my dad insisted I open a checking account at the bank and start building my credit. The checking account came with a Visa card. It was a good thing, because this shopping spree would probably wipe out the balance in my account. Ellie resisted each purchase I made for her, worried about the cost. After getting jeans, shirts, and sweatshirts, I saw some shorts on the clearance rack.

"Hey, how about some shorts?"

She cast me a look of disdain. "Surely you are joking, Mr. Harper. I long for the moment I can shed this dreadful pair your sister has been kind enough to loan me."

Coming from a culture where long skirts were the fashion, wearing shorts might be a big leap. But they had to be more comfortable. "Here, at least try them on."

"No, thank you," she replied.

I swished my hands in front of my legs, imitating her skirt. "Come on. You've got to admit these would be a lot more practical in the heat than having all that fabric around your legs. And no one will think less of you for wearing them around here. Everybody wears shorts."

Ellie took the shorts from my outstretched hand and let out a huff of air. "My, but you are persuasive. I'll try them on, but I don't want them. I can't believe I let you talk me into this."

I chuckled at her grumbling. With my hands shoved in my pockets, I waited for her outside the dressing rooms. My mom would die of shock if she knew I was willingly at the mall. It frustrated her that I refused to go shopping with her for my clothes. I left her to either guess at what I'd like or look at me in my tattered jeans and ratty T-shirts. I checked the time on my cell phone. This had to be a record for me: three hours and ten minutes at the mall.

"Ellie, how do they fit?" I called over my shoulder.

"They look hideous."

"I didn't ask how they look. How do they fit?"

"I don't like them."

"But they fit you, right?"

Ellie left the dressing room and scowled at me. "They fit fine."

"Good, let's buy them and get going. I'm hungry."

"I'll never wear these." She held the shorts in front of her.

I grabbed them and pulled my wallet out of my pocket. "Well, I'm buying them. I think when it's a hundred degrees outside, you'll change your mind and thank me."

She followed behind me. "You're wasting your money, Mr. Harper."

I dropped the shorts on the counter by the register and glanced at Ellie. "For ten bucks, that's a risk I'm willing to take."

Loaded with packages, we left the mall. I tossed our bags in the backseat of the crew cab and opened the door for her. She caught me off guard when she extended her hand to me and waited expectantly. I stared at her hand before realizing she expected me to help her step into the truck. Interesting . . . and different. Although she handled the wilderness like a pro, her mannerisms were more formal than what I was used to. Maybe she had plans to turn me into a gentleman.

Once I climbed in and closed my door, she touched my arm with her fingertips. "Chase, thank you for the clothes. It's very kind of you, but I do feel terrible you spent so much money on me. You shouldn't have to do that. My grandfather stashed away some money in his cabin. I'm sure it isn't much, but I'll pay you back what I can."

"Don't worry about paying me back. I don't think we'd be able to keep our little secret about the counter quiet if all you had to wear was your long dress. It doesn't exactly blend in with the times."

I tried to talk her into going straight home, but she still insisted on finding me trousers and boots that would pass as frontier clothing. I took her to a thrift store, where we scoured racks and racks of pants and shirts. She found tan pants for me to try on. They were a little big and made out of wool. I kept scratching my legs. They looked awful to me. But Ellie insisted, with some suspenders and the right shirt, they would be perfect. We bought the pants, some beat-up, square-toed leather boots, and a pair of old suspenders. Ellie couldn't find the perfect shirt, but she got two cotton dress shirts and claimed she could make something out of those.

We drove home, and I carried the shopping bags into Jessica's room. I glanced out the window at the sound of a car. My dad stepped onto the driveway.

"I better go," I said to Ellie. I tossed my wallet into my room and ran downstairs. "Hey, Dad, how's it going?"

"Good, where are you off to?"

I pointed to the note my mom had left on the counter—the note I had forgotten about until now. "I've got to mow the lawn. Then I've got a date with Kim."

EIGHT
The Date

I spent forty-five minutes driving the riding lawn mower and dumping grass clippings. I caught sight of Ellie watching me from Jessica's window. *What thoughts are running through her mind?* I wondered, because my mind was a planet, and Ellie was the sun around which it orbited. The date I'd looked forward to all week now seemed like an inconvenience.

I parked the lawn mower and ran inside. I threw on a cowboy hat and boots. I might as well look the part for my date. I jetted down the hall past Jessica's room. "Hey, cowboy, where you off to so fast? Hot date with Kim?" she yelled.

"Whatever, Jess," I said, realizing Ellie must've heard her comment.

I jumped down the steps to the porch and jogged to the barn. Red, the sorrel gelding my mom had bought for Jessica and me, stood waiting by the gate. I pulled him out, along with Smoke, my dad's big gray horse.

Moments later, Kim drove up in her sporty Nissan. She had shoulder-length, dark brown hair and brown eyes—the kind of look that would make any guy do a double take. She was one of those perfectly put-together girls: perfect hair, perfect complexion, perfect makeup, and perfect manicure. She wore high-heeled boots, light blue designer jeans, and a white tank top. Smiling, I shook my head. *Totally impractical for riding horses. Definitely a city girl.*

She threw her arms around me and kissed my cheek. "My goodness, Chase, what happened to you? How awful. That looks painful!" Her fingertips traced the outline of the bruise on my face.

"It's nothing. I'm fine. I just crashed my bike at Zion."

"I'm glad you're back. Last week was so boring without you. Well, do you like my haircut?" She turned her head from side to side, giving me a flirtatious look.

I leaned back to check out her new 'do, but I couldn't tell the difference. "Yeah, it looks great."

She talked nonstop as she watched me saddle the horses. I helped her mount up, then shortened the stirrups for her. We rode up our gravel road and through the neighboring vineyards. Three times Kim disrupted the peaceful ride by dropping her reins and panicking over it. After getting off my horse for the third time, I crossed them over the horse's neck.

"Just hold them with two hands, like this, and keep them crossed," I said. "That way they can't fall to the ground."

Red pranced his way onto a recently harvested grass seed field. "Do you want to try going a little faster?" I asked her.

"Sure." She gave her horse a big kick.

Obviously startled, Smoke took off like a horse out of the gate at the Kentucky Derby. Kim bounced up and down, hair flying out behind her, screaming for the horse to stop. I galloped alongside her. She had dropped the reins, opting to hold onto the saddle horn with both hands. Luckily, with the reins crossed over the horse's neck, they weren't dragging on the ground where he could trip himself.

I motioned with my hand. "Pick up your reins and pull back."

Her white-knuckled fingers squeezed the horn even tighter. "I'm scared to let go!" she screamed.

My horse running alongside hers only made matters worse. Smoke picked up his pace, anticipating a race. I pointed again. "Pick up the reins and pull back!" I yelled.

"No, I can't."

Edging Red closer, I reached over and grabbed her reins in my right hand. The stunt guys made this look easy in the movies. Not so in real life. After a few jolting strides, I managed to slow both horses to a walk. I turned them toward home.

I tried not to laugh but failed miserably. "Why'd you kick him so hard?"

"Don't laugh at me, Chase! That was scary. I didn't think he'd run away. Maybe I should walk."

I flipped the reins over Smoke's head and led the horse behind mine. "Kim, we are walking. I'll hold the reins for you the rest of the way back."

Her fingers still held the saddle horn in a death grip. "Maybe I should get off."

"Don't worry, you're fine."

We didn't say much on the way home. I could tell Kim wasn't happy. When we dismounted, Old Smoke turned his head and chose that instant to rub his sweaty, dust-covered face and green, snotty nose across the front of her white tank top. I stifled a chuckle and turned my head away.

Kim groaned when she tried to brush off the front of her shirt. "Oh, I can't believe this. I better go, Chase. Be at my house at 6:30 PM. I'll see you then." I held my breath until she got in her car. Her tires spit gravel as she gunned the engine. Then I busted out laughing.

Mom walked out of the barn to take one of the horses from me. "What's so funny? You weren't gone that long. Is everything okay?"

"Everything's okay for me, but I don't think Kim will be climbing back in the saddle anytime soon."

Seeing an empty saddle, my mom couldn't resist and mounted up. "Let's ride a little, and you can tell me about it."

We rode around our circular driveway. Involuntarily, I glanced at Jessica's window. My eyes met Ellie's. She had been watching, and I wondered how much she'd seen. She quickly turned away from the window.

My mom laughed pretty hard when I told her about the horseback ride. "I can see why Kim wouldn't want to go riding again, especially after you were laughing at her. Chase, you should be nice. Not to mention you shouldn't be going faster than a walk with a novice rider. It isn't safe."

"Mom, I was nice."

"I hope so."

We put the horses away, and I went in to shower. An hour later, I pulled into Kim's driveway.

She answered the door perfectly clean and composed. Stepping through the doorway, she wrapped her arm around mine. "Let's go in my car. We'll meet my family at the restaurant. We can reserve a table while they pick up my grandma."

Soon, we sat with her family, sipping raspberry lemonades and eating appetizers. The dinner conversation jumped from the family's next planned vacation to the new living-room furniture Kim's mom wanted. With an upcoming trip to Hawaii, Kim's brother needed a new surfboard, Kim needed to go to the tanning salon, and her little sister needed new swimming suits. It went on and on. After the intriguing conversations with Ellie, this was torture to me.

I thought of all the inventions and social changes I'd enlightened Ellie about. The results of the women's rights movement fascinated her. The volume of people she saw amazed her. The brightness of electric lights was a wonder. I'd learned she'd taken piano lessons in Boston for the past four years and dreamed of owning a piano someday. I'd learned about her great-aunt Lydia, whom she had lived with in Boston. Aunt Lydia had been sick off and on over the past few months, and Ellie worried about her health. She'd told me more about her grandfather, too. Now that I had the counter, I was naturally curious as to the life history of the man who had it before me. I gazed out the window of the restaurant, wondering what was happening at my house. I had so many unanswered questions bouncing around my brain.

Finally our food came. The waitress looked young and nervous. She worked her way around the table, placing everyone's plate in front of him or her. I got my food and picked up my fork. When the waitress reached over Kim's shoulder, she fumbled the hot plate of ravioli, and it fell into Kim's lap. Kim screamed and jumped to her feet. Out of the corner of my eye, I saw the heavy plate falling toward the tile floor. I leaned over, and with lightning-quick reflexes I didn't know I had, I snatched the plate out of the air.

I stared at my hand, holding the hot plate inches above the black and white tile. I glanced up, but there was no need to worry about anyone noticing the inhuman speed with which I had moved. Kim had the attention of everyone within hearing distance.

"What were you thinking?" she shouted at the waitress. "These jeans are new, and no doubt marinara sauce stains. I can't believe this." She brushed at the food with her napkin.

Give me a break, I thought. *It's not like the waitress dropped the plate on purpose.* Marinara sauce splattered down my arm as Kim shook her sweater. I set the plate on the table.

Kim's mom led her toward the front of the restaurant. "Come on, Kim, let's go in the restroom."

The manager apologized to Kim's father and offered to pay any cleaning bills. The poor waitress looked near tears as she cleaned up the mess. Everyone else at the table began to eat.

Between bites of food, I helped the waitress clean up. After sliding my chair out of her way, I used my napkin to scoop up some of the spilled food. "Don't let what she said bother you," I whispered to the waitress. "She can be a little irrational at times."

The waitress kept her eyes focused on the floor. "I'm so embarrassed. I can't believe I did that. It's my first week, and I'll probably get fired after this."

"Not necessarily. Keep smiling, and it'll blow over and be forgotten soon enough."

I had eaten half of my food when Kim returned from the bathroom.

"Come on, Chase, let's go."

Her father looked across the table. "Kim, sit down and let's finish our dinner first. They're getting you another plate. It should be here any minute."

"No, I can't stay here looking like this. Chase, I'll be waiting in the car." She spun around on her high heels and marched toward the exit.

Her mother whispered something to her father, and they went back to eating. The conversation died after that. I slammed down a couple more bites of food, leaving more than I wanted to on my plate, and said my goodbyes to her family.

I passed the waitress on my way to the exit. "Good luck," I said.

Kim sped home, grumbling the whole way about the waitress and how humiliating it was to have food dumped in her lap. I tried to convince her it was an accident and that there was no reason to be humiliated, but she cut me off every time I started to speak. I finally gave up and stared out the window, counting the miles until we got home. Until that night, Kim's physical beauty and popularity had masked how self-absorbed and spoiled she was.

She slammed the door to the Nissan and stomped up the steps to her front door. "Good night, Chase. I'll see you later," she called over her shoulder, leaving me standing by her car. I locked it for her and walked to my truck. I'd be getting home earlier than I thought.

NINE
Decisions

A shaft of light escaped a crack in the door from the garage to the house. Someone hadn't closed it all the way. The sound of my parents' arguing in the kitchen greeted me as I silently pushed the door open. I hesitated, listening.

"Joe," my mom said, "I know we don't know her yet, but that doesn't mean we can't help her. This is the perfect opportunity to get to know her. Jessica says she'll need to move to Boston and live with her great-aunt if she's not able to find a home here. You know how I feel about bouncing teenagers around from school to school. I hated that as a kid. It was awful. I lived with four different foster parents during high school and went to four different schools. This is her senior year. She's such a sweet girl. I hate the thought of her having to put down new roots so far from home when we can easily accommodate her. Remember, we always did want to have more kids. We even talked about adopting."

My dad raised his voice. "Jen, that was fifteen years ago! I'm used to our two now. I like our family how it is."

"I like our family too, but we can add one more. It will only be for a year, and then all of them will be off to college. Plus,

Jessica wants her to stay. Every girl needs a sister. I never had one, and neither does Jessica. I think this could be really good for her. Please, Joe, I feel like this is the right thing to do."

"What about Chase?"

"What about him? He's so busy with his sports and his girlfriend, I doubt he'll even notice her."

"Oh, he'll notice," my dad said. "He already has."

"Oops," I muttered to myself. I would have to be more careful or I'd mess this up.

"Well, shouldn't we at least give it a try? When was the last time we went out of our way to do something nice for someone else? Remember the parable of the Good Samaritan? Perhaps this is our opportunity to serve, to open our home to someone in need. I can't help but ask myself, will we be like the priest and the Levite who walked by on the other side of the road and ignored the wounded man? Or will we be the Samaritan who bound up the man's wounds, cared for him through the night, and then left money for his lodging?" My mom paused for a moment before softening her voice and continuing. "Joe, if it doesn't work out for some reason, we'll cross that bridge when we get there."

My mom, in her soft-spoken way, could always guilt us into seeing things her way.

After a long pause, my dad said, "You're probably right. We should do something charitable now and again."

"Thank you, Joe. Oh, I'm so excited to tell Jessica."

"Wait! Hang on, Jen. Before you say anything to Jessica or Ellie, I want to talk to Chase. I don't feel right about deciding something this big without getting everyone's input."

"Okay, then, we'll talk with him when he gets home."

I smiled. Jessica had been busy. Evidently she'd decided Ellie wasn't so bad after all. I closed the door loudly behind me and walked into the kitchen. I poured a bowl of cereal and sat across the table from my dad. It seemed like a millennium before they brought up the subject I wanted to talk about.

"Chase, we have something we want to discuss with you," my mom finally said.

"Your mom and Jessica want to invite Ellie to stay with us this year," my dad said. "I wanted to know what you thought about that."

Trying to act as nonchalant as possible, I kept my voice devoid of any emotion and shrugged my shoulders. "I don't care."

"If she can't find a good home here, she'll need to move to Boston with her great-aunt," Mom added. "You know how I hated moving and changing schools every year as a teenager. Living in foster care was miserable, and we all know how my brother turned out as a result." Mom was obviously trying to convince me to see her point of view. I chewed my cereal intently, trying to avoid cracking a smile. If my mother only knew how convinced I already was.

Her younger brother Roy had been in and out of jail for as long as I could remember. Not a year went by that he didn't call my mom, begging for money. His laundry list of crimes included dealing drugs, burglary, and identity theft. As a result of how her brother turned out and her negative experiences growing up, Mom worked hard to provide Jessica and me with a steady home life.

I glanced up from my cereal to my parents. "Yeah, I know, Mom. I said I didn't care. It's fine with me."

Dad stared at me for a minute before saying, "We'll give it a try, then. Go ahead and tell Jessica."

My mom pushed her chair back. "Good, I'll go let them know."

My dad chuckled. "This means we'll be outnumbered by the girls."

I smiled back at him. "I think we can handle it, Dad."

Mom came downstairs a few minutes later. My parents were about to start a movie I'd already seen in the theater, so I said, "I guess I'll go to bed. Good night."

As I turned toward the stairs, my mom's words stopped me in my tracks. "Chase, I forgot to ask when the funeral for Ellie's grandfather is."

Thinking fast, I picked a day I thought Mom would be at work. "I think it's on Tuesday."

"Should we be going to that? I have to work, but I may be able to change shifts with someone."

"No, Mom, you don't need to go. I know Jessica is planning to go with her."

"Are you sure?"

"Yeah, I'm sure. I heard Ellie telling Jessica it wasn't going to be any big deal, just a few friends."

"Okay. Good night, honey."

"Good night."

The sound of giggling escaped Jessica's room as I walked past. I glanced down the stairs and heard my parents' movie starting. With my knuckles, I tapped lightly on the door. Jessica opened it and pulled me in. "Take your shirt off."

I looked from Jessica to Ellie, who blushed and then glanced away. "Why?" I asked.

Jessica held up the altered dress shirt from the thrift store. "Look at this shirt Ellie made for you. And by hand, too. I want you to try it on." The shirt now slipped over the head and had a short, straight collar, completely different from what we'd bought earlier today. She had altered the cuffs so they matched the short collar. I pulled my T-shirt over my head and tossed it on the bed, then reached to take the shirt from Jessica. She snatched it away from me and squeezed my bicep. "Wow, Chase, I didn't know you were weightlifting. Are you trying to impress Kim?"

Feeling my face flush at her teasing, I lunged for the shirt, and this time she wasn't fast enough to keep it away from me. I caught Ellie's amused smile just before I slid both arms into the shirt and pulled it over my head. I stepped in front of the full-length mirror and looked at myself.

"I'm impressed. You really made this?"

Ellie walked over to me. "Yes." She raised my arms and examined the extra fabric hanging around my torso. Her fingertips brushed against my rib cage and slid down to my waist, gathering in the fabric as she went. My heart raced, and I held perfectly still while she studied the fit of the shirt. "I think I should take it in a couple inches through here," she muttered.

Mesmerized by her touch, I stared at her reflection in the mirror. She must have showered while I was gone, because her hair was damp. She had twisted it into a bun, and a few wayward curls framed her face.

Next she lowered my arms to check the fit of the sleeves. I fought the urge to reach out and tuck the loose hair behind her ears.

Ellie stepped in front of me and waited expectantly. Once she touched me, I hadn't heard a word she said. Startled out of my daydream, I stumbled over my words. "What . . . what did you say?"

"I'll take it in a little here," she repeated, tucking the fabric between her fingers and sliding them down my sides. "But how does it feel?"

I moved my arms, checking to see if I had good range of motion. "Good. I mean great. It's really great. Thank you, Ellie."

She glanced at Jessica, who sat talking on her phone, and lowered her voice. "Well, you'll look more natural walking through the Utah Territory in this than you would in your shorts and T-shirt. I hope it doesn't bother your mother that I looked through the cupboard and used her sewing things."

"No, that won't bother her. She never sews anyway."

Ellie took hold of the shirt and pulled it up to my shoulders. "Let's take this off so I can fix it." I leaned forward and raised my arms, letting her pull it over my head. Then I stuck my hands in the pockets of my jeans and stood there watching Ellie thread the needle.

Jessica slid her phone closed and threw my T-shirt at the back of my head. "You can put your shirt back on. What are you going to do now?"

I picked up the T-shirt and put it on. "I guess I'll go to bed."

"Did Mom tell you they decided to let Ellie stay here?"

I sat on the bed next to Jessica. "Yeah, thanks. I'm glad you talked to Mom. There's only three more days until school starts. Do we have to register her or something?"

"Of course. I'm sure she'll need a birth certificate to get signed up. Does she have anything like that?"

"No. But I'm thinking about calling Uncle Roy. Maybe he can get her a fake ID."

Jessica lowered her voice. "Chase, are you serious? How many times has he been in jail? If you're not careful, you'll end up in there with him. Plus, if you're going to do something that stupid, don't you want to use someone who's good enough not to get caught?"

Little Miss Perfect annoyed me sometimes. "That's a good point, but we don't really know any other criminals, do we, Jess?"

"Mom's going to be mad if she finds out. You know she forbade Uncle Roy from having any contact with us. He may not even take your call."

"I know, but I've got to try."

The three of us spent the next hour crafting Ellie's fake life story. Thankfully, Jessica was willing to go along with what I'd told her about Ellie. I couldn't have done all this alone.

Ellie finished her alterations on my shirt and hid it in the back of Jessica's closet with the pants and her dress. We decided she'd lived on an Indian reservation in Arizona with her grandfather before they moved to Oregon. We incorporated as much truth as possible, including her being orphaned as a young girl. We had told Adam she went to Glencoe High School last year, but that wouldn't work. My mom assumed she went to Hilhi. Mom's willingness to let Ellie stay was based on the presumption that she would have consistency in schools. The school would undoubtedly ask for copies of her records, and there wouldn't be any. There was nothing to do but hope they didn't compare notes and catch us in the lie. We'd have to tell the school she'd been homeschooled.

After working through all the details, I left the girls' room and went down the hall to mine. Sound effects from the movie playing in the family room floated up the stairs as I drifted off to sleep.

Ellie and I were feeding the horses Sunday evening when I asked, "You said you like horses, right?"

"Yes, I do," she answered.

"Do you like to ride?"

She smiled at me over the trough. "Oh yes, I love to ride. My grandfather and I often rode up the canyon when I was younger."

At the mention of her grandfather she turned away and took a deep breath. Hoping to cheer her up, I said, "Then we should go for a ride tomorrow."

"I'd like that."

At practice on Monday afternoon, I dominated on the soccer field. My speed, endurance, and agility were at another level altogether. And the urge to fight for the ball was overpowering. An hour into practice I forced myself to back off. What was going on with me? Coach stared, while the assistant coach whispered in his ear. Ellie had alluded to the magic of the counter. Was it that?

Coach blew the whistle, then came over and slapped me on the back. "Great practice today, Chase. I didn't notice before, but you must be weightlifting."

I pulled a water bottle from my backpack and took a swig. "I just worked construction all summer."

"Keep playing like that, and you'll be starting."

I began to wonder if I did look different. "Thanks, Coach."

After dinner, with the sun throwing long shadows across the ground, Ellie and I walked to the barn together. Mom and Dad were at a PSU faculty retreat, so we had the place to ourselves. I had looked forward to horseback riding with Ellie more than I expected.

We fed all the horses, then got out the two we planned to ride. I handed her the lead rope on my dad's horse and showed her which saddle and bridle to use. By the time I saddled Red, Ellie was already leading Smoke out of the barn.

She climbed into the saddle and said with a smile, "Where now? Do you want to lead the way?"

"Sure."

"Did I tell you about the vaquero lassoing me that night when I tried to escape?"

"No, tell me."

"I was asleep when they took an ax to the front door. I climbed out the back window and jumped on a horse, bareback. I rode away, but one of them followed me—Ortiz, the one you fought with. He lassoed me from behind and yanked me off the horse. I landed flat on my back. It plumb knocked the wind right out of me."

My blood boiled. A stunt like that could have killed her. I wished now I'd hit the man harder when I had the chance. I tried to keep the anger out of my voice. "I'm sorry, Ellie. It's lucky you weren't hurt."

She laughed lightly. She appeared relaxed and confident on the back of a horse. And the conversation with her soothed me, like a cool breeze on a hot afternoon. The road meandered between two sprawling grape vineyards. Bunches of grapes hung plump and heavy on their vines, while brown cottontail rabbits darted between the rows. Across the valley, a tractor mowed a wheat field, sending up a haze of dust. I took a deep breath, savoring the smell of the harvest in the air. The rocking sensation of my horse's gait lulled me into a trance. I would be content if this moment never ended.

The grass seed field lay ahead. Before I could warn Ellie, Smoke started trotting. I jerked myself to attention as Kim's disaster flashed before my eyes.

Ellie grinned at me over her shoulder. "Do you want to race?"

She pushed Smoke into a gallop before I had a chance to answer. Unlike Kim, she rode as smooth as silk. The only thing I needed to worry about was losing this race.

Red jumped ahead as I released the pressure on the reins and dug my heels into his sides. Ellie's horse moved at an easy gallop, and I quickly caught her. Her horse looked at mine and went faster. Leaning forward, we rode at near break-neck speed, the horses' hooves thundering across the hard-packed earth. I scrambled to keep my hat from flying off my head. With the reins in one hand, I pulled the brim down on my forehead with the other.

I glanced at Ellie and smiled at her obvious enjoyment. When we'd circled the field, she sat back in the saddle and eased her horse into a trot. I followed suit, and our horses pranced side by side.

After a deep breath and a sigh, Ellie said, "That was exhilarating. This field—it's wonderful compared to the rocky trails I'm used to."

I chuckled. "You're hard to catch."

Her melodic laugh rippled through the evening air. "I love this. Thank you, Chase. I'd fancy riding again sometime, if you're willing."

"All right. I have a great place in mind for next time."

The light of day faded, and bats began to dart erratically through the evening sky. We walked our horses back in an easy silence, interrupted only by the chirping of crickets.

When we got to the barn, I flipped the switch, flooding the arena with light.

"Land sakes, it's hard to believe all this light can be had by simply moving that tiny thing. And in a barn of all places," Ellie said as she dismounted. "Grandfather and I never lit a candle or lamp in the barn unless it was absolutely necessary, because of the fire risk."

I loosened the cinch on Ellie's horse's saddle. "I never thought much about that before."

We brushed the sweat off the horses and turned them loose in the pasture. Elbows resting on the top of the fence, we watched as both horses walked, noses to the dirt, searching for a place to roll. In turn, each walked a tiny circle, inspecting the ground before lowering his sweaty body into the dust, then vigorously rolling from side to side. After standing up, the horses shook themselves, sending the fine dust of late summer floating on the breeze.

I glanced at Ellie's profile as she watched the horses. Loose curls fanned the side of her face, and she tossed her head to get them out of her eyes. Impulsively, I reached over and slid a stray wisp of hair behind her ear. My touch startled her.

"Sorry," I mumbled, looking back at the horses. They seemed content as they ate their hay. I felt Ellie's gaze on me for a minute before she leaned forward and rested her chin in her hands.

Not wanting my time with her to end, I resisted going inside the house. I knew what was happening—I was starting to like this girl. But I couldn't. It would never work, especially after what I'd overheard my dad saying. I didn't understand why, but the urge to protect her was undeniable. And I couldn't do that if she wasn't here. So she had to be Jessica's friend, not mine. Ellie would simply be an acquaintance to me, nothing more. I stole another glance in her direction. She didn't seem all that into me anyway. When it came to me, all she probably thought about was the counter and her sense of duty to ensure I took care of it.

Ellie rested her hand on her stomach. "That made me hungry. If you don't mind, I'd fancy some of those Cheerios again."

I laughed "You like those, huh?"

"Oh yes. When the crusts of bread dried out we used to crumble them into a bowl and pour milk and honey over them. But your Cheerios are so much better."

"Okay, Cheerios it is."

We walked inside and sat together at the kitchen table with

our bowls of Cheerios. Jessica and her boyfriend Ryan came in a few minutes later with a quart of ice cream.

"What have you guys been up to?" I asked.

"We saw a movie and brought home ice cream," Jessica said. "Do you want some?"

"Sure."

I introduced Ellie and Ryan to each other while Jessica scooped ice cream. I handed Ryan a bowl and walked back to the table with two bowls of double-fudge brownie ice cream. I sat next to Ellie and set a bowl in front of her. I leaned over to whisper in her ear. "If you like Cheerios, try this."

The icy cold caught her off guard at first. But a few bites later, she looked at me with appreciation. "This is good."

Soon, Jessica dropped her bowl in the sink and filled two glasses with water. She looked out the window. "Parents are home," she said, glancing in my direction. In spite of all the teasing, I knew my sister had my back.

"Okay." I stood up and cleared our cereal bowls from the table, then rinsed them off in the sink. After grabbing the TV remote, I jumped over the back of the sofa. I had just turned on ESPN when our parents walked in the door from the garage. They visited with Jessica and Ryan for a few minutes before going to their bedroom to change out of their nice clothes.

That night in the bathroom, I checked the bruises from my fight. They had all faded, and only a few sickly yellow spots remained. I flexed my muscles in the mirror, admiring the definition across my chest and down my arms. I had definitely changed—it wasn't my imagination. I pulled the gold counter out of my pocket and set it by the sink, smiling. I liked the counter. This Keeper job wasn't too bad.

It was Tuesday, the last day of summer vacation. Jessica, Ellie, and I pretended to get ready for the funeral, but we went to buy school supplies instead. Then we ate lunch and dropped Jessica off at the pool.

When I turned the car onto the highway, Ellie said, "Let's go back today."

I looked at her hopeful expression. "What? You mean back to your cabin?"

"Yes, let's go right now. There's no one at your house, so it's the perfect time to go."

"I've got soccer practice in an hour."

She leaned closer. "That doesn't matter, we'll only be gone a moment. When we come back, it will be as if we were never gone."

"Are you sure?"

"Of course I'm sure."

I thought for a second and shrugged my shoulders. "Okay. Why not?"

TEN
Going Back

Once we got home, Ellie dug our old-fashioned clothes out of Jessica's closet. After handing me my pile with the leather boots on top, she scooted me out the door. I undressed and pulled the new white shirt over my head, then donned the ugly brown pants and the boots. The suspenders were tangled behind my back when Ellie knocked. "Come in," I said.

She opened the door and walked in. Smiling, she took the suspenders from my hand and untwisted them. "I can help you with those. There." She centered each strap on my shoulder and fastened it to the waistband. Then, she picked up my cowboy hat and set it on my head. Her gaze lingered on me for a moment. "You make a nice-looking frontiersman."

I rolled my eyes. "Great, just what I always dreamed of."

"Where's the counter?"

"In my pocket." I pulled it out and handed it to Ellie.

"Touch it so it will light up," she said softly. I cradled her hand in mine as I slid my thumb onto the counter. The magical light appeared at my touch. Ellie studied the symbols on the dials. "You haven't moved anything, have you?"

"No."

She made a slight adjustment to one dial and the globe. "When you were in 1863, were you there for one or two days?"

"One day. I was probably there for a little over twenty-four hours."

"Good. I'm hoping this setting will take us back to the same time we left, only we should appear down the canyon to the southwest, hopefully at the cabin."

"That sounds like a plan. If we're lucky, those guys will still be up the canyon, looking for us."

"Here you go," she said, handing me the open counter. "Press Shuffle, then Go. That's the middle button, then the one on the right."

I held it in the palm of my hand. Ellie rested her hand lightly on my forearm, and I smiled. "Ready?"

She raised her other hand. "No, wait. I remember something. My grandfather said he pictured the place he wanted to go in his mind. So I think you need to imagine the cabin."

"Hmm. That could be a little difficult seeing as how I've never seen your cabin."

"It's a two-room log cabin with a small, plank-sided barn and a corral behind it. It's near the river, but not too close to it. The front door was smashed in by the Mexicans, and the animals are loose in the yard."

"Okay, I'm trying to picture that. Are you ready now?"

"Yes."

I touched the buttons. My bedroom shimmered away, and my insides felt like they were in motion. I dreaded the shuffling-through-time part. We appeared on a remote beach on the western shore of Mexico. I took her hand off my arm and slid it into mine, intertwining my fingers with hers. After all, it was the perfect excuse to hold her hand.

"Ellie, why can't we skip the Shuffle button and go straight to the cabin?" I led her to the wet-packed sand on the water's edge.

She looked into the endless expanse of rolling waves. "I don't know, exactly. But Grandfather insisted it was safer. He said it made him harder to track."

A strong west wind blew in off the Pacific. "Who was tracking him?"

She shook her head. "I don't know. But whoever they are, they may now be tracking you."

I didn't know what to say to that and glanced at her profile before the air shimmered in front of me. Next, we appeared in a dense northeastern forest, I guessed somewhere in Massachusetts by the location of the light on the globe. We pushed through the underbrush, emerging onto a footpath. I followed it until we shimmered to the Deep South. Instantly, we sank up to our ankles in a watery bog. Ellie let go of my hand to lift her skirt out of the mud. I wrapped my fingers around her arm, not wanting to risk being separated from her. While we looked for higher ground, we reappeared in a bustling, turn-of-the-century town. Horse-drawn carriages moved down the street, and a few early automobiles weaved between them, honking their horns.

I stared at the scene playing out in front of me. Ellie let go of her skirt and took hold of my hand. She pulled me to the edge of the street, toward an alley. "We should get out of sight before we disappear," she said.

I hustled to follow her. "Oh yeah."

Stepping into the shadows between two buildings, we disappeared. I felt the bitter cold before the shimmering haze cleared. Snow and ice swirled in the wind, stinging my face. I pulled my cowboy hat lower on my head. I looked at the counter and saw we were somewhere in Canada. The dark of night was descending. The vast tundra took on an ominous feeling as the howls of a wolf pack echoed around us. I turned my back to the wind and pulled Ellie's shivering body next to mine. I wrapped my arms around her back, and she buried her face in my chest. The temperature had to be well below zero, especially with the wind chill. I tucked my head next to her hair, breathing in the delicious smell of her for the first time.

The howls grew closer. Glancing up, I watched the shadowy figures of the wolf pack. A shudder ran down my spine. I looked at the counter. What button could I push to get us out of here?

My eyes smarted, the cold wind triggering tears. Everything blurred. Blinking, I lost track of the wolves. I wiped my eyes with the back of my hand, but the blur I now saw was the shimmer of our next shuffle. The temperature warmed instantly, and the cramping muscles in my back loosened. I breathed a sigh of relief when a cabin surrounded by farm animals appeared before my eyes.

Surrounded by the warmth of the dry, southwestern air, I felt Ellie relax in my arms. Reluctantly, I relinquished my hold on her. "Is this it?" I asked with a smile, feeling proud of myself.

She looked around. "Well, not quite. This is the Johnson's place. My cabin is a mile upriver, but it's not bad for your first try." She reached down and scooped up a handful of dirt. She let the dusty earth slide through her fingers, then rubbed her hands across my chest and down my arms.

I didn't mind her touching me, but I frowned at the mess she'd made of my new shirt. "What did you do that for?"

"You never see a settler this clean unless he's going to Sunday meetings. And today is not Sunday." She finished off by brushing her fingers over my face. "There." She smiled. "That's much better. Follow me."

I stiffened at the creak of a door opening behind me. I stood between Ellie and the cabin. My heart raced when I heard the familiar slide of a shotgun shell entering the gun chamber. A deep voice bellowed, "Boy, what you doin' 'round here?"

I spun to face the man with the shotgun, trying to keep myself positioned between him and Ellie. But she stepped next to me and slid her arm through mine.

"No need to worry, Mr. Johnson. He's with me. Our animals got loose last night, and we're still looking for a couple of goats. I'm sorry. I reckon I should have knocked, but I didn't want to disturb you. We took a quick look to see if they got in with your livestock. But" —she waved her hand toward the corrals— "it looks like we'll need to keep looking."

Smiling, he released the shell and leaned his shotgun against the doorframe. "Why, Miss Ellie, I didn't see you there. Sorry to startle you like that, but a man can't be too careful." He walked toward us. "Are you new to these parts, young man? I haven't seen you around. I'm Benjamin Johnson." The man extended his hand, and I reached out to shake hands with him.

"It's nice to meet you, sir. I'm Chase Harper."

"Let me saddle up a horse, and I'll give you a hand roundin' up those critters."

Ellie shook her head. "No need to bother, Mr. Johnson. Since they aren't here, they're probably upriver from our place. We can look there first, and I'll let you know if we need some help. We barely started looking, and I can't imagine they would have gone far."

He nodded, still eyeing me curiously. "Well, you let me know if there's anything I can do to help. Sure nice to meet you, Mr. Harper."

"Thank you," I said.

Ellie led the way up the rocky drive. I glanced over my shoulder and saw Mr. Johnson still watching us from his doorway.

The midmorning sun sent the mercury rising. Sweat soon dampened my long-sleeved shirt, and my woolen pants were stifling.

"We should have thought to bring water," I said.

"There's water at the cabin. Look there." Ellie pointed to a brown horse on the hill up ahead. "That's our old gelding."

A few minutes later, the gelding followed us as we walked up the trail. My first look at Ellie's grandfather's cabin revealed a neatly stacked woodpile, tools organized and hanging along the wall of the barn, and a mess of loose chickens and goats. A bellowing milk cow and a sorrel paint horse stood in the meager shade of the barn. As Ellie had described, the gate to the corral was open. The old gelding lowered his muzzle into the water trough and slurped the last of the water. Ellie grabbed a metal pail and a small T-shaped wooden stool and walked over to the cow.

"Oh, you poor Molly, let me help you." She plopped the bucket down under the cow's udder and began to milk her. "Chase, do you mind throwing some hay out for the animals, and grain for the chickens? The grain is in the barrel to the right of the barn door, and the hay is stacked along the wall."

I walked into the dim interior of the barn. Slivers of sunlight streaked through the cracks in the wooden planks. I found an old tin can in the grain barrel and filled it. Then I piled my arms with hay. Ellie still sat milking the cow when I finished feeding the other animals.

I stood behind her and eyed the frothy white liquid filling the bucket. "That's impressive."

Without breaking her rhythm, Ellie said, "It's only milk."

"I know. But it's the job you're doing milking that's impressive."

With a start, she looked over her shoulder at me. "I wouldn't consider milking a cow impressive."

I shrugged. "It is to someone who doesn't know how."

She stood and handed me the milk stool. "I can change that. Here then, you have a go at it. I'll show you how."

I wobbled around on the stool, trying to balance my tall frame on something so tiny. When Ellie leaned over my shoulder, I became acutely aware of her cheek next to mine. "Grab a hold of her, and squeeze each finger in turn, starting from the top, like this—one, two, three, four—and then give a little tug." A stream of milk hit the side of the bucket, making a pinging noise. "Now you try."

I took hold with both hands and began the one-two-three-four-tug routine. At first I coaxed only a dribble of milk out of the cow, so Ellie wrapped her fingers around mine, helping me get the feel of it. "Like this. Squeeze a little more firmly."

A few minutes later, a strong stream of milk shot into the bucket. I grinned with pride once I got the hang of it. It wasn't long before Ellie interrupted my concentration. "That's enough milking for her. She needs to start drying up, since there may not be anyone to milk her from now on." Ellie looked around wistfully, as if saying goodbye with her eyes. "I will certainly miss my grandfather and this old place."

"I'm sorry, Ellie. He was like a father to you, wasn't he?"

She sighed. "Yes, he was."

I gave her a few minutes alone with her thoughts, but my impatience sprouted like weeds. This should have taken only a few minutes, but with ending up at her neighbor's and feeding the animals, we'd been here much longer. I looked over the horizon. We seemed to be alone, but I wanted to get moving. I glanced back at Ellie. "We should get the journal and get outta here."

We pumped water into the trough and drank our fill before walking to the cabin. Ellie stepped over splintered sections of the front door. Her attackers had left the ax blade buried in the wood-plank flooring. I pulled it out and leaned it against the doorframe. A small table and three chairs stood against one wall, and a stone hearth and fireplace filled the opposite one. A packed bag sat on the floor inside the door. There was a small bed in the corner and a narrow doorway leading into a back room.

I followed Ellie into the room. A large trunk lay at the foot of the bed, a rustic chest of drawers with a bowl and pitcher on top adorned one wall, and a blurry mirror hung from a nail. Ellie pushed the bed aside. I contemplated this glimpse into the past—Ellie's past.

"Chase, can you help me pry this board up? I think we'll need the ax."

I got the ax and knelt next to her. All the floorboards except one were nailed down. I wedged the blade between the boards and pried up the loose one. Ellie peered into the hole, scrunching her face at what she saw. "Spiders."

"Is the journal down there?" I asked.

"No, but Grandfather's money bag is."

"Here, let me see."

She moved away, and I looked through a mass of cobwebs. A small leather pouch lay in a tin bowl surrounded by dirt and mice droppings. Pushing away the webs, I reached into the hole. "You need a cat," I said.

"We used to have one, but Grandfather said he disappeared last winter."

I pulled my arm out and brushed the cobwebs and mice droppings off the bag before handing it to her. The heavy bag jingled with the sound of large coins.

She leaned away from me, pointing at my elbow. "Thank you. Um, spider—on your arm."

I brushed the spider and the cobwebs off my shirt and stood up, then reached my hand down to Ellie and pulled her to her feet. "We should hurry," I said. "What about the journal?"

"It's buried under the blue hearthstones."

I followed her into the main room. Remembering the tools I'd seen hanging on the side of the barn, I asked, "Should I get a shovel?"

Ellie picked up a broom and swept away the ashes. "Yes, thank you."

I walked to the barn, taking in the sight of the animals eating. The air buzzed with the sound of flies, and the horses swished their tails at their tiny tormentors. I broadened my view as I walked back to the cabin with the shovel. I looked over the surrounding hills and the trail leading toward the breathtaking Zion Canyon.

"No. It can't be," I muttered when I saw a plume of dust following a rider down the canyon. I sprinted toward the cabin and leaped over the wreckage of the front door. "We've gotta hurry. We're going to have company."

Ellie's face paled. "Dig up these two stones." She pointed with her foot. I pried two large blue stones loose with the shovel and lifted them out of the way, then removed three shovel's full of hard, packed dirt. Ellie watched out the window. "It's one of the vaqueros," she whispered.

My shovel hit metal as I heard his horse trotting into the yard. He would realize someone was here when he saw the fresh feed spread out for the animals. Ellie watched my progress. I dropped to my knees and scraped the dirt away from the top of the box.

Ellie laid her hand on my arm. "We should go. We'll have to come back. He's here now."

I grabbed the fire poker and dug the dirt away from the sides. "We can't go now. He'll find the journal if we leave it like this. I've almost got it."

Ellie picked up a smaller shovel. "Let me finish, then, and you go watch him." She sounded nervous. Wedging the tool into the crevice of earth alongside the metal box, she worked to free it.

With the fire poker in my hand, I stood near the window. I peered through a crack in the muslin curtain. The older vaquero, Miguel, dismounted his horse and pulled his rifle out of his gun scabbard. His eyes scanned the barnyard and then settled on the cabin. He stood behind his horse while he loaded his weapon. Then, holding the rifle at his shoulder, he darted to the corner of the cabin. He worked his way along the outside wall to the opening left by the battered door.

I wiped one sweaty palm at a time across the front of my shirt. My first priority: get the rifle away from him. I tiptoed to the entrance, afraid my thundering heart would betray me. I pressed my back against the wall and waited.

His shadow paused at the window before moving on. The black barrel of the rifle came through the doorway. Once his left hand cleared the doorframe, I shoved the barrel away from Ellie. The rifle exploded, blasting a hole through the roof of the cabin. My ears throbbed, and for a moment the world fell silent. I fought for the rifle with my left hand while I battered his arms with the iron poker. Finally breaking his hold on the rifle, I yanked it away from him.

But as soon as the rifle fell from his grasp, Miguel drew his sword. It flashed in my face. I stepped back again and again. It was all I could do to parry his blows with the butt of the rifle and the fire poker. I retreated as far as I could. Behind me, I heard Ellie working frantically to release the box. When I found a rhythm to Miguel's swinging, I began to block the sword with the rifle while jabbing at him with the fire poker. After a few solid blows, I gained ground, slowly forcing him across the room.

I heard Ellie's frustrated grunt as she pounded on the metal box, trying to free it from its earthen grave. Miguel cursed me in Spanish. When I backed him into the wall next to the table, he picked up a chair and threw it at me. I flung my right arm up to block the blow. The chair hit me, and pain shot down my arm—my funny bone. Miguel grabbed the next chair and threw it. I started to turn away, but I didn't react quickly enough, and the chair slammed into my side.

I staggered away, keeping my focus on the flash of his sword blade. It frustrated me that I held a rifle but didn't have the time or the know-how to load it. It obviously wasn't one of the modern rifles I was used to—it looked like a muzzleloader. With numb fingers, I struggled to hold onto the fire poker. Apparently sensing my weakness, the vaquero advanced with increased fury. I gave way as he backed me toward Ellie, relentlessly attacking with his sword. I kicked the chairs away from my feet, nearly falling over them. My breathing came in ragged gasps now. And so did his.

Miguel spoke with a heavy accent. "Why are you fighting me, señor? My fight is not with you, amigo. I only wish to speak with the girl."

The pain in my hand lessened, and the feeling came back. I growled at Miguel. He and Ortiz had kidnapped Ellie, and Ortiz would've taken advantage of her if I hadn't stopped him. Neither of them would ever touch her or speak to her again if I had anything to do about it. "Then your fight *is* with me, amigo," I said to Miguel.

With renewed determination, I stabbed at him with the fire poker and swung the butt of the rifle toward him. His sword glanced off the knuckles of my right hand, slicing through the skin as I slammed the rifle into his head. He stumbled backward and went down on one knee. He looked dazed but kept his sword at the ready.

I stared in shock at the deep gash. Blood spilled across the top of my hand and down my fingers, dripping onto the wooden floor.

I heard movement behind me but couldn't risk taking my eyes off our attacker to see what Ellie was doing. "Ellie, can we go yet?"

"I've got it," she said excitedly. She ran behind me, slid her hand in my pocket, and pulled out the counter, then flipped it open.

The sight of the counter clearly infuriated Miguel. Rushing toward us, he yelled, "You have it? How can *you* have it?"

I backed Ellie toward the cabin door and threw the fire poker at him. I pushed the Shuffle button and then the Return button. In the shimmer of the upcoming shuffle, I saw Miguel's sword come toward me. Again I raised the rifle to intercept the blow, but it never struck. A wave of motion sickness twisted my gut as Ellie and I appeared in another desert. We were welcomed by the sight of dusty, brown dirt dotted with sprawling eucalyptus trees and kangaroos.

"Australia," I mumbled, pocketing the counter. No need to check our location this time.

Ellie looked wide-eyed at the blood dripping from my fingertips. "You're hurt." She lifted my hand, and her face paled. "There's so much blood! I'm sorry. We should have left when he first came." The distress in her voice deepened. "We need to stop the bleeding. Hold on to me."

I put the rifle in my bloody hand and took hold of her arm with my clean one. She bent over and began ripping a piece of fabric from under her skirt. She glanced at my bleeding hand as she worked. I nodded toward the bag she set on the ground between her ankles. "What's that for?"

"It's nothing really, just my traveling bag from Boston. I never had a chance to unpack it."

I enjoyed watching her fuss over me until a look of guilt and anguish crossed her face. "Chase, I'm so sorry. It's my fault. I shouldn't have wasted time with the animals. And we should have left when we saw Miguel coming. Or perhaps I shouldn't have made you go back there at all. How selfish of me."

I interrupted her. "Ellie, it's nothing but a scratch. It might need stitches, but that's no big deal. Quit apologizing. As I remember, it was me who wanted to stay and get the journal, not you."

She stood with a piece of fabric torn from her skirt as the familiar shimmer surrounded us. Next, we appeared in the mountains—maybe the Rocky Mountains, from the looks of the scenery. We stood in a grove of aspen trees while Ellie wrapped my bleeding hand and tied the cloth in a knot. She still looked worried but had at least stopped apologizing.

"Thanks," I said. "Where's the journal?"

"It's in my bag."

We shuffled through a dense jungle, sending the monkeys hanging from the trees into fits of screaming. Next, we walked along a cold beach in the dark, listening to the roar of the crashing surf. Our final shuffle placed us next to a modern highway on the edge of a cornfield. A harvester roared toward us, gobbling up the cornstalks in huge swaths. I looked down the road and saw a line of cars headed our way. Not wanting anyone to get a close-up look at us, I pulled Ellie into the field. The roar of the harvester grew louder. We walked farther into the corn, bending over to conceal our movement. The engine on the harvester shut down as it pulled alongside the spot where we'd entered the field. But I wasn't worried. I expected to be gone any second, and the counter didn't disappoint me.

My bedroom materialized, and I stood up straight. Releasing my hold on Ellie's arm, I breathed a sigh of relief. Then I collapsed on the edge of my bed. "That was intense."

Ellie left my room, calling over her shoulder, "I'll return in a moment." I lay back on the bed, resting the rifle across my chest. I let my eyes close for only a second.

ELEVEN
A Stitch in Time

I ran through the dark, surrounded by trees. Someone was chasing me, closing in. To stop meant certain death, so I kept moving, clutching the old rifle as I ran. Was it even loaded? Panic struck me—I didn't know where Ellie was. I'd lost her. I struggled to remember what had happened. Where was I? I searched the darkness, trying to make sense of things, but my memory failed me.

I felt someone near, watching me. I heard footsteps coming closer. Whipping the rifle to my shoulder, I bolted upright.

"Whoa there, cowboy. It's only me."

Blinking my eyes in the afternoon sunlight, I saw Ellie standing in the doorway of my bedroom, holding a bowl and a towel, her other arm thrown in front of her in a defensive position. She stared back at me with a shocked expression.

The gun barrel came into focus, and I realized I had the rifle pointed at her. I lowered the weapon and shoved it behind me on the bed. "Sorry about that." I rubbed my eyes and rested my forehead in my good hand. "I was dreaming. How long did I sleep?"

She stayed in the doorway. "Maybe twenty minutes. I can take care of that hand for you if you'd like."

I waved her into the room. "Thanks."

She unwound the blood-soaked cloth from my fingers. The last layer stuck to the bloody flesh. She lowered my hand into the bowl of lukewarm water. The water softened the clotted blood, and she eased the fabric out of the wound and then gently cleaned it. In spite of the painful throbbing in my hand, I melted at her touch. She gave the wound a thorough inspection once she'd cleaned it.

She pointed to the deepest part of the cut. "Do you want me to stitch it closed? I think it would heal better if it were stitched."

"You know how to do that?"

"I do hate the sight of blood, but I've stitched up my grandfather before. There were a few times he came back injured after using the counter."

Blood oozed from the cut, and I knew it needed stitches. I wrapped the clean towel around my hand, applying pressure. I considered all the questions I would have to answer at the emergency room. Plus, I'd have to face my mom's scrutiny. They would undoubtedly page her when I checked in. If I'd been working construction today, it would have been an easy lie. The sheets of metal we used for siding and roofing could slice skin as easily as a blade. But today I had supposedly run a few errands and attended a funeral. Only a complete idiot would accidentally cut his own hand this badly. Not one plausible excuse for the injury came to mind.

I decided. "Okay, stitch it up."

"Certainly. I'll get a needle and—"

I rose to my feet. "Wait. I think we've got something in the first-aid kit." Over the years, my mom had accumulated quite a collection of medical supplies, one of the perks of working in a hospital. With my good hand, I rummaged through the plastic container. At the bottom, I found it: a package containing one sterile needle and some suture thread. I returned to my bedroom and handed it to Ellie.

"Do you have any laudanum or whiskey? You'll want something to dull the pain."

"No, we don't drink," I answered, "but I've got Tylenol or Advil."

She shrugged her shoulders. "Get whatever you have. You're going to want it."

I went to the medicine cupboard and popped two Tylenol in my mouth. I stuck my head under the faucet and swallowed the pills. I dug through the first-aid kit again and pulled out some alcohol wipes, antibiotic ointment, and Band-Aids before returning to my room.

I handed her the alcohol wipes. "The needle's sterile, but you should clean your hands."

Ellie looked at the small packets. "What do you mean? What's this?"

I ripped open one and wiped it across her fingers. Civil War horror stories spun through my mind: wounded soldiers treated in unsanitary conditions with the same instruments that had been used on every other soldier that day. It was another reminder of what a vastly different world Ellie had come from. Tidbits of knowledge I took for granted would be lifesaving revelations in her day. "Sterilize. Kill the germs. Clean it," I said. "The needle was sterilized before it was packaged. But our hands carry germs. Alcohol kills the germs that cause infection. You know, like gangrene."

"Oh, I see." She took the alcohol wipe from me. "I can do that," she said, scrubbing both her hands.

When I started opening the packaging around the needle, she took that too. "Allow me."

Holding the needle, she picked up my wounded hand. "You might want to look away while I do this. Are you ready?"

I clenched my teeth and vowed not to scream. "No, but yes."

My hand involuntarily pulled back as the needle pierced my skin, each stitch tugging on my tender flesh. Sweat beaded on my forehead. I clamped my mouth shut, battling the urge to yank my hand away from her. Despite my best efforts, a few errant groans escaped my clenched teeth.

Ellie finished quickly, although it had felt like forever. She exhaled a breath I hadn't noticed her holding, and her face looked pale when she released my hand. "There you go. Should be good as new in a couple of weeks."

I explained the purpose of antibiotic ointment while I squeezed a generous portion from the tube across the long cut. I showed her how to open the Band-Aids. She covered the cut with them, hiding the injury.

She glanced at the clock. "What time is your soccer?" She said the word "soccer" like it was in a foreign language.

"Shoot! I need to leave in ten minutes." I started trying to unbutton the suspenders, but the throbbing pain in my hand and the mass of crisscrossing Band-Aids made it difficult to bend my fingers.

"Stand up, and I'll help you," she said.

I pulled my aching body upright and watched her unfasten the suspenders. She pulled my shirt over my head and slid it carefully off my bandaged hand.

"Oh my," Ellie gasped. "Does that hurt?" She touched the reddish-purple bruise spreading across my rib cage. I held perfectly still as a shiver shot through my body.

I smiled at her. "Yeah, it hurts . . . a little."

A concerned frown darkened her expression. "Chase, I'm so sorry. I always seem to be causing you injury."

"Ellie, you've got to stop apologizing. I didn't see you swinging swords and chairs at me. You can't take the blame for everything on yourself. Don't worry about it. It's nothing a little time won't heal."

She let out a deep breath and nodded. "I won't mention it again." She set my shirt on the edge of the bed. With a twinkle in her eye, she glanced at my pants. "That's all the help you get. You can leave the dirty clothes on your bed, and I'll put them in that washer contraption for you while you're gone."

I stared after her as she left, then shut my door and took off the cursed wool pants. I tossed them on top of the bloodstained shirt, wondering how long it would take for my legs to stop itching. I pulled on gym shorts and a sleeveless T-shirt I had taken a pair of scissors to. Sitting on the edge of the bed, I put on soccer socks and my cleats. I checked my bag for shin guards and my ball, and then dropped in the counter and my cell phone. I jogged downstairs and grabbed my keys. "See you later," I called as I pulled the door shut behind me.

I couldn't wait to get home and see Ellie's grandfather's journal. After all that effort, I still hadn't gotten a look at it. I went through the monotony of practice. The throbbing in my hand never relented. I put in minimal effort and played conservatively to protect my battered body. My coach yelled at me in frustration, no doubt disappointed after my brilliant display of talent the day before. Two hours later, he announced the end of practice with a shrill blast of his whistle.

My fight with Miguel haunted me while I drove home. Scenes from the encounter had flashed through my mind all afternoon. I marveled that I'd walked away with so few injuries. I would bet he was an accomplished swordsman. Likely only my enhanced strength and quickness from the counter allowed me to momentarily get the upper hand and escape.

Kelly Nelson

—◆—

"How was the funeral?" Mom asked as we sat down to dinner that night.

Jessica, Ellie, and I exchanged quick glances before Jessica answered. "It was nice. Funerals are always sad, but I thought it was nicely done. Didn't you think so, Chase?"

I looked down at my plate of food. "Yeah, it was a really nice funeral. I'm glad we went."

Ellie nodded her agreement, and we all breathed a sigh of relief when Mom and Dad moved onto the next topic: the need to repaint the house next summer.

The rest of dinner passed uneventfully until we began clearing off the dishes. My mom grabbed my wrist. "What happened to your hand? Is that a bruise on your arm? What happened to you?"

"It's nothing," I lied, pulling my hand away from her. "Coach had me play goalie today, and somebody's cleats got my hand, then I got kicked. Don't worry, Mom. I'm not that good of a goalie, so he won't play me in that position again."

A stab of guilt sliced through my gut. I didn't lie. I never had. But in the last five days, I'd told more lies than I could count, and I didn't like it.

She walked to the sink and started on the dishes. "Gosh, I didn't think soccer was supposed to be such a rough sport."

I sighed. "It usually isn't, Mom."

"What do you have planned tonight?" she asked. "I guess the girls are going to a movie."

I put the salt-and-pepper shakers in the cupboard. "I've got a book to read."

Mom stopped doing the dishes and turned around to look at me. "It's the last night of summer vacation, and you're going to read a book? Are you feeling okay?" She reached her hand out to touch my forehead, but I ducked under her arm. She chuckled. "What is this great book that's got you reading the night before school starts?"

I rolled the tablecloth into a wad. "It's sort of a sci-fi, time-travel Western, I think."

"What's it called?"

"Um . . . *The Journal.*"

My mom returned to loading the dishwasher. "Hmm. Sounds interesting."

The girls were upstairs getting ready to leave. My mom was right—Jessica had invited Ellie to go to a movie with her and her friends. My sister's initial distrust of Ellie had faded, and the two of them now acted like friends. As I walked past their room, Ellie came out with a tattered, water-stained, leather-bound book.

"I heard you talking to your mom. Here it is." Her lips curved into a hint of a smile as she handed me the journal. "I looked at it this afternoon. It's packed with information. I think you'll find it quite useful."

I raised the book in salute. "Thanks. Have fun at the movie tonight."

"I reckon I will."

TWELVE
The Journal

I walked into my room and locked the door. After stacking my pillows on the bed for a backrest, I turned on my reading lamp. The book in my hand looked ancient. Two stiff leather straps tied the cover closed, and when I opened the book, the yellowed parchment inside crackled at my touch. The handwritten title on the first page read, "Journal of Amyot Williams, born March 19, 1783."

Turning the title page, I began to read.

I, Amyot Williams, do make a record of my past history and travels. I do also endeavor to leave instructions concerning the magical counter which came into my possession when I was but a lad. I leave these instructions lest my future posterity should endure the tribulations of being lost in time as I was.

I skipped over the lengthy family history, hunting for information on the counter.

I contemplated the curious device. Upon touching the buttons, I found myself transported to a strange place. That one action began a series of life-and-death struggles as I found myself lost. I continued to spin the dials and push a combination of buttons, but no action on my part returned me to my home. I bounced from place to place. Food and shelter became my primary concern. You can't imagine my relief when I appeared in a populated section of the world. Upon inquiring as to my whereabouts, I determined I had been transported to another time. I was in 1650, whereas I was born in 1783. I studied the symbols on the counter, isolating one dial at a time. Thereby, I discovered the first four dials represented the year, the next two the month, and the last two, the day of the month.

I estimate my wanderings in time spanned a year. During that time, I feared for my mother and worried she would be distressed at my disappearance so soon after my father's death. When I had identified the English equivalent of each symbol on the counter, I found my way home to 1796. I returned myself to the same day I had departed. I expected to have grown older, but other than my tattered clothing and longer hair, I had not aged during my absence. However, I found after using the counter that I was stronger and faster than ever before. While lost, I had gotten myself out of scrapes with men twice my age. I later learned the magic encased within the counter transfers to its Keeper and enhances the Keeper's abilities.

As soon as I returned to my own time, I began increasing in both stature and strength. Soon, I did the work of a full-grown man. I took over providing for my mother and sister. When I was not working, I explored as many time portals as I could, never tiring of the new sights and sounds around me.

I paused in my reading, leaning back against the headboard. That explained what I suspected about my increased speed, my superior strength, and other changes to my physique. Credit for escaping Miguel's sword should definitely go to the magic of the counter, not me. I buried my nose in the book and continued.

Some months later, the Master Keeper summoned me to his fortress. It was there I received comprehensive training in the history of the counters. The Master revealed that I am a Keeper—the Protector's Keeper. I feel I am forbidden to write more on this matter, but it suffices me to say that each new Keeper of the counter will be summoned to meet the Master, as I was.

I swallowed. *Interesting. Ominous.* I didn't know how I felt about the prospect of being summoned. What did Amyot mean by Protector's Keeper? And what couldn't he say? In this modern age, where could you hide a fortress? Had the Master Keeper summoned Amyot to another time? Maybe someday I would discover what he meant.

I turned my attention back to the scrawl of words on the page.

December 24, 1815: I married Prudence West in 1804. Our first child was a son, George, born May 2, 1805. We had four other children, daughters, all of whom died in infancy.

I skipped ahead, looking for anything related to the counter.

I built a cabin near the Virgin River and irrigated a small patch of earth on which to grow a garden. So far, I have successfully avoided detection. During my lifetime, I have either been hunted by or helped to hunt three different Sniffers, whose sole purpose was to kill a Keeper and steal his or her counter. We, the Keepers, defeated each one in turn, escaping with our lives and our counters, which was no small feat.

The more I read, the more questions I had. What was a Sniffer? Were there more of them? Who and where were the other Keepers? A name caught my eye, and I continued reading.

October 3, 1855: George grew into a fine young man, although neglecting to marry until he was thirty-eight. His young bride delivered a beautiful baby girl almost two years later on May 28, 1845, named Ellen Elizabeth Williams. She was at once the light of both her father's and grandfather's lives. Unfortunately, her mother passed away while she was quite young.

It came as a bitter blow when George, my last remaining child, fell ill. No amount of doctoring on our part could turn the tide of fate, and I lost him to the ravages of typhoid fever. It was fortunate I had Ellie. Had the responsibility of her care not fallen on me, the grief of my loss may have drowned me. Instead, I showered my affections on my dear granddaughter, who was left an orphan at the age of eight. The prospect of raising her delighted me, although I felt uneducated in how to properly nurture and care for a young girl.

January 18, 1860: Years have passed since I've written. Ellie is growing into a fine young lady. Fearing that she wouldn't receive a proper education from an old man in the western territories, I sent her to spend time with my sister, Lydia, in Boston. There Ellie will attend four years of formal schooling. Unable to bear the thought of being separated from her for so long, I use the counter each week to visit her in Boston, as I used to frequently visit her and her father in New York when she was young. I am quite fond of the meals we share each Sunday evening.

Before Ellie left for school, I told her about the counter and my life's mission and obligation to protect it, for only by keeping it safe would I keep myself, and our way of life, safe as well. She has agreed to take the counter at my death. I made arrangements to stow it for safekeeping in an emergency, and there she can retrieve it at a later date. I have included at the back of this book the meanings of the ancient symbols found on the counter. I do this for my dearest Ellie and whomever may follow her in keeping the counter.

Now I realized why she was so upset when she first learned I'd used the counter. Her grandfather had obviously meant for her to have it, not some stranger.

May 19, 1863: I fear this may be the last time I write. I am an old man now, at least eighty years old in my own time, plus all the time I spent in other time portals, during which my physical body did not age. It has been a long life, and at times I feel to welcome the quiet of the grave. My little corner of the world has seen an influx of settlers, and I long for the solitude I once enjoyed. I look forward to my dear Ellie coming home in two weeks.

Unfortunately, rumor has it there are some Mexicans looking for me. I am uncertain if these men work for my longtime rival, Chavez, or if it is the work of a Sniffer. In St. George they were inquiring as to my whereabouts, and a friend passed them false information regarding someone sighting me in Texas. I hope they move on before Ellie returns. If not, I'll leave her the counter and lead them as far away from her as possible. She won't like my plan, but my first priority must be her safety as well as the counter's. I reckon I'll encourage her to return to Boston in that event. But for now I seal up this record, hoping it finds its way safely into the hands of my dearest Ellie.

I love you, Ellie, and wish only for your continued safety and happiness in the years to come.

With love,
Grandfather

I closed my eyes to rest for a moment, sobered by the life that had passed before me as I'd read the words of the journal. Amyot had lost four children and then his wife. He'd watched his only grandchild lose both her parents. He had probably built with his own hands everything I had seen in and around his cabin.

My phone vibrated in my pocket. It was probably Kim. I'd answer her later. I turned to the back of the book. Now for the crucial information: the symbols and their meaning. I removed the counter from my pocket and flipped it open. The eerie blue light illuminated the symbols. As he had promised earlier in the journal, Ellie's grandfather had drawn a diagram of the counter at the end of the book. Each button and symbol was labeled and explained.

The symbols on the three buttons were described in detail.

The first button on the left, denoted by double arrows pointing left, is the Return button. Pushing this button will return you to the last place the counter was used at approximately the time it was used—in other words, the time and location you came from.

The middle button, denoted by two circular, interlocking arrows pointing in opposite directions, is the Shuffle button. Pressing this button randomly shuffles you through five different locations and times. I find I am in each time and location from one to five minutes. Shuffling is especially important if you are concerned about being followed. The counter leaves a signature in the time portals you travel through. When you shuffle before going where you want to end up, you make it more difficult for someone to track you—not impossible, but difficult. The less time you are in a particular time portal, the less distinct is the signature of your counter. After the unpleasant experience of being chased for the first time, I made a resolution to always shuffle my travels. You never know who might be watching you. Another method I've found for disguising my tracks is shuffling through different times in the same location. This overlaps the signatures, leaving a garbled mess that is difficult for a Sniffer to decipher. I would impress upon you the importance of erring on the side of caution, as a Keeper's life is irreversibly connected to the safety of his counter.

The final button on the far right, denoted by an outline of an eagle's head, is the Go button. It will take you to the date highlighted on the number dials and the location pinpointed on the globe. Always push the Shuffle button before pushing either the Go or Return buttons.

The place where you intend to arrive can be influenced by your thoughts. Considering the smallness of the globe, it is nearly impossible to place the light on the exact location desired; therefore, you must picture the place in your mind. By adding the energy of your mind to the power of the counter, you will gain more control over your destination.

Finally, the number dials. Each symbol corresponds to a number.

- *Zero is one raised dot.*

∪ *One is a curved line in the shape of a half circle, in a bowl-shaped position.*

< *Two is two curved lines forming a V tipped onto its side, with the point to the left.*

\\ *Three is three straight lines of varying lengths lined up from smallest to largest to form a triangle.*

☐ *Four is four straight lines joined in a square.*

■ *Five is a square with a raised and darkened center.*

⌒ *Six is one curved line in the shape of an upside-down half circle.*

❯ *Seven is two curved lines joined to form a V pointing to the right.*

⚡ *Eight is three lines joined to form a lightning bolt with a small arrow pointing downwards.*

⟁ *Nine is four straight lines joined to form the shape of a ladder.*

The first four dials represent the year. The next two dials are the month of the year, with January denoted as "01," and so forth. The final two dials are the day of the month. Timing within a particular day can be controlled with your mind, the same as location, or you can make an adjustment in the day dial. Putting the dial halfway between two numbers will place you in the middle of that day. As you picture the location you desire, picture it at the time you wish to appear.

Don't worry if at first you are unsuccessful. With a little practice, it becomes a natural part of using the counter. However, I would offer a suggestion to you: practice now to become comfortable with all of its properties. You need to be proficient in using the counter before you are actually called on to use it for your protection or to protect and save another.

What did Amyot mean by "save another"? Maybe there was more to this than I thought! I studied the symbols and their meanings, committing them to memory. I spun each dial and practiced setting it to different dates. But I was too tired to actually go anywhere. Each trip back in time had been a physically exhausting experience, ending in a fight. As long as I could find the Shuffle button in an emergency, I should be able to get away.

The phone vibrated again. This time I slid it open to respond. *Kim. Just as I thought.* I read the text. "Where r u? We r getting ice cream. Do you want 2 come? I can pick u up."

I thought for a minute. I was tired, I was sore, and I expected Ellie and Jessica to be home soon. I'd rather talk to Ellie when she got home than go into town with Kim and our friends. I texted her, "Go ahead w/out me. I have 2 get stuff ready 4 school tmrw. C u then." I knew she wouldn't be happy.

Sure enough, my phone instantly buzzed with a reply. "Party pooper. Oh well, I'll c u tmrw. Look 4 me @ lunch. Goodnite Chase." That didn't need a reply, so I slid my phone shut.

Might as well get ready for school. I opened my closet and dug through the piles of jeans, shirts, and shoes until I uncovered my school backpack. I put in my school supplies. The shopping trip this morning now seemed like a distant memory—so much had happened since then. I packed my soccer gear and zipped the backpack closed. I'd get my water bottle in the morning.

I paced a semicircle, back and forth, around my bed. What should I have Ellie do tomorrow? Would my parents notice if she stayed home? Would the school let her attend classes if she showed up? I weighed the different options, finally deciding to take her to school. I'd talk with the office staff and explain the situation. Well, not the real situation, but a good, convincing situation that would hopefully have them registering her on the promise of a forthcoming birth certificate and Social Security number.

With that settled, I got Ellie's things ready for school. I found an extra backpack and put in a binder, notebook paper, pencils, and pens. I set her pack next to mine. The flash of headlights moved across my wall as a car pulled into the driveway. I shoved the counter and my phone back in my pocket, hid the journal under my pillow, and walked down to the kitchen.

Ellie and Jessica walked in with big smiles. I couldn't resist grinning back. "You liked the movie?" I asked.

Jessica hung her keys on the rack and opened the fridge. "It was awesome."

Ellie shook her head in amazement. "I've never seen anything like it. So big, so lifelike. It felt like the screen would swallow me up, and I'd be right there in the movie. And the sound was everywhere." She lowered her voice and leaned closer. "It's a far cry from the opera house in Boston, where one is always straining to hear clearly."

I chuckled. "I'm glad you liked it." Before she could leave, I kept talking. "I think you should come to school with us tomorrow. I'm hoping we can get you registered even though we don't have everything they'll need. Maybe if we tell them a good story, they'll let you start. What do you think?"

She smiled. "It sounds like you have it all planned out."

"I hope so. What do we have to lose? The worst they could say is no, right? If that's the case, I'll bring you back here. By then my parents will be at work, so they won't ask questions. They need to think you're at school or they'll get suspicious."

THIRTEEN
High School

I woke up twenty minutes before my alarm was set to go off. For the first time in years, I felt nervous about starting school. I listened to the birds outside my window while I tried to unravel the nervous twist in my gut. I wasn't nervous for myself but for Ellie. My worry over her had caused me to wake up suddenly, my heart racing.

I thought of all the things I hadn't told her about. The biggest one: computers. She would never pull off the charade of a high school senior without knowing about e-mail, Microsoft Word, and the Internet. What about all those lost years between 1863 and 2011? She'd asked me who won the Civil War and when. But what high school senior doesn't know about World War I or World War II? I didn't even think she knew who the current president of the United States was. The list went on and on. Maybe it wasn't such a good idea to take her to school. What if people asked too many questions? It could be a nightmare for her.

It didn't take long before the overprotective part of my personality won out over the worried side. I wanted to be able to see Ellie and know she was all right. Besides, she would never learn to be comfortable in 2011 if she hid at my house all the time.

Kelly Nelson

With that settled, I sat up and turned off the alarm. I wouldn't need it. Running my fingers through my messy hair, I winced as the movement sent a throb of fresh pain through my hand. I would have fun trying to write today. After showering, I popped two Advil and grabbed four more Band-Aids and the antibacterial ointment. I pulled off the soggy, old Band-Aids and studied the neat stitches in my skin. I thought about putting on the Band-Aids with my left hand, but it was too good an excuse to go bug the girls. A minute later, I knocked on the bathroom door.

"What?" Jessica said.

"Is Ellie in there?"

"Yeah, what do want?"

"Tell her I need her help," I said quietly. "Please."

I faintly made out the sound of Jessica saying something through the second door leading to the shower. "She said she'll be right out."

"Thanks, Sis."

Soon, Ellie opened the bathroom door, drying her hair with a towel. Her cheeks had a rosy glow from the hot shower. She shook her head, and damp curls rippled around her shoulders, framing her beautiful face.

"I love your shower. All that hot water is utterly divine. It sure beats heating water over the fire and hauling it in buckets to the tub." She paused, looking me in the eyes. When I didn't say anything, she asked, "Are you all right?"

I finally looked down at my hand and remembered what I was doing. I stumbled over my words, wondering how she managed to leave me so dumbstruck. "I . . . uh . . . Could you put on these Band-Aids for me, again . . . please . . . and this too?" I said, dumping the Band-Aids and ointment into her hand.

"Certainly. Let's sit down."

I followed her into Jessica's room and sat next to her on the edge of the bed. The effect she had on me was downright embarrassing. How often had she left me speechless, grasping for words? She held my wounded hand and began with the ointment.

Pulling myself together, I said, "I packed some school supplies for you in a backpack. I realized there are a lot of things I haven't told you about. Like computers and—"

"Oh, that's all right," Ellie interrupted me. "Jessica started showing me how to use it. She set up a mail thing for me, and I've even practiced a bit."

"She did?"

Ellie smiled. "Yes, and she borrowed books from the library for me to read. I've been learning my history, or should I say, what might have been my future. She's teaching me the names and faces of movie stars and singers. She went through everyone in her yearbook and told me what to expect from the people I'll meet at your school. I already feel as if I know some of them."

I watched Ellie's self-assured expression as she gently pressed the last Band-Aid into place. "My sister really did all that?"

"Yes, she's been wonderful."

I stood and walked to the door. "Good. I guess you're better prepared than I thought." I paused, leaning back into the room. "But who's the president?"

"Barack Obama," she said.

I smiled and gave her the thumbs-up sign before I left to let her finish getting ready.

I drove the truck into the school parking lot a half hour before we needed to be in class. Jessica, Ellie, and I went straight to the office. Jessica had worked in the office as an aide last year and agreed to be the spokesperson for our crusade.

I watched in amazement as she spun a vibrant tale of Ellie's past that would tug at anyone's heartstrings. The woman in the office, who had obviously appreciated all Jessica's hard work the year before, didn't stand a chance. Jessica's story sucked her in, and before we knew it she had Ellie added to three of Jessica's classes and two of mine. And Ellie had one class on her own.

The counselor handed Ellie her schedule. "Now, don't forget to bring in your birth certificate and Social Security number as soon as you can find them. We'll need to have them soon." We left multiple promises with her that the birth certificate and Social Security number would be located.

Hilhi has an outdoor campus with each department in a separate building. We gave Ellie a tour of the school and helped her find her locker. It took her a few tries to get the hang of when to turn the knob left and when to turn it right.

I left Ellie with Jessica and went to find my locker and my first-period class. Jessica and Ellie had advisory, first, and third periods together. Ellie had second and fifth period with me. For fourth period, she would be by herself.

During first period, I watched the clock tick by the time. When the bell rang, I rushed out the door. I worked my way through the crowded breezeway and met Jessica and Ellie coming out of their first class. "How did it go?" I anxiously asked them.

"It was IB math studies," Jessica said. "How exciting can that be?"

Ellie smiled. "It went fine, Chase. Now where?"

I pointed down the hall. "This way."

That morning I had added Advanced U.S. History to my schedule, replacing Automotive Technology. I needed a better grasp of history if I was going to be using the counter, plus it gave me another class with Ellie. The teacher assigned seats based on our last names, so I sat two rows away from Ellie. We left class with a heavy textbook and an assignment to read the first chapter. I walked her to the gym for her third-period class.

When I opened the door for her, I said, "You're going to have to wear shorts in there."

She sent me a confused look. "What? Shorts?"

"Yup, I thought I'd warn you." I chuckled. "Good luck with that."

She huffed. "Oh, Chase." With her head held high, she marched into the gym.

My third period was English. At the end of class, I had a copy of *The Grapes of Wrath* and an assignment to read the first two chapters in the next week.

As I walked into the lunchroom, I located Jessica and Ellie sitting at a table with Jessica's friends. I got a tray of food. But before I could walk across the room to Ellie, Kim intercepted me. She steered me toward a table where Adam sat with our group of friends. Seeing their faces pricked my conscience. I had neglected my friends the past week. Kim wrapped her arm around mine. "We're sitting over here. We missed you last night."

I set my food down next to Adam. "Yeah, sorry. I had some stuff to do before school. Adam, how you doin'?"

He picked up his burger and pointed across the room. "I'm great, dude. Does Jessica still have that girl staying at your house?"

It annoyed me that he called her "that girl." "Yeah, but her name is Ellie."

Kim gave us a questioning look. "Chase, you didn't tell me you had company. Who's staying with you?"

I swallowed my bite of food. "A friend of Jessica's."

Kim looked across the room at Jessica and Ellie before changing the subject. "So, the homecoming game is in four weeks."

That got Adam's attention, and he launched into an analysis of the team we would be playing. I ate my food in relative silence, occasionally staring across the room at Jessica and Ellie's table. I could see Ellie perfectly. She looked at ease and even contributed to the conversation.

"What are you looking at?" Kim asked.

I turned my head toward Kim. "Just thinking," I said. I gave her my full attention, flashing my best smile in her direction. "Are the cheerleaders going to come to any of our soccer games, or are you only football fans?"

She took the bait. "We'll have to see about that. If you make it to state, we'll be there for sure, I promise."

"Done. I'll be watching for you on the sidelines."

The first bell rang, and we cleared our trays. I pulled out my schedule. Fourth period: Strength Training. Should be an easy A. Fifth period: Human Anatomy—one of my classes with Ellie. I walked Kim to her next class, figuring I needed to keep up the appearance of a dutiful boyfriend. But I only thought of Ellie.

Strength Training ended, and I hurried across campus to Human Anatomy. I waited outside the classroom for Ellie. When she came through the door into the hall, Randy, football quarterback and class president, held the door open for her. Chagrined, I watched her flash him a smile. I shoved one hand in my pocket and leaned against the wall. Watching her lips, I saw her thank him. I averted my gaze as they walked down the hall. When they were close enough to hear me, I stepped in front of them. "Hey, Ellie, how's your first day going?"

She looked up and smiled. "Chase, I didn't see you. It's great. I'm enjoying it. I can't believe how big this school is. Pardon me, where are my manners? Chase this is Randy. Randy—"

"We know each other," Randy interrupted her. "Hey, Chase, how was your summer?"

My answer lacked enthusiasm. "It was great. How about you?" I found the guy arrogant and condescending. But every girl I knew, including my sister, found him to be, and I quote Jessica, "the hottest guy in the senior class."

"It was awesome, but I'm glad to be back." He turned to Ellie and said, "We'd better get into class."

I followed them into the room. Rows of tables, three chairs at each, began filling with students. In front of each chair was a piece of paper. The teacher stood at the front, trying to talk over the sound of chairs scraping across the floor and the noise of thirty teenagers. "Everyone take a seat quickly and begin working on the pretest in front of you. By the end of this semester, you should know all the answers, but I want to get an idea of what you already know."

Randy pulled out a chair for Ellie. Before she sat down, she turned and motioned for me to sit by her. I plopped my books on the table and sat down, feeling deflated about the seating arrangement. Ellie sat with Randy on one side and me on the other. We finished the pretest and got our homework: read chapter one of the textbook. I let out a sigh. I couldn't wait until summer vacation.

The bell rang, dismissing us from class. It was a relief when Randy went the opposite direction. I tried to sound casual when I asked Ellie, "So, how did you meet Randy?"

"He's in my English class. We were assigned to work as partners today."

"Hmm."

I held open the door to the MS—math and science—building for Ellie. Before I could step out into the brilliant sunlight, Kim ran up from behind me and wrapped her arm around my neck, brushing her lips across my cheek. "Hi, Chase," she said as she let go and walked out the door.

My eyes met Ellie's, and I felt my face flush. "That must be Kim," she said.

I wished she hadn't seen that. "Yeah," I muttered. "I have soccer practice after school. Do you mind hanging out for a couple of hours?"

Her eyebrows furrowed. "You want me to hang?"

"I mean wait. Can you wait for me? I'll be on the soccer fields—the grassy area to the west of the buildings."

She smiled. "Oh yes. I'll wait for you. Is there someplace I can study?"

"Sure. I'll walk you to the library."

She waved goodbye as I held the door to the library for her. "See you later, Ellie."

I jogged to the locker room. If I wanted to make a habit out of walking her to the library, I'd have to hustle. Coach wouldn't like it if I was late to practice.

Toward the end of soccer, Ellie walked across the grass and sat on the bleachers. I turned my game up a notch when I realized she was watching. We finished off our practice with a scrimmage game against the junior varsity team. I scored two goals for her in the final minutes. After practice, I picked up my water bottle and backpack and jogged to the bleachers.

"So, your kicking the ball into that net was good, right?" she asked.

I nodded, fighting the urge to laugh. Just like everything else about Ellie, her naivety drew me in. I picked up her backpack. "Yes, kicking the ball into the opposing team's net is definitely good. But if their team kicks the ball into our net, that's bad."

"I see."

146

As we walked to the truck, I tried to keep my distance, self-conscious of the sweat dripping off my forehead, and my T-shirt sticking to my back. Ellie didn't seem to mind, though, and stayed right at my side. I tossed our bags into the backseat and opened her door. Again, she put her hand out to me before she stepped into the truck. Smiling, I held her hand while she placed her foot on the step bar and climbed into the cab. I closed her door and jogged around to the driver's side. The diesel engine roared to life, and we headed for home.

Ellie turned to me. "It amazes me how much leisure time everyone takes. In 1863 there's too much work to do simply to have food to eat, fuel to stay warm, and a roof over your head. There's hardly a bit of time left for leisure, unless, of course, you are wealthy enough to employ a house full of servants. Sometimes I feel guilty being here."

I took my eyes off the road to look at her. "Ellie, that's how it is, and you're here now, so you shouldn't feel guilty."

We rode in silence until I said, "Hey, what did you think about high school?"

Ellie smiled. "I liked it. Some students are quite peculiar-looking, though. Everything in our English class has to be typed, so I've got to keep learning the computer. Your friend Kim was in Physical Education with Jessica and me. Human Anatomy is most interesting. I reckon I'll learn things that people didn't even know about in my time."

"I'm glad you had a good day. I was hoping you'd like it."

The next two days passed much the same as the first. I settled into a comfortable routine. The only hiccup in the daily schedule was sharing Ellie with Randy in Human Anatomy class. He always showered her with his attention, and I didn't like it. But what could I do about it? I had Kim as my girlfriend, and I couldn't afford to lose that cover. In fact, I couldn't afford to care about Ellie any more than a friend or brother would. It shouldn't matter if Randy liked her. I was responsible to keep her safe. That was all. But I couldn't do that on my own. Treating her like a sister offered me the best chance of success. I needed to ignore what I felt and think of her as I did Jessica.

So, I bit my tongue and stared at my textbook when Randy put his arm around the back of Ellie's chair, or when he leaned over to whisper in her ear. I looked the other way when he walked her to class. But deep inside, it infuriated me. Randy was scum. He wasn't good enough for her.

FOURTEEN
Summoned

Labor Day found me with a list of chores. How appropriate for the day! Dad left the house early to work in his office at the university. Mom and Jessica went shopping or running errands—I didn't know where, but they were gone. Ellie saw my list of chores and went to work on it with me. She fed the horses and cleaned stalls while I mowed the acre of lawn around our house. As I drove the lawn mower back and forth, I watched her walk from the barn into the house. She returned ten minutes later with a plate of sandwiches, a pitcher of water, and a tentative smile. It didn't take more than the sight of food to get me moving, and I turned off the mower. The angry engine sputtered and backfired when I jumped off the seat too fast. I walked to the picnic table in the shade of a giant cedar tree.

"Are you hungry?" Ellie asked.

"I'm starving." I took the glass of water she offered and downed it in a few long swallows. "Thanks."

"Thirsty too, I'd say."

"Yeah, that too." I devoured one sandwich in silence. When I reached for another, I finally had the common sense to say, "These are really good. Thanks for making them."

"You're welcome."

"What do you want to do after I finish mowing?"

She looked like she had something to say, but hesitated.

I studied her beautiful face. "Tell me," I urged. "If you could do anything you wanted right now, what would it be?"

She dropped her gaze. "You're going to think I'm silly, but I loved riding the horses with you. I was thinking . . . if you wanted to . . . perchance could we go this afternoon?"

I laughed. "That sounds like something my mom would want to do. But I loved riding with you too, so it's a plan. I'll finish mowing, and then I'll take you to the ravine. That'll be the perfect ride for a hot afternoon."

Ellie smiled when I picked up the last sandwich. She watched me eat, and I watched her watching me. She occasionally dropped her gaze, making a trivial comment about the yard or the horses. How had I become so infatuated? Trying to clear my thoughts, I shook my head and stood up. "I'll be done in a few minutes. Thanks again for lunch."

The monotony of driving the riding lawn mower allowed me plenty of time to watch Ellie. She took the dishes inside. She saw me looking and waved. I waved back and halfheartedly glanced at where I was going. She left the house and walked to the barn for two halters. Then she wandered up the pasture and returned with the same two horses we'd ridden last time.

I glanced at the lawn, checking to see if I was done. Hmm. Four strips of long grass glared back at me from the neatly cut lawn. Should've watched where I was going. I drove back and forth, cleaning up my sloppy rows. I dumped the grass clippings and parked the mower in the shop, then pulled the door closed with a bang. After jogging into the house, I scribbled a note on the back of my list of chores. "Ellie and I went riding. Be back soon. Chase."

Both horses were saddled when I got to the barn. I took off Red's halter and replaced it with a bridle. We mounted up and walked our horses along the road.

Ellie looked over at me. "Chase, I was curious. Have you gone anywhere yet, with the counter, that is?"

"No. In your grandfather's journal he said I should practice, but I haven't really wanted to go anywhere." I glanced down at the dark leather reins in my right hand. "I suppose I have everything I could ever want right here in 2011. I haven't wanted to leave."

"I see," she said.

I eyed the two-foot stubble left after the wheat harvest. "We could cut across this field."

Ellie nodded, and I steered my horse to the edge of the road. I kicked him into a lope as soon as he hopped the ditch. We galloped in single file where the tractor wheels had flattened the stalks against the dry soil. When the tractor trail veered in the wrong direction, I plunged into the thick stubble. Our horses were breathing heavily by the time we reached the top of the hill. We slowed them to a walk as we went down the back side.

"Let's stop for a minute," I said, pulling out my cell phone. "Smile. I'll take your picture."

Ellie reined her horse to a stop. "With that tiny contraption?" The golden wheat field and evergreen-covered hills made a perfect backdrop. She turned in the saddle, flashing her smile at me over her shoulder.

I snapped the picture. "Yeah, you look good up there. A lot better than my dad does on big Smoke." Happy with the result, I slid my phone shut as Ellie's melodic laugh floated on the air.

We followed a dirt road through a nursery, its trees and shrubs standing in neat rows like tin soldiers ready for battle. The horses crossed the railroad-tie bridge, their hooves echoing loudly in the sultry air. Flies buzzed overhead, and sweat trickled down my spine. I studied the thick wall of trees. A moment later I found it: the almost imperceptible trail leading into the forest. We followed the creek into the shady ravine. The silky threads of spider webs reflected the trace of sunlight filtering through the leaves. I swatted the webs out of my way. From time to time, a bird squawked and rustled the branches. Other than the sound of the gurgling creek next to us, Ellie and I rode in silence.

The trail veered away from the creek to a grassy path, skirting the base of a large knoll. When the trail came to an end a quarter of a mile later, I led the way up the steep, forested side of the knoll. Our horses weaved between large fir trees and stepped over branches. My horse labored up the hill. It was steep, and Red's back was slick with sweat. I grabbed a handful of mane and leaned forward, worried about the saddle slipping.

"Are you okay, Ellie?" I called back to her.

"I'm fine."

I glanced behind me to see her leaning over her horse's neck. She held her reins in two hands, each hand also full of her horse's mane. We finally reached the grassy summit. Relaxing as my horse stepped onto flat ground, I let out a sigh. I turned Red and stopped to wait for Ellie. She emerged from the trees. I made eye contact with her for a brief moment before plummeting into utter darkness.

FIFTEEN
Algonia

Like a kitten picked up by the scruff of its neck, I felt an unseen force tugging at me. Encased in the darkest darkness, I waited. Finally released into the hands of gravity, I fell, and a low grunt escaped my lips as I hit the ground. Startled by the sound of my voice amid such oppressive silence, I froze, alert for danger. I put my hand in front of my face, blinking, but there was nothing. The absence of light freaked me out. I could not remember ever being surrounded by absolute darkness. Usually some glimmer of light was present, either from the stars or the distant lights of a city. Here, there was nothing. Above me, not a single star brightened the sky.

Listening to the thundering of my own heart, I wiggled my fingers. They closed around moist leaves, and my fingernails dug into soil. I felt my way across the ground, and soon my hand brushed over a large root. I followed it to the base of an immense tree. With a start, I remembered the counter. I sat on the root and pulled the device from my pocket. Its eerie blue light was never more welcomed than it was now. I spun the globe to the northwestern U.S. and adjusted the date dials to September 5, 2011. I pressed the Shuffle button and then the

Go button. Nothing happened. "Ahh! You've got to be kidding me." I pressed Go again and again, feeling more frustrated. I tried the Return button also, which was stupid, since the last place I'd been by way of the counter was Ellie's cabin with the sword-swinging Mexican. But now nothing on the counter worked except the pale light.

I turned the counter so it illuminated my surroundings. Thick mists of fog hung limply in the air, and my skin already felt clammy from the moisture. As I panned the dense forest and expansive root system of these strange trees, the glimmer of light fell on a man. My sharp intake of breath broke the smothering silence. He was short, probably less than five feet tall. He wore a dark cloak, with the hood pulled over his head. He tapped his staff on the ground three times. On the third tap, a glowing orb appeared at the top of the staff. It was the same bluish light as the counter emitted, only brighter.

In a heavily accented voice that sounded neither young nor old, the curious fellow said, "The Master will see you now." The cloaked figure tilted his head to the side, implying that I should follow him. Pointing his staff into the trees, he turned and walked away. He moved quickly over the rough terrain of tangled roots and leafy plants. As the radius of light from the staff threatened to abandon me to the darkness, I jumped up and followed. Sensing this was not the time for questions, I kept quiet. But after walking a couple of miles through chest-high brush and stumbling over a maze of roots, I couldn't keep from asking, "Where is the Master?"

Without looking back, the man answered. "You shall find him in the fortress."

"How far away is the fortress?"

"Not far now."

"How much longer do we keep walking?"

"Not much longer."

Trudging behind the little man, I shook my head. *That really cleared things up.* I wondered what Ellie had seen, and if she would worry. Then I wondered if this was even real. Maybe it was a vision or dream.

"What's your name?" I asked.

"I am called Quirus, but this is not the time or the place for talking. The forest—it has ears."

I started to nod, but he wouldn't see that. I barely heard him moving through the underbrush, while I seemed to be crashing through like an elephant. At the mention of ears in the forest, I tried to mimic his movements. I partially succeeded, but I would never be as quiet as Quirus. At least trying to move silently gave me something to pass the time as I blindly followed this stranger through the woods.

We continued our steady upward trek, the night sky indiscernible above the thick tree canopy. The fog left my clothes damp, and only the exertion of the climb kept me warm. If I had any remaining doubts as to the authenticity of Ellie's explanation or her grandfather's journal, they rapidly disappeared. Although bizarre, this definitely felt real—it was no dream.

Still wrapped in darkness, we finally climbed above the fogbank, stepping into crisp, clear air. The trail rose up before us. I bit my tongue to keep from asking, "Are we there yet?" Quirus didn't look like the type to appreciate—or even understand—the humor in that question. But we had hiked for over an hour, and I was tired of this.

My head shot up when we stepped out of the trees into a clearing bathed in pale moonlight. Simultaneously, I saw two things: a tall stone wall rising up in front of me, and a vast number of stars hanging low in the night sky. The fortress, as I remembered it being called, impressed me, but the star-filled sky captivated my gaze. Never before had stars appeared so close to the earth. Never had they looked so large and luminous. I reached my hand skyward, feeling for a moment as if I could touch one. Quirus's staff darkened again, but the brightness of the stars more than compensated for it. I longed to lie on the grass and lose myself in the constellations.

Quirus followed the stone wall for a time. Then, he stopped in front of an oversized double door made of heavy wood planks and iron rivets. He tapped on the door with his staff. A slat, no bigger than a man's hand, slid open, and Quirus whispered something I couldn't make out. I expected the large doors to open, but a moment later, a rope ladder flew over the side of the wall. He indicated I should go first. I looked up the sheer wall and wrapped my fingers around the thick, coarse rope. He nudged me from behind, and I stepped onto the ladder.

When I had climbed ten feet off the ground, he started up behind me. With both of us on the ladder, the ropes swayed and bounced erratically with each step. My foot slipped once, drawing a grunt of disapproval from Quirus. The higher I climbed, the more carefully I placed each foot on the rope. I forced myself not to look down, focusing on my hands instead.

Two guards, clad in leather tunics and carrying swords at their waists, met me at the top of the wall. They each took me by an arm and pulled me onto the six-foot-wide walkway along the top of the wall. I turned to watch them help Quirus in the same manner. The guards studied me as Quirus led the way. They looked skeptical and even exchanged whispered comments. We descended a narrow flight of circular stairs to the ground floor below. Flickering orange flames danced atop torches mounted on metal posts. Once we left the wall and moved through the courtyard, Quirus visibly relaxed. I glanced over my shoulder and met the serious eyes of the two guards, who shadowed my every step.

Hoping it was safe to speak, I asked, "Where am I?"

Quirus smiled proudly, his crooked teeth visible in the torchlight. "Algonia. You are in Algonia, although, more specifically, Cadré Unair, the fortress city of the Master Keeper. We are striving to keep your identity a secret, even from those who live in Cadré Unair, hence the cover of darkness. During the day, this courtyard bustles with the activities of those who live within the walls of the fortress. We will make certain you leave here before morning. Only the Master's most trusted guards were placed on duty tonight, so you can be assured this visit will remain secret."

Not knowing how to respond, I said nothing. The fortress had a medieval look to it, only larger and more organized than what I'd seen portrayed in history books. We passed small buildings, maybe houses, some made of stone and some of wood. A large castle loomed ahead of us. The stone-paved streets wound endlessly in a labyrinth around the castle.

Ultimately, we made it to the center and entered the castle through a heavy wooden door. Once we stepped inside, another guard followed us through the corridors and up two staircases. The corridors were lit with bluish orbs, like the one on Quirus's staff, attached to sconces on the walls.

I glanced behind me at the sound of heavy footsteps. I wondered if the armed guards were here to guard me, or to guard the Master from me. They were big, burly fellows. The new guard had a full beard, and a long sword strapped to his back. The other two were dark-skinned and clean-shaven. The new guard wore the same leather tunic and skeptical look as the other guards. I shoved my hands in my pockets and wondered what I'd gotten myself into.

We entered a large room with two fireplaces, a roaring fire in each. Quirus walked to a table in the center of the room and picked up a goblet, draining its contents in one gulp. He slumped into a stuffed chair. I licked my lips, my throat aching for a glass of cold water. Turning around, I saw four more guards, two on each side of the door we'd just come through. I noticed their grim expressions and hoped this didn't end poorly.

I stood in an uncomfortable silence until a door in the opposite wall opened. Quirus jumped to his feet, at full attention. Two more guards entered the room, followed by a middle-aged man. He wore a neatly trimmed beard, and his dark hair was flecked with gray. He carried himself with a self-confident grace I'd never seen in any other person. He had a kingly presence, but his clothing and robes were not extravagant. Two guards flanked him as he walked across the room toward where I stood.

"I am Archidus, a sorcerer and a seer. I am also the Master Keeper and the king of Algonia. I believe you have acquired something of mine?" He extended his hand, palm up, and waited.

I pulled the counter out of my pocket and placed it in his hand. "Uh—here it is."

His eyes lit up as he examined the gold counter. But his brow furrowed when he saw the dent in the back. He whispered something under his breath, and upon further examination of the device, his smile returned. "As I said, I am a seer. I can see things that have been, things that are, and some things that will be. Before I can return this, I need to see you."

The Master slid the counter into the pocket of his robe and placed one hand on my shoulder. He closed his eyes and lifted his finger, making a motion like flipping through the file folders in a filing cabinet. Instantly, my head hurt. I fought the pain, trying to keep control of my mind. But the pressure built inside my skull, behind my eyes, making it difficult to see, difficult to think. Everything around me blurred, and I felt nauseous from the pain. I tried to speak, but nothing came out. Random thoughts and images from my past flashed through my mind, and I realized, through the haze of agony, that he was in my head, searching my memories. I pressed the heel of my hand to my forehead and gave up on watching what happened around me. It was all I could do to stay lucid amid the chaos inside my brain.

The pain lessened slightly as I remembered finding the counter in the cave. I remembered burying Ellie's grandfather, saving her from the Mexicans, trying to give her the counter, and watching her point the gun at me and tell me she'd have to kill me if she wanted to use it. I gasped. A sharp stab of pain, like a jolt of electricity, shot through me when I watched as Ellie and I used the counter to go to 2011. I saw us at school together, riding horses, fighting off Miguel in her cabin, the journal of her grandfather's, and her bringing me sandwiches. Lastly, I saw the distressed look on her face as she dismounted her horse atop the knoll and picked up my horse's reins. Abruptly, the Master slammed the door closed on the filing cabinet of my memories. *He must have found what he wanted,* I thought.

I staggered sideways, nearly losing my balance. I could barely formulate a coherent thought. The Master paced back and forth in front of me. My first rational thought was that the last thing I'd seen wasn't my own memory at all. He had shown me what Ellie did *after* I disappeared. Whether he had done so intentionally or by accident, I didn't know.

Sounding agitated, the Master said, "Quirus, put our Keeper in a chair before he falls over."

Quirus placed a chair behind me, shoving it into the back of my knees. I collapsed and held my throbbing head. The Master stopped pacing and faced me. I squinted up at him. Before he could speak, an urgent knock sounded at the door.

Furrowing his brow at the interruption, the Master motioned to his guards. I strained to look behind me as the guard opened the heavy wooden door. A haggard-looking soldier rushed into the room, dirty and covered in what looked like dried blood. We made eye contact before he dropped to one knee and bowed before the Master. In that moment, I glimpsed the soul of a battle-weary soldier, one who had seen and experienced things he wished he could forget but never would.

"Captain Marcus Landseer, rise," the Master commanded. "You may speak freely."

The soldier rose to his feet and squared his shoulders. "Sire, Arbon's troops have attacked our northern border. The village of Radnor—it's gone." The soldier shook his head in obvious dismay.

"Gone? What do you mean, Captain?"

"Destroyed. Burned to the ground. Arbon's troops left no one and nothing alive. The women, even the children, and the herds—they burned them all. The stench of it sours a man's stomach. It taints the land for miles." The captain seemed to lose his train of thought, probably reliving the horror of the story he told.

"What of Barculo and his thousand soldiers? Were they not stationed near Radnor?" the Master demanded.

"I know not. We were a day's ride west when we saw the smoke from the fires. When my men and I arrived on the outskirts of Radnor, it was overrun with Arbon's troops. There were signs of a great battle. Everywhere, the earth runs red with blood, and smoke darkens the sky. It was butchery! I saw no prisoners. We searched the outlying regions by night, hoping to discover what had transpired. We found three men, severely wounded, hiding in the woods. I think they are Barculo's men, but two of them died on the journey here, and the third has not yet spoken.

He is with the healer. If he recovers, we may yet learn what happened. I had hoped to discover the direction Arbon's troops would move next, but on our second night of surveillance, a small squadron of his soldiers discovered us. I lost four men in the scuffle, and three more were wounded. Not one of Arbon's soldiers escaped to reveal our presence. After that we returned immediately to sound a warning."

Still holding my throbbing head in my hands, I was shocked at the horrors the soldier had described. I glanced from Captain Landseer to Archidus. Master Archidus raised his thumb and forefinger to his chin before responding.

"We must assume Barculo and his men were destroyed. Quirus, send messengers to all the captains. We meet at sunrise. Captain, we are fortunate you have returned safely. If Barculo's man recovers, I want word of it sent to me at once. Thank you, Captain. You are dismissed."

The captain bowed quickly. "As you wish, sire." He retraced his steps out the door, Quirus hot on his heels.

Turning his attention to me, the Master said, "Chase Harper, do you know it is a crime punishable by death, if I so deem, for a Keeper to take someone out of his or her proper time?" He shook his head and frowned. "But of course not, for that was the first thing you did as Keeper of the counter, wasn't it? Do you realize I have every right to terminate your existence? And the girl's?" He paused a moment before resuming his pacing.

I couldn't think of an answer. True, I had taken Ellie with me, but initially I hadn't known it was forbidden. I wanted to say something to defend myself, considering my life was on the line—and Ellie's, as well. But I'd never felt pain like this before, and I couldn't make any words come out.

Again the Master stopped to stand in front of me. "But I won't. I've waited too long for the Protector to find a Keeper, and I'm not about to wait again. There are things that need to be done, so you'll simply have to do. I've seen you coming for many years. During that time, I've sent two other Keepers to protect this counter for you, keeping it safely hidden. But what I didn't see was you getting involved with Amyot's granddaughter. If conditions were different, I'd do away with you both right now. But although your future is strangely indiscernible, I have high hopes for you. And the girl is the granddaughter of one of the best Keepers I've known. Therefore, I will forego justice in favor of mercy."

He gazed off in the distance as if pondering. "I am willing to overlook your error. In fact, I see circumstances arising where I will need to overlook it in the future, as well. Since I perceive that your intentions—as well as the girl's—are pure, I will return this to you." He handed me the counter.

"Thanks, I think," I muttered, turning the device over in my palm. The counter reflected the flickering light of the fire. The Master had polished it to a high sheen—and repaired the dent.

"Let me tell you something of our past so you will understand the significance of your calling as a Keeper and your duty to protect our future. Hundreds of years ago, our worlds were one and the same. When religious fanatics began burning witches at the stake and striving to exterminate anything they suspected as supernatural, we determined to separate ourselves. We formulated a plan to split off into another dimension. Seven of the greatest sorcerers pooled their unique talents and powers to generate the magic necessary to form a new dimension—a new world, actually. The new dimension would draw on the natural resources of earth, but exist separately. We felt it necessary to preserve our way of life. You see, the power of magic is regenerated by the belief of those around it. Increasingly surrounded by unbelievers, our magic was being smothered. It would have disappeared completely had we not acted when we did.

"At the time of the division, seven counters were forged and each instilled with the magic of one of the seven sorcerers. These seven paid the ultimate price to preserve our way of life, for once they completed the separation, they were no more with us. All that remains of their power and greatness is contained within the counters they left to our safekeeping. Each counter was named based on the unique contribution of the original sorcerer from whence it came. Yours is the Protector. Along with the Guardian, these two skilled and valiant sorcerers were charged with protecting the other five individuals while the division took place.

"The magic necessary to keep the two worlds separate is contained within the seven counters. We feared if one person had complete control over the magic, the temptation to abuse that power would be too great. Although young at the time, I had obtained much skill in the art of magic and was asked to hold one of the counters in safekeeping. My older brother Arbon, an exceptionally skilled sorcerer, was also chosen to hold a counter. When it came time to choose a Master Keeper, Arbon aspired to the calling. Being a natural-born leader, I expected he would be chosen. However, the other Keepers voted and selected me for the honor. This infuriated Arbon. I spoke with him at length and thought we had reached an understanding.

"Our people lived in peace for nearly a hundred years before we realized Arbon had spent that time studying and plotting his evil designs. He planned to steal the other six counters and bring their magic back together. Using the combined magic, he intended to cause our worlds to collide, with the goal to destroy all humankind who wouldn't follow him. He allowed his bitterness and anger over a trivial disappointment to fester until his desire for revenge was insatiable. With all seven counters, Arbon would be the most powerful sorcerer our world or yours has ever known. Under those conditions, if our two worlds were merged as one again, he would be unstoppable. In addition to the unique powers of the individual counters, he would control the movement of time. To have power over time is to control everything.

"When Arbon murdered a Keeper and stole her counter, his evil plot came to light. He assumed, with the increased power attained by holding two counters, that it would be easy to overpower the remaining five Keepers, one at a time. Being a seer, I discerned his plan, and the five remaining Keepers met in secret and formulated an alternate plan. Arbon's power in our new world was now so significant that the risk of keeping the counters here was too great. Considering the higher population in your dimension of earth, which we call the old world, we planned to find the most noble and responsible humans we could and entrust the care of our counters to them. As Master Keeper, I would retain the power to override a counter held by a human.

"To this day, Arbon hasn't given up his quest for the counters. The source of his magic is here. When he goes to earth, he is little more than a human. Remnants of his strength and magic go with him, but they are minimal in comparison. He prefers to bribe, deceive, and lead on other humans with his flattery so they will hunt the Keepers for him. As the Protector's Keeper, you are endowed, from the magic within your counter, with strength and speed. Your senses are enhanced beyond those of a mere mortal. Some of these changes you have experienced. You must work to develop those skills necessary to save your life and protect the counter. The peace and safety of your world, as well as ours, depends on your success and that of the other four Keepers."

"Where are the others?" I asked, finally able to articulate the most basic of questions.

"They are scattered throughout the continents of earth. Some of them prefer to live a nomadic lifestyle, traveling from place to place, from time to time, whereas others choose to never use their counters, but simply keep their existence secret, thereby safeguarding them. Eventually, you will meet all of the Keepers."

"Can you go to the future with the counter?"

"The portals of time stay open for a long while, but not indefinitely. Your range of travel is roughly 350 years into the past and 50 years into the future. However, I leave you with a strong word of caution concerning the future. There is little good that comes from knowing one's own future. Should you discover undesirable future events, it will taint the joy you experience in the present. Most people focus all their energy on trying to change the outcome. As a result, they miss out on an otherwise enjoyable present. On the other hand, if they learn of something spectacular in their future, they tend to look for it to happen. The simple act of looking for or expecting something alters one's actions, ever so slightly, and can jeopardize the outcome."

The Master sat down across the table from me and drank from one of the gold goblets, studying me in thoughtful silence.

"What's being done to stop Arbon?" I asked, hoping I hadn't overstepped my bounds with such a pointed question. But after the tragic report from the soldier, Marcus, it sounded like they were getting their butts kicked.

"My people and his have battled for hundreds of years. At times it seems as if we are winning, while at other times Arbon appears to be gaining ground. However, little has changed. Arbon is entrenched in his stronghold, deep within the boundaries of

Shuyle. He has amassed large armies of violent and bloodthirsty humans. He has also bent the will of the two remaining dragons to do his bidding. On the other hand, we have a substantial army of humans who fight to keep the peace. The elves—other than the few who have turned rogue and are working as Sniffers for Arbon—are with us, as well. The dwarfs, entrenched in their mountain hideout, have adamantly remained neutral, firmly refusing to join either side. Those who help us, continue to battle Arbon and his evil forces with valor."

I worked to digest all the Master had told me. "How do you and Arbon have human armies? I thought you left the humans on my dimension of earth when you separated."

"There were many humans who respected and believed in magic. They valued and relied on its existence. Those who did were brought here with us. Only the unbelievers were left. Although those of us who are considered magical beings live incredibly long lives, we cannot replenish our kind as quickly as humans can. The humans who came with us are now numerous. Those who live within the borders of Algonia are valiant in their fight to defend right and protect their peaceful way of life. Even though at times it feels as if Arbon's forces are undefeatable, we will persevere in faith as we defend ourselves and search for an opportunity to overthrow him once and for all."

My head still throbbed, and I closed my eyes for a few seconds. The sound of a sword being drawn from its sheath echoed through the great hall. My eyes shot open. The Master, examining a narrow-bladed sword, ran his thumb over the jeweled hilt.

He stood and walked around the table, then presented the sword to me. "You'll need a blade. I've seen Balcombe, one of Arbon's Sniffers, bribe the Mexicans with gold bullion in exchange for your life and the counter. Even as we speak, they are hunting you."

With reluctance, I accepted the sword. "Thanks."

For the first time since I'd met him, the slightest of smiles touched the Master's mouth. When he had again seated himself at the table, he continued. "As Protector, you need to learn how to use the sword. I don't wish to see that wild, backwoods hacking I witnessed in Amyot's cabin. This is too fine a blade to be handled in such an ignorant manner. Those men—the Mexicans—must be destroyed."

"What, you mean killed?"

"Yes, you must acquire the skills necessary to kill them before they can kill you and take your counter."

I shook my head. "I don't know if I can do that."

The Master slammed his fist on the table and raised his voice. "Chase Harper, you are a Keeper now—the Protector. You must learn to do it, or perish. We are at war. There is no other alternative."

An ominous silence hung in the air before he went on. "Your most dangerous enemy, other than Arbon himself, is a Sniffer. Sniffers are outcasts. They are rogues of elfish background who, through their inherited magic, can jump through the portals of time without assistance from any external devices. These rogues are trained to sniff out the signatures left by a counter when it leaves or enters a time portal. Sniffers will follow your counter's signature through time. The most experienced Sniffers are able to pull humans through with them. If you have a Sniffer on your tail, it is critical that he or she be destroyed. In situations involving a Sniffer, I'll make every effort to send another Keeper to assist you. But Sniffers are slippery creatures who usually run at the first sign of resistance. They are inherently cowards and prefer to save their own skin.

"To follow a Sniffer, immediately roll all the dials on your counter to zero and press the Go button as you follow in their footsteps. You will appear wherever they choose to reappear. If you've been around a Sniffer or suspect one is lurking near, it is vital that you hide your counter's signature with rapid jumps through time in the same location or by using the Shuffle button. Keeper, do you understand all that I'm saying?"

I pulled myself upright and chanced a glance at the Master. The hard, cold steel felt heavy in my hand. I couldn't do what he wanted: run around killing people with this sword. "I don't think I'm the right person for your job. I'm not a soldier. I can't kill people. That's not who I am. You'll have to take these back." I stumbled across the room and set the sword and the counter on his table.

A distinct frown turned down the corners of his mouth. "The choice is yours, but you can do it. The counter would not have chosen you if you could not. Perhaps, my young friend, you have not fully considered the consequences of the choice before you. Allow me to enlighten you."

My mind spun away like a twirling top dropping off the edge of a table. I saw myself turning to leave, abandoning the sword and the counter on his table. Before I left his room, the Master said, "I'll have to give this to another." Fog blurred the vision, clearing a moment later to show me Ellie. She ran through a dim alley, glancing over her shoulder, her eyes wide with fear as she pulled the gold counter from her pocket. Her hands trembled. In a wave of emotion, I felt her terror as someone grabbed her.

Still locked in the Master's vision, I heard Ellie repeat what she'd told me when I offered her the counter in Zion Canyon. "You can't give it away. Once you've used it, you are the Keeper of the counter until you're dead. It won't work for anyone else. I'd have to kill you first if I wanted to use it."

Next, I watched myself beat a hasty retreat from this room, running like a coward from the call to duty. "Kill him," Master

Archidus said to his guards, his voice filled with regret. Fog settled in again, clearing to show me a fencing lesson. I saw myself fencing. And I was winning. Then, as quick as popping a balloon, my mind came back to me. I stood staring at my hands, resting on the Master's table next to the sword.

I may not want this, but I wouldn't wish it on someone else, either. Instead of asking, why me, shouldn't I be asking, why not me? Was I entitled to a life of ease any more than anyone else? I didn't think so. Better me than Ellie. If my counter went to Ellie, who would be there to protect her? I'd be dead, and she'd be left alone. I had to trust that this strange twist of fate came my way for a reason, and that if I did my best, I would live to tell the tale.

I grabbed the sword and the counter and slumped back into my chair. "I'll do it," I said.

Master Archidus nodded once in approval.

My splitting headache had only intensified. "What did you do to me?"

The Master chuckled. "Never fear, you'll return to normal soon enough. I'll admit I wasn't pleased at first, so I stirred your brain when I viewed your past. Also, I added a few memories that you may find useful in the future. They are making themselves at home even as we speak."

I looked at the Master, assuming he'd made a joke, but he appeared quite serious. He walked to me and reached out as if he would shake my hand, taking hold of my wrist instead. I squeezed my hand around his wrist in return, and he pulled me to my feet.

"Welcome, Chase the Protector. It has been an honor making your acquaintance. In the future, I will require your services. When that time arrives, you'll receive a message. Now, it's late, and I need to prepare for the meeting with my captains. I'll have Quirus show you out." The Master nodded toward the door.

I glanced over my shoulder. Quirus stood waiting for me; he must have returned while the Master had control of my mind. "My services? A message . . . how?"

"There will be no mistaking the message," the Master replied. "I will make it quite clear." With that, he turned on his heel and left the room, his guards flanking him.

SIXTEEN
Return

Quirus bowed in my direction. "Follow me, Keeper."

When I walked through the door, each of the remaining guards bowed as well. Evidently I'd passed the test and now deserved their respect. Quirus led the way through the corridors of the castle and into the labyrinth of houses and shops. He walked quickly, and I struggled to keep pace as the migraine symptoms intensified. More than once, I reached out to grab the wall as pain shot through my head. When the sword clanged against the stones, Quirus took it from my hand and buckled it around my waist. After wrapping my arm around his shoulder, he dragged me alongside him.

"We must hurry," he said. "Daylight isn't far off."

We climbed the narrow staircase and retraced our steps along the catwalk. The same two guards followed us. They tossed down the rope ladder, and Quirus began his descent. About four feet down, he paused and looked up at me. "Keeper, concentrate," he whispered. "It would not be wise to meet such an untimely death as this."

I nodded back at him, then rubbed my eyes, trying to clear my vision. The guards took my arms and lowered me over the edge. Focusing all that remained of my mixed-up brains on maintaining a firm grip, I lowered myself one rung at a time down the face of the wall. Quirus stood tapping his toe at the bottom before I made it halfway down. It took all my strength to keep both hands on the rope. Finally, my feet touched solid ground, and the rope slithered through my fingers and up the wall. Quirus dragged me toward the cover of the trees as the first hint of the coming dawn appeared in the east.

The little man seemed to glide over the terrain, while I staggered along behind him. I had no idea what we were running from, but I didn't feel up to finding out just then. We went back the way we had come. The dense forest canopy blocked all the early-morning light, leaving us to stumble through the underbrush in darkness. I tried to ignore the pain in my head and focus on placing one foot in front of the other. We both breathed heavily from the exertion of the run, and sweat dripped from my forehead.

Abruptly, Quirus stopped. Faint light seeped through the trees. "Witches Hollow," he said, waving his arm in a circle. "We're safe now. The magic is thick here. It hides the signs of our comings and goings. There aren't many places where one can pass from the new world into the old. Witches Hollow is the closest."

I found the same upraised root and sat down, lowering my head into my hands. The throbbing behind my eyes beat in tandem with the rhythmic pulse of my heart. "Now what do we do?" I asked between ragged breaths.

"We wait. Master Archidus will send you back shortly."

Soon the same lifting sensation pulled me by the scruff of my neck through the dark abyss. The addition of interdimensional travel to my already-splitting headache left me groaning in agony. Once released, I dropped five feet to the ground, jarring my shoulder on impact. My eyes clamped shut against the bright sunlight, and I clutched my head, desperate for relief. I tried to roll over and climb to my feet. I didn't make it past my knees.

Ellie ran to my side and dropped down next to me. "Land sakes! Chase, what happened to you? Are you hurt? What's wrong?" Her voice quivered.

"My head . . . It's my head . . . Oh dang it!"

I staggered to my feet. She wrapped her arm around my waist, and I draped my arm over her shoulder.

"Do you need a doctor?"

I moaned. "No. He said it would go away."

"Who? Who said it would go away? Who did this to you?" Now her voice had a sharp edge to it. Was she angry I was hurt? It felt satisfying to think she was angry—that maybe she really cared. The dizzying pain overwhelmed me, and I fell to the ground. My weight was too much for Ellie, and I dragged her down with me. I tried to crawl, but her hand on my cheek stopped me.

"Chase, lie down for a minute. Perhaps a little rest will clear your head. Do you know what happened? Who hurt you?"

I collapsed onto the yellow stubble of late-summer grass and forced myself to speak. "The Master did it."

With that exertion, I must have passed out. The events of the past few hours repeated themselves in my dreams. At a rapid pace, I saw and heard everything the Master had said again and again, until it burned itself into my memory as if with a hot branding iron.

At last I slipped into a restful slumber. My first waking sensation was the absence of pain. In fear of it returning, I lay still. Without opening my eyes or moving, I examined my surroundings. I felt Ellie's fingertips stroking my hair away from my forehead. Over and over, she ran her fingers through my hair in an absentminded way that left me feeling peacefully calm. I felt her other hand resting on my arm, just below the sleeve of my T-shirt. My head rested in her lap. Pretending to still be asleep, I luxuriated in the tenderness of her touch.

A horse whinny jerked me back to reality. What time was it? How long had I slept? Fearing the return of pain, I opened my eyelids ever so slowly. Ellie was leaning against a tree, her eyes closed. I wondered about the tear that hung from her eyelashes. The bright orange glow of sunset cut through the trees above us, spotlighting specks of dust dancing with insects in the air above.

My parents would worry if we weren't back before dark, and we had a good forty-minute ride ahead of us. We would make it home in time if we hurried. I sat up slowly, testing myself for remnants of the headache. Once I was sitting, I climbed to my feet. Relieved to find myself pain-free, I turned and pulled Ellie up. Smiling at her, I wiped away the tear from the corner of her eye. "How long did I sleep?"

She glanced away. "Maybe a couple of hours," she said, stuttering a little. "I don't know for certain."

Reluctantly I let go of her hand and stepped away from her, looking for the horses.

"Red is tied to the tree over there," she explained. "I let the horses take turns grazing while I waited for you."

"Thanks for waiting."

She picked up Smoke's bridle and walked toward him. "You worried me, Chase. You disappeared. Then you were absent for hours. I began to think you had died somewhere."

Her voice sounded strained. I untied Red and faced Ellie. "I'm sorry. I didn't have any control over it. The counter didn't work. This sorcerer dude—the Master Keeper—got in my head, searching my memories. He threatened to kill both of us for taking you out of your designated time. Then they ran me for miles through the forest in the dark and sent me back here with a splitting migraine."

Her mouth turned down in a frown. "I'm sorry, Chase. I knew I wasn't supposed to go with you, and I did anyway. Oh, I had no idea it would cause so much trouble. Can you ever forgive me for being so selfish?"

"Hang on. I didn't tell you that to make you feel bad. It's no big deal. Plus, I wouldn't want it any other way. And in the end he said it was fine."

She turned away from me and pointed to my bridle. "Your horse ran off when you disappeared. He stepped on one of the reins and broke it. I tied it back together, but it'll need to be repaired."

The tone of her voice, the way she wouldn't look in my eyes—what was going on with her? I took hold of her arm and turned her to face me. "Ellie, are you okay? Talk to me."

"I'm not usually of such delicate emotions," she said, her voice cracking, "but you were gone so suddenly, gone for so long. My grandfather disappeared at times, but he always told me he was leaving and came back quickly. You scared me. I kept thinking, What would I do if you never came back? Then when you did come back you were writhing in agony. I didn't know what to do for you. I didn't know what was wrong. I felt so helpless."

Wrapping my arms around her, I tucked her head next to my neck. "You did everything I needed. You watched the horses, and you waited for me. What more could a guy ask for? Huh? I'm fine. Everything's fine."

Seeming embarrassed, she pulled away from me and wiped her eyes. I watched her turn and climb into the saddle. "I reckon you're right," she said. "I don't know what got into me. I suppose we ought to go."

She walked her horse down the trail. I mounted up, content to follow her home, keeping company with my own thoughts.

I worried over what I'd heard and seen from the Master and the haggard soldier who had witnessed the slaughtered village. I contemplated telling Ellie more, yet I didn't want to burden her with what I knew.

When the narrow trail through the ravine ended, she pulled up her horse to wait for me. In her usual self-assured manner, she asked, "Where did the sword come from? I've never seen you wear one before."

Glancing at the sword I'd almost forgotten about, I smiled. "You're right about that. I've definitely never worn a sword before. Master Archidus gave it to me." I chuckled at the memory, then continued with the story. "He said I should learn how to use it. He didn't want to see that 'backwoods hacking' I was doing in your cabin."

Ellie looked perplexed. "He said that—called you a backwoods hacker?"

"Yeah. I didn't think it was all that bad. At least I got out of there with nothing more than a scratch."

"A scratch? It did need stitches," Ellie reminded me.

I shrugged, answering her with a half smile. I had serious doubts about my ability to use this sword to kill a man, and I hoped it wouldn't actually come to that. It wasn't in my nature to be a killer, or even a fighter, for that matter. I thought Master Archidus was being overly optimistic, thinking I'd be killing the Mexican vaqueros.

I pulled out my cell phone and called home, taking a proactive approach to avoiding trouble with my parents. Luckily, Jessica answered.

"Hi, this is Chase," I said.

"Where are you guys? You've been gone for hours."

"It was a long horseback ride. Are Mom and Dad worried?"

"No. You are the luckiest guy I know. Dad asked Mom to meet him at his office, and they went out to dinner. I dropped Mom off at PSU hours ago. They don't even know you've been gone."

"Good," I said, feeling the apprehension of a few minutes ago melt away. "We're heading back now. I'm guessing we'll be there in thirty minutes."

"Sounds good," Jessica said. "I'll see you then."

We followed the same trail back home, galloping along the dirt road and across the wheat field in an effort to make up lost time. When we passed the house, my dad's car was still absent from the driveway. Jessica walked out to meet us, and the three of us fed the horses.

When my sister and I were alone in the grain room, she pointed at me and laughed. "What's with the sword, Chase? It's not Halloween yet."

"I've got to learn how to use it. Remember the explanation I gave you at Zion's? It's all true. Ellie was absolutely right. There's weird stuff going on that I never dreamed existed."

Jessica's look blared skepticism. "When are you going to take me with you so I can see this time-travel miracle for myself?"

"Never. That's strictly forbidden. I learned the hard way that you don't take other people with you," I replied in all seriousness.

"Chase, I can't believe we're having this conversation. I would think you're crazy if it weren't for Ellie. She's either a really good actress or else she really is from the 1860s like you say. I'm going to feel stupid for believing you if I find out you two are making all this up."

"Don't worry, Jessica. We're not making anything up."

"Well, I'd still like some proof, but either way I've got your back."

SEVENTEEN
Chinatown

Once the horses were fed, we went in to find dinner for ourselves. I scanned the contents of the refrigerator. "There's nothing to eat. Let's go out to dinner."

Ellie laughed at me. "What do you mean, there's nothing to eat? I've never seen so much food in one house at one time in my entire life. You have potatoes and carrots, meat in the freezer—we could make stew. You have bread and Cheerios. There are bananas and apples. You have milk and ice cream. Plus, there are cans in your pantry full of foods I've never even heard of before."

"You're right, Ellie, but let's go out anyway. Jess, if you drive, I'll buy."

"That's a deal," my sister said.

I smiled at Ellie while I stuffed my wallet in my back pocket. "Ellie, you're in 2011. People randomly go out to eat, regardless of how much food is in the house."

Catching on to my carefree mood, Ellie laughed. "As you wish, Chase."

After enduring excruciating pain all afternoon, it energized me to simply feel good again.

Jessica walked to the front door. "Come on, let's go. I'll be in the car."

I opened the car door for Ellie, then walked around to the passenger side and got in the backseat next to her. Jessica turned to scowl at me. "What? You're making me chauffeur you around now?"

"Yes, ma'am," I teased.

"Chase, you're incorrigible!"

"You and your big vocabulary. What's that supposed to mean, anyway?"

Jessica threw an empty paper cup at me and flipped on the radio. "You're impossible."

I knew I shouldn't do what I was thinking about, but I did anyway. I couldn't withstand the impulse. I picked up Ellie's hand and tucked it under my arm, intertwining my fingers with hers. I glanced at her, and she squeezed my hand.

Once we were seated at the restaurant, Jessica leaned forward and asked, "Did you call Uncle Roy?"

"No. I need to do that this week."

"Good. There was a message from him on the answering machine. I worried you'd called him and he was going to rat you out to Mom. I got his number off the caller ID if you need it."

"Thanks. I do need the number."

It was two days later before I found time alone to dial Roy Burgess's phone number. On the fourth ring, he answered. "Yeah?"

"Uncle Roy?"

"This is Roy. Who's this?"

"It's Chase. Chase Harper. Your sister Jennifer's son."

"Your mom know you're callin' me?"

"No, and I'd better keep it that way. I need something, and I thought maybe you could help me."

"Kid, I'm not in the business of doing favors."

"I could pay you," I added quickly.

"What kind of favor are you talking about?"

"I need to get a fake ID for—"

Roy interrupted me. "Kid, shut up! Meet me Friday night at seven in Chinatown on the corner of 4th and Couch Street. We'll have dinner."

"Uncle Roy?" There was no answer. He was gone. Friday at seven in Chinatown—downtown Portland. Did that mean he would help me? I'd have to cancel my date with Kim. I'd be going out with Uncle Roy instead.

Friday afternoon I told Jessica and Ellie about my plans to meet Uncle Roy.

"Do you want Ellie and me to come with you?" Jessica asked.

"Um . . ." I paused, thinking. It would be nice to have the company, especially Ellie's, but Uncle Roy wasn't the type of person I was anxious to introduce her to. I imagined he hung out in some sleazy places, not the kind of places I wanted to take Ellie or my sister. "No, that's okay. I'll go see what I can find out on my own. Can I take your car, though? It will be a lot easier than driving the truck downtown."

"Sure," Jessica answered.

That evening I took her keys off the key rack and called, "Bye, Mom."

"Where are you going?" she asked.

"I've got a date—for dinner."

"Okay, have fun. Tell Kim I said hi."

Guilt stabbed my conscience. "Yeah, Mom," I muttered, closing the door behind me.

I turned onto 4th Avenue under the archway marking the entrance to Chinatown. The first intersection I came to was

Couch Street. I scanned the streets for an open parking space. A block later, I parked Jessica's car and walked back toward Couch and 4th. The weekend crowd populated the area, and a homeless beggar slouched in an empty doorway, hounding passersby for their loose change. I shoved my hands in my pockets and stared straight ahead, looking for any sign of my uncle Roy. I stepped into the road to avoid confronting a tough-looking group of teens, maybe gang-bangers, who monopolized the sidewalk.

At the corner of 4th and Couch, there wasn't a familiar face in sight. Nothing. I'd wait. He was probably late. Actually, I'd never known him to be on time to anything. I crossed Couch Street several times while I awaited his arrival. It was 7:30 PM. before I saw the rough-looking dirty blond that was my uncle Roy, walking down 4th Avenue. He slinked down the road, glancing around furtively as he walked. I shook my head, pitying him for the rotten mess he'd made of his life. How could he live like that, always feeling like he had something to hide? But then I smiled. Hopefully, he would put all his criminal mischief to good use on Ellie's behalf.

"Uncle Roy!" I yelled from across the street.

His head shot up, and he looked in my direction. I waved before I crossed the street.

"Chase? Is that really you? Wow, you've grown. How many years has it been, kid?"

"It's probably been at least four years since we've seen you."

"And that's no fault of mine. Tell your mother to invite me over. It's rude of her not to let old Roy see his niece and nephew once in a while."

"Yeah, I'll see what I can do. But I need your help with something. You're the only person I know who might be able to help me."

He wrapped his arm around my shoulder and led me toward the Chinese restaurant. "Hold yer horses, kid. Buy me dinner first, and then we'll talk business."

I held my tongue and followed Roy into the restaurant. "We'll sit at the bar," he told the hostess. But the hostess cast a skeptical glance in my direction and hesitated. "How old are you now, anyway?" Roy asked me.

"Seventeen," I mumbled.

"Never mind—a booth's fine."

She led us to a booth in the back corner. We sat on red vinyl benches across from each other and took menus from the hostess's outstretched hand. Soon, a waitress set tiny bowls of steaming soup in front of us. I sipped the nearly flavorless broth before sliding the bowl away. The lighting was dim, perfect for camouflaging the run-down interior of the restaurant. A single flame, glowing from a small candle in a red glass bowl, accented the meager table decorations. I scanned the contents of the menu, quickly deciding, then pushed the menu aside and waited impatiently for Roy.

The waitress returned a few minutes later. "What'll it be?"

Roy answered first. "A Bud Light and the sweet & sour pork."

She turned in my direction. "And for you?"

"Sprite and the orange chicken, please."

She scratched some notes on her pad of paper and flipped two paper coasters onto the table before leaving.

"Sorry for cutting you off the other night. That wasn't the kind of talk I could have over the phone. Now what does a good kid like you need a fake ID for? You wantin' to crash the clubs and put some moves on the college girls?" he said with a wink.

"No, Uncle Roy—"

"You got some buddies who want you to buy their beer for 'em?" he interrupted.

"No, I—"

"You got a scheme worked out? You wanna follow in your old uncle Roy's footsteps?"

"No," I answered emphatically. "If you'll listen, I'll tell you."

He leaned back. "Ah, you're no fun. If it ain't for any of those reasons, you've got me stumped. Why on earth does a good kid like you need a fake ID?"

"It's not for me. I need it for a girl who—"

Again he leaned forward and interrupted me. "Ooh la la! I see now. You've got yourself a little dark-eyed beauty from south of the border, huh? You want me to make her legal?"

"No. Well, it is sort of like that, only she's not Hispanic. She's as American as they come, except she doesn't have any identification and no way to come by it legally." Remembering what the registration secretary at Hilhi had asked for, I said, "I at least need to get her a birth certificate and a Social Security card."

"Well, that's interesting. Where are her parents? How come you can't get her birth certificate if she's American?"

The waitress returned with our drinks, and Uncle Roy started on his beer.

Feeling frustrated, I waited for our server to move away before I continued. "Actually, she is an illegal alien, but she looks American. Can you help me or not?"

"The quickie IDs I make won't fool anyone for long. She'd probably get caught if she used it very often."

My heart sank. The last thing I wanted to do was get Ellie into trouble. "That's no good. I've got to have something that's as realistic as possible for her."

"Then I can't help you, but I do know someone who can. I work for this guy. He's shrewd and tough, but he's good. I'll warn you, though—he's not cheap."

"Who is he? Where do I find him?" I asked.

"I can't tell you that. I'm sure he won't see you, either, but I'll take him the message and call you when I hear anything."

Not seeing any other options, I agreed. Then I stopped the waitress as she tried to hustle past our table. "Can I borrow your pen for a minute?"

She tossed her pen on our table and left. I quickly scribbled out my name and cell-phone number on the napkin in front of me. I slid it across the table to my uncle. "Here's my number. How long do you think it will take to hear back from this guy?"

Uncle Roy folded the napkin and slid it into the inside pocket of his worn leather jacket. "I don't know, but at least a week or two."

The waitress set our food in front of us and retrieved her pen. She scrawled a quick "Thank you" across the bottom of the bill and set it face down on the table. We ate our food with minimal conversation, though Uncle Roy did ask about Jessica and my mom. I gave him short answers. He knew my dad didn't like him, so his name never came up.

When we finished, Roy nodded to the bill and said, "I'll let you get that."

"Thanks." I pulled out my wallet and turned the bill over.

"Do you have a car here?" he asked as I tossed five dollars on the table to cover the tip.

"Yeah," I said, standing up.

"Good, you can give me a ride home."

"I can," I muttered sarcastically. I paid for the dinner, and Uncle Roy followed me to my car.

We drove across the Willamette River on the Burnside Bridge, and he directed me to a dilapidated apartment complex.

"I'm in apartment 213. Stop over there." He pointed across the parking lot. When he got out of the car, he said, "Thanks, kid."

"You've still got my number, right?" I called after him.

He laughed and patted the front of his jacket. "Sure do—right next to my heart. See ya later, kid."

"Bye, Uncle Roy."

The next two weeks passed with agonizing slowness as I waited for some word from him. What was taking him so long? If he didn't call by the end of the week, I decided, I would call him.

EIGHTEEN
Fencing

Thursday night I stared at my plate: salmon, baked potato, and broccoli. The dinner conversation between Ellie and Jessica buzzed around me.

"I signed up for fencing lessons today," I said, before shoving another bite of salmon and potato in my mouth.

The room fell silent. I swallowed my food before raising my eyes. My dad had stopped chewing with a wad of food in his cheek. Mom held her fork suspended in front of her open mouth. Ellie didn't look surprised and was the only one still eating.

Jessica spoke first. "That's random."

My mom set her fork down. "Where on earth did you get that idea? Were you watching *Zorro* or something?"

I scooped up another bite of food. "It's just something I want to try."

"If it's what you want to do, I guess it's fine with me, but only if it doesn't interfere with your schoolwork," Dad said, then resumed eating his dinner.

My mom still looked concerned. "Chase, isn't that a dangerous activity?"

"Not any more dangerous than anything else I've been doing lately."

"Well . . . okay, I guess," she said.

On Sunday morning, Uncle Roy finally called. The news wasn't as bad as it could've been. He said his boss had agreed to make a fake ID for Ellie, but it would cost us.

I watched for an opportunity to talk with Jessica and Ellie alone. Sunday night after my parents had gone to bed, I walked down the hall to the girls' room and knocked softly.

"Who is it?" Ellie called.

"Chase," I answered her. Since holding her hand on Labor Day, I'd backed off. It wouldn't do either of us any good to lead her to believe we were more than friends. We had an easy, comfortable friendship, and I didn't want to ruin it.

When the door opened, she stood in front of me in a Hilhi Spartans basketball T-shirt and a pair of Jessica's flannel pajama pants. "I like my shirt on you," I said.

Ellie instantly blushed and turned to my sister. "I thought you said this was an extra shirt."

"It is. All his T-shirts are extras. He's probably got fifty of them," Jessica answered flippantly.

I laughed and winked at Ellie. "She's right. That one is from freshman year. It's too small. Looks better on you than on me, anyway."

After doing so well at keeping the relationship casual, I go and say something stupid like that! I could have kicked myself. Glancing down the hall, I hoped my parents hadn't overheard. Ellie stood blushing directly in front of me, blocking the entrance to the girls' room. I shifted my voice to a more businesslike tone. "Can I come in and talk to you two?"

She recovered her composure and stepped aside to open the door. "Oh, certainly. Forgive my lack of manners."

I sat on the edge of Jessica's bed and told her the news from Uncle Roy. When I finished, no one spoke at first.

"So, we get the money, somehow, and then give it—along with two passport photos of Ellie and her personal information—to Uncle Roy, and he takes care of the rest?" Jessica finally asked.

"Yup. That about sums it up. Whoever this guy is, he's wary of a trap and wants Uncle Roy to be the middleman."

A heavy silence pervaded the room. Ellie cleared her throat. "Do I really need a birth certificate? I don't see why I can't get by without one. I can't see spending a small fortune on a piece of paper. I have the silver dollars my grandfather left me, but there's not more than twenty or so. It's so disheartening how expensive everything is."

Jessica leaned toward Ellie, her eyebrows lifting. "Did you say *silver* dollars?"

"Yes," Ellie answered with a sigh.

A plan started to form in my mind. "Made with *real* silver, right?"

"Of course," Ellie said.

I looked at my sister and smiled. "Jess, are you thinking what I'm thinking?"

"Those coins could be worth a fortune by now," Jessica said.

"How?" asked Ellie, looking confused.

"Silver is too expensive now to use in coins," I said. "I don't know what year they quit making them out of silver, but it was a long time ago. Antique coins—especially those made of real silver or gold—would be worth a lot of money today. I have no idea how much, but it's got to be a good start. All we need to do is find the right buyer."

Ellie retrieved her grandfather's money bag from the closet and offered it to me. "In that case, you can have the coins. All of them."

I took the bag. "Thanks, Ellie."

I dumped the contents of the leather pouch onto the bed and fingered one of the heavy, antique coins. Jessica moved to her desk and searched the Internet for coin dealers. Ellie and I counted the money. She had twenty-three silver dollars and eight paper bills.

"What year were the coins minted?" Jessica called from her computer desk.

I started naming off the dates. "In 1797, 1799, 1860, 1845—"

"Wait," Jessica interrupted. "Tell me how many were dated between 1794 and 1803. It says here they are selling for up to $2,000 per coin if they're used."

Ellie and I laid them out in chronological order. "Three," I answered.

"Okay," Jessica said, writing down the value on a piece of paper. "Now, how many are dated between 1804 and 1839?"

"Eight," Ellie said.

"Those are worth up to $1,000 a piece. Are the rest of them dated between 1840 and 1873?"

"Yes, there are twelve left," I said.

"Those are worth up to $500 a piece. Do any of the coins look new? If so, they could be worth a lot more, like up to $5,000 each."

"One of them might pass for new, but I don't know how picky they are," I said.

Jessica pulled her calculator out of her backpack and did the math. "If we can sell these, we might have found the money we need." She typed while she talked. "There are three coin dealers within a three-hour radius of Portland. I'll e-mail them each for a bid on the coins, and we'll see what kind of response we get." After a few minutes, she hit "Send" on her e-mail, and it was done.

Over the next week, Jessica and I sold the coins to different dealers in Portland and Salem. The two coin dealers I dealt with required my personal information, along with my Social Security number, before they could complete the transaction. I hoped this didn't come back to haunt me later on.

We didn't get top dollar for Ellie's coins, but we got enough to pay Uncle Roy. I called him from my truck before school and left a message—a vague message. I didn't want him angry because I'd said too much over the phone.

Later that night, Uncle Roy sent me a text. "Dinner again. Chinatown. Same time." I was anxious to be rid of the wad of cash I had stashed in my closet. Four more days until Friday.

I had fencing lessons twice a week. The instructor, Coach Bill, had fenced on the Olympic team twenty years ago. He worked everybody hard, but I think he took great pleasure in pushing me to the limit. I didn't mind, though. Every time the sword blades flashed, I remembered Miguel coming at me from across the cabin, and my motivation to learn was sky high. If the Master really saw the future, I'd better be ready for another encounter with my Mexican nemesis. I doubted I would kill him, but I needed to know enough to keep myself alive.

Bill usually stayed after class and dueled one-on-one with me. He seemed to find my speed intriguing. During one of these duels, he asked, "Are you sure you haven't taken any lessons before?"

I parried his cut and lunged forward in a counterattack. "Yeah, I'm sure."

My blade grazed his. Sliding down, it glanced off his hand guard. Quickly disengaging, I feinted, attacked into one line, then switched at the last moment. He was tricked by my feint, and I put his foil in a bind. The button on the tip of my foil scored a perfect hit on his chest.

Breathing heavily from the exertion, Coach Bill lowered his weapon and stepped back. He smiled proudly at me. "You're like a cheetah. You have incredible quickness, and your reflexes are impeccable. You're a natural. With a little more experience, you could be really good, maybe even Olympic material."

"Thanks, Coach," I muttered, reminding myself to take it down a notch for our next engagement. I was pretty sure the Master didn't have Olympic fencing in mind when he told me to learn how to use my sword. My job was hiding the counter, not flaunting my skill set for the whole world to see.

My life seemed to be falling into place nicely until I got home. I walked into the kitchen and saw a large vase sitting on the counter, filled with a dozen long-stemmed red roses. "Who got the flowers?" I asked my mom.

"Ellie got asked to homecoming."

I stopped mid-stride and tried to keep my voice indifferent. "By whom?"

"I think she said his name was Randy something."

While my blood came to a boil, I dug through the freezer for the ice cream. "That idiot. I hate him," I mumbled to myself.

"What did you say?" my mom asked.

"Nothing. I've just never liked Randy all that much."

"Well, Jessica sure seemed excited about him asking Ellie."

I felt extremely irritated and said the first thing that popped into my mind. "Yeah, well, I think Jessica likes about every boy out there. But what I want to know is what Ellie thought."

My mom turned away from the dishes and looked at me. "Why are you so worried about what Ellie thinks?"

I plopped the carton of ice cream on the counter. "I'm not worried, just curious."

My mom watched me. "She was excited too. What about you? Have you asked Kim yet?"

I dropped a scoop of ice cream in my bowl. "No, but I guess I'd better."

"Yes, you should, before someone else asks her and you have to ask me."

I looked up and saw my mom grinning at me. I rolled my eyes. "Yeah, right."

The next day I asked Kim to the homecoming dance. After saying yes, she harassed me for waiting so long.

Day after day, I kept Ellie under subtle surveillance. Randy walked her to class, talked with her in the hall, and ate at her table during lunch. And Ellie actually seemed to like it.

Although fun and bubbly, Kim was as overbearing as ever, and I found it increasingly annoying. I went through the motions of school and soccer. I was having the best soccer season of my entire life, and I should have been ecstatic. Instead, I found myself in a state of discontent. I still enjoyed my daily drive to and from school with Ellie. But like my mom said, she was excited about the dance and all the attention showered on her by the superstar football quarterback, and I got tired of hearing about him.

Friday night arrived, and it was a ditto of my previous experience. I slipped out the door with a backpack full of cash and the keys to Jessica's car. I stashed an envelope in the backpack with Ellie's personal information and her passport photos. I drove to Chinatown and parked on Couch Street. I shouldered the backpack and leaned against the side of a building to wait for Uncle Roy. Again, he was late, and again, we ate dinner at the Chinese restaurant.

The conversation was sparse, so I asked, "What have you been up to lately?"

"Not much, kid, just trying to stay out of the slammer."

"You know, if you got an honest job it wouldn't be so hard."

"Yeah, but where's the fun in that?" he joked. "This guy I work for—he keeps me busy. I make deliveries. Sometimes, I do his dirty work."

"You should be careful, Uncle Roy."

My uncle Roy was cocky, and it showed in his answer. "Always am."

Roy took the backpack, and I picked up the bill from the table. Soon, I drove him to the same dilapidated apartment complex.

"When will I hear back from you?" I asked when he opened his door.

"It's gonna be at least a month. The boss is busy."

NINETEEN
Homecoming

Soccer, homework, and the fencing lessons nearly swamped me, and I almost forgot about homecoming. Fortunately, I intended to double with Adam. He planned and replanned the day's activities for us.

When I went to the football game Friday night, I was smugly satisfied. Randy couldn't sit with Ellie during the game, since he was playing. And Kim's cheerleading left me free to roam the bleachers until I found Ellie. She sat with Jessica and Ryan and some other friends. "Excuse me," I said, looking down the crowded row of students. Normally I wouldn't push my way into the middle of a row, but that's where Ellie sat.

She saw me coming and asked her friends to slide over. By the time I got there, she had cleared a space. "Hey, Ellie," I said as I sat next to her.

She smiled back at me. "Hello, Chase."

Never having watched a football game before, she struggled to follow the ball in play. Within minutes, I was giving her a play-by-play account of what happened on the field. She smiled at me, listening intently while I educated her on the strategies of modern football.

Adam had a great game. He caught and ran the football into the end zone for two of our team's five touchdowns. Hilhi won by ten points—a great way to start homecoming weekend.

Saturday evening, I walked out of my bedroom and paused in the hall to finish fastening the bow tie on my tuxedo. The door to the bathroom was wide open, and I listened in on Jessica and Ellie's conversation.

"Jessica, thank you. I like it," Ellie said.

"You look gorgeous," Jessica gushed. "Randy is going to go crazy over you."

"Thank you for loaning me the dress. Are you sure this slit up the leg is okay? It feels a little revealing."

I bit my lip to keep from laughing. I knew the dress they were talking about. Jessica's prom dress from last year—a long, navy blue gown with a slit up one side, ending just above the knee. Nothing too revealing about that in my opinion, but it amused me that Ellie worried about it.

"It's not, so don't worry," Jessica said.

Abruptly, they both exited the bathroom, and I tried to look like I hadn't been eavesdropping.

"Chase, you look pretty good in a tux," Jessica said, adjusting my bow tie as she passed me in the hall. Ellie followed close on her heels.

"Just pretty good?" I called after her.

Once Jessica passed me I got a look at Ellie. *Stunning.* I'd never thought much of the dress when it was on Jessica, but on Ellie—wow! Immediately, I reversed my opinion on the revealing nature of the slit. It wasn't that the slit revealed too much, but the realization that I didn't want even an ankle revealed to Randy.

The now-familiar flame of jealousy heated up my insides. It must have shown in the anguished expression on my face.

"Is something wrong? Does this gown look bad?" Ellie asked as she smoothed the dress over her hips. Her ringlets were piled on top of her head with rhinestone hairpins. Wisps of hair strategically escaped, curling around her beautiful face. She continued to ramble. "Jessica did my hair and makeup. She assured me it would be appropriate, but maybe it's too pompous. You think it's too much, I can tell." Ellie bit down on her bottom lip and averted her gaze.

Disappointment clouded her once-radiant expression, and I quickly changed my grimace to a smile. "Ellie, no, that's not it at all. You look beautiful! Your hair is perfect for homecoming, you'll see. And the makeup—wow, it looks really good on you." I smiled down at her and risked exposing too much by saying, "I just wish it wasn't Randy picking you up, that's all. I'd better go. I'll see you there." Abruptly, I turned and walked down the hall.

"Why? What's wrong with Randy?"

I waved off her question. "It's nothing. Hey, have fun tonight," I called over my shoulder.

I walked downstairs and picked up my keys, but one look at the clock stopped me in my tracks. I had another hour to go. I couldn't show up at Kim's this early. Sounds of the Seattle Mariners game playing on the television drew me in. I sat on the couch to watch with my dad while I waited.

Within minutes the doorbell rang. I jumped up to answer it for the girls. I might have scowled when I saw it was Randy, but I managed to invite him in. I hovered while he presented Ellie with a corsage and she pinned a white-rose boutonniere onto the lapel of his jacket. And then I stood on the porch and watched him open the car door for her. She looked back and gave me a little wave before she stepped into his car. I halfheartedly waved back, unable to smile, and kept my eye on her date. Randy shot me an annoyed look before he got behind the wheel and backed out of the driveway. Once they left, I sulked back inside to watch the game.

Five minutes later, the doorbell rang again. It was Ryan. Dad got up to talk with him and say goodbye to Jessica. I didn't feel the need to watch the flower exchange and focused on the game.

While driving to Kim's, I forced myself to snap out of my sullen mood and try to have a good time. I owed her at least that much. After I picked her up, we met Adam and Rachel at Hilhi for the dance. Ellie and Randy weren't on the dance floor. Looking for her was the first thing I did.

My eyes repeatedly darted to the entrance—a red carpet leading under a decorative archway. Potted plants from one of the local nurseries, decorated with small white lights, strategically lined the edge of the gym floor. Large black cutouts of the Eiffel Tower and other Paris wonders hung on the walls. A banner read "Paris—A Night to Remember."

Jessica and Ryan arrived, holding hands and looking as happy as ever. I pulled Kim over to talk with them for a minute. The melody of a popular slow song floated across the gym. Turning to Ryan, Jessica said, "Let's go dance. I love this song."

I watched my sister dance away with her boyfriend before I noticed Kim's attention focused on the arched entrance. I turned and glanced over my shoulder to see whom she was staring at. There in the archway stood the most stunning couple I'd seen all night: Randy and Ellie. She looked poised and elegant. He looked as proud as a peacock with her draped on his arm.

Kim turned and looked at me. "They sure are a cute couple, aren't they, Chase?" She pulled her hand up to her hip and waited for my reply.

"What? Oh yeah, I guess they are." No doubt Kim had seen the admiring way I'd looked at Ellie.

I couldn't change the past, so I refocused my attention on Kim. It took a Herculean effort to keep my eyes on my own date. We danced and talked with friends until the student body president called for everyone's attention. The students gathered around the stage for the announcement of the homecoming royalty.

After an introduction the principal took the microphone and raised his hand for silence. "Hilhi's 2011 homecoming queen, based on popular vote by the student body, is . . . Kim Stanton." Applause, whoops, and hollering exploded through the gym. I leaned over and gave Kim a congratulatory hug and then walked her to the front of the gym. Two girls on the student council placed a silver tiara on her head and presented her with a bouquet of roses.

When the applause quieted, the principal said, "Hilhi's 2011 homecoming king is . . . Randy Jones." Applause again exploded through the gym, accentuated by the excited screaming of girls. Randy hopped up onto the stage next to Kim. *How convenient.*

I didn't watch what happened after that. All I noticed was the opportunity to spend a few minutes alone with Ellie. I worked my way through the crowd of people, whose attention was riveted on the homecoming royalty.

The principal continued talking. "Our king and queen will lead the next dance, after which we'll play the last song of the night. Thank you all for coming, and remember to drive safely." More applause rocked my eardrums as music filled the gym.

Finally, I made it to Ellie's side. She was looking the other direction and didn't see me coming. Wrapping my hand around hers, I whispered in her ear. "Can I have this dance?"

She turned, looking surprised. "Certainly."

I rested my hand on the small of her back, pulling her as close as I thought I could get away with.

"I declare, this is the strangest sort of dancing I've ever seen," Ellie whispered in my ear.

I lowered my head to brush my lips against her ear as I whispered back, "Why's that?"

She swallowed once and took a quick breath. "Well . . . I mean . . . You don't do any *real* dances. For example . . ." She raised her eyes and pulled back to look me square in the face. "Do you know how to waltz?"

"A little. My mom tried to teach me once."

"I feel like waltzing." Ellie nodded toward the side of the gym where it wasn't so crowded. "I'll help you. Let's go over there."

She proceeded to give me a lesson on the waltz. "Hold your arm like this. Now put this hand here. Step like this—one, two, three, one, two, three. Good. Now keep doing that as we move around the dance floor." After stepping forward when I should have stepped back, she said, "Maybe you'd better follow me."

I smiled down at her and muttered the cadence to myself: "one, two, three," over and over. Soon, I let out a contented chuckle. "Hey, I'm waltzing."

"Why, yes, you are, Mr. Harper," Ellie said with a flourish. With such an adept partner, it was much easier than I imagined. Much too quickly, the song ended, and she let go of my hand, dropping into a deep curtsy. I bowed slightly, hoping that was the correct protocol when you finished waltzing with a girl from 1863.

She graced me with her incredible smile. "Thank you, Chase. That was most delightful."

I saw Randy moving through the crowd behind Ellie and shoved my hands in my pockets. "You're welcome, Ellie." When he stepped next to her, I added, "Congratulations, Randy."

"Thanks," he said.

I danced the last dance with Kim, but I couldn't restrain myself from watching Randy and Ellie. It looked like Randy held her in a crushingly tight embrace. The hot surge of jealousy in me threatened to boil over. Luckily, Kim's nonstop chatter about being voted homecoming queen kept me distracted enough until the last song ended.

After the dance, Adam and Rachel wanted to go out for ice cream. We talked with them in the booth at the ice cream parlor for almost an hour. I halfheartedly listened while my mind revisited the sparse minutes I'd shared with Ellie on the dance floor. Those three or four minutes made it the best dance I could remember attending.

When I kissed Kim good night on her front porch, I was just going through the motions. Yet, not wanting to tip her off to my lack of feeling, I put my best effort into it. I traced the outline of her cheek with the tip of my finger while she told me how much fun she had. As I tipped her chin up, she stopped talking. I cupped her cheek in the palm of my hand, then slid my fingers around the back of her neck and wrapped them in her dark hair. I bent down, lower than I'd have to if I'd been kissing Ellie, and brushed my lips against hers. That was all the invitation she needed, and the next thing I knew, she had both arms wrapped around my shoulders. I breathed in the sweet aroma of her rose bouquet as it brushed against my neck while she kissed me back. After a minute, I gently pulled away, wrapping my fingers around her arms to untangle myself from her.

"I'd better go. Thank you for the great day, Kim, and congratulations, homecoming queen!"

"Good night, Chase. Thank you."

Feeling guilty, I shoved my hands deep in my pockets and walked back to the car. That night's sleep entrapped me in a dream that looped back and forth between enchantingly waltzing with Ellie and kissing Kim on her porch. When I woke up, I didn't feel the least bit rested.

TWENTY
Tortuga

After homecoming, it appeared Ellie and Randy were officially a couple. I analyzed their relationship from a distance. Randy's feelings were obvious. It may have been wishful thinking, but Ellie's actions left me confused as to how she really felt about him. Ultimately, I tried to ignore their relationship and focus instead on the friendship she and I shared on a daily basis.

The school sent Ellie several reminders regarding her missing documents. Hopefully Uncle Roy's boss would come through with the IDs, and soon. I would die if Uncle Roy took our money and split.

Ellie made huge strides in adjusting to life in 2011. Rarely did things catch her off guard like they used to. And she'd even picked up some of our modern slang. Her grateful nature didn't change, though. She never took the ease of anything for granted, like I always seemed to do.

She played the piano every Saturday and Sunday morning. Invariably, if I went downstairs to watch her, she finished the song and then slid the cover closed over the ivory keys. If I urged her not to stop on my behalf, she would say she was finished anyway. It was always the same. Nowadays, I opened the door to my room, letting the melodies of Bach or Mozart drift in, while I climbed back into bed. If left undisturbed, she played for an hour or more. I found her music enchantingly beautiful.

Soccer was a cakewalk. The practices didn't exhaust me like they had in prior years, and I dominated the field if I chose to. Since I was now the fastest member of the team, Coach played me exclusively as a forward. Occasionally he yelled at me for loafing, but better that than attracting too much attention by playing my hardest. I got in the habit of scoring enough goals to win the game, while acting like I'd exerted myself. They ranked our team first in the district, and we would play in the state championship tournament in two weeks.

The latest buzz around school was the upcoming Halloween costume party and dance. All the girls I knew excitedly planned their costumes. All the guys I knew, including me, would undoubtedly wait until the last minute to find something. With only three days left until the dance, an idea popped into my head during my fencing lesson: I'd be a pirate. I already had the sword from Master Archidus. All I needed were some clothes.

That night I researched pirates on the Internet. Barbados, Port Royal in Jamaica, and Tortuga were all famous pirate hot spots. Piracy had run rampant in the Caribbean from the 1650s to the 1690s. Port Royal sounded like the biggest pirate hub, playing host to nearly five hundred ships. It was even compared to the bustling city of Boston. Too big, I decided. I wanted something less populated.

The notorious pirate Henry Morgan started out in Tortuga, a small island off the coast of Haiti. *Tortuga.* The name really rolled off the tongue nicely. I studied the map of the Caribbean and compared it with the markings on the tiny globe in my counter. I found the dot I thought was Haiti and positioned the pinpoint of light where Tortuga would be. I picked a random date in 1659—July 18—and set the dials of the counter.

I threw on the clothes I'd worn with Ellie to her cabin, thinking they'd blend in with the times better than my basketball shorts and Hilhi soccer T-shirt. I shuffled through five time portals, jogging at each stop to spread out the counter's signatures. It pleasantly surprised me to find I didn't feel as much motion sickness as I had before. Maybe the running helped, or perhaps my body had adjusted to the sensations of time travel.

I meant my final destination to be the main port in Tortuga, but I ended up somewhere in the center of the island, surrounded by thick brush and low trees. After I bushwhacked for a mile, the foliage thinned, giving way to a rocky landscape leading down to the aqua blue of the Caribbean.

Once I reached the coastline, I needed to figure out which way to go. I scanned the horizon. A ship tacked into the wind, heading directly for the island. I turned to the right and went the direction the ship was heading. The rough, porous rocks made the walking difficult, and I cursed my bad luck, wondering where all the exotic beaches were. It wasn't until I rounded the northern tip of the island that I saw a beautiful, white-sand shoreline, virtually untouched by the human hand. In my own time, this would likely be the site of a five-star resort. I jogged along the hard-packed, wet sand, hoping to make up for lost time. It was after midnight for me, and I felt tired.

The port town came into view, and I crouched near the tree line to avoid detection. The wharf bustled with people, most of whom were men, and many looked like they could pass for pirates. Now all I had to do was borrow a set of clothing. The problem was they all looked dirty—I bet not one of these men even owned an extra pair of clothes. This would be harder than I thought. Not only did I have to take the clothes, I had to get them off a pirate. Guilt burned my conscience, but I doused the flame with a clever rationalization. I would only borrow the clothes. It wasn't a theft, and I would return them immediately. They would only be gone for a minute or two. With the counter I'd make sure of it.

Even after my pep talk, I considered abandoning the mission until I spotted a bathhouse at the end of the dock. Two big kettles hung over fires. A large black lady dumped steaming water from one of the kettles into a washtub. I crept closer for a better look at the process. The men went behind a curtained area and stripped down, tossing their clothes to the lady. She collected the clothes and dunked them in the washtub. After slapping soap on each piece of clothing, the woman scrubbed it against the washboard at a furious pace. When she finished scrubbing, she rinsed the clothing in one of the pots of boiling water. Then she twisted the fabric in her hands, wringing out the water, and hung the items up to dry behind the curtained partitions.

I smiled to myself at the sight of all those clothes fluttering in the breeze, like ripe fruit hanging from a vine, begging to be plucked. When she turned her back, I walked as inconspicuously as possible behind the partitions and scanned the clothes. I found a billowy white shirt with full sleeves. It fit the pirate profile perfectly. I found a pair of black pants that looked like my size and pulled them off the clothesline. I counted my good fortune as I watched someone set his boots and hat outside the partition around his tub. Sneaking closer, I listened. The man splashed in the bathtub, singing like a drunkard. I put his hat on my head and picked up his boots. With my arms loaded, I beat a hasty retreat to the trees. To further appease my conscience, I glanced over my shoulder and muttered, "Thanks, buddy. I'll have these back before you're out of the tub."

Before I left, I tried on the boots and pants, wanting to make sure they fit. The boots were a bit snug but not terribly uncomfortable. The pants were definitely a size too big, but that could be fixed with a belt. Shouts from the bathhouse interrupted me. "Cursed be! Who took me boots? Where the devil's me hat?"

"Shoot! Time to go," I said to myself. I picked up all the stray clothing and held the waistband of the pirate pants before I touched the Shuffle button and then Return. Carrying everything was awkward, especially when one of my stops put me on the edge of a steep mountain face. I slid and stumbled around, trying to get my footing in the loose shale. I dropped a boot and was lucky to grab it a split second before I disappeared again.

I reappeared in my bedroom at 10:02 PM—one minute later than when I'd left. How satisfying. I didn't think it would ever cease to amaze me that I could be gone for hours and then suddenly be back in my bedroom as if nothing had happened. I jumped when a knock sounded at my door. "Who is it?" I asked, looking to see if the door was locked.

"It's Dad. Can I come in?"

I kicked the extra clothes under my bed. "Sure." I unlocked the door, wearing the shirt Ellie had made me, the hat I'd borrowed, the pirate pants, and the tall, brown leather boots. I still held the pants up so they wouldn't fall down to my knees.

"Hi, Dad. I'm working on my costume for the Halloween dance. I'm a pirate."

He seemed preoccupied. "Do you want to go salmon fishing with Uncle Steve and Adam on Saturday morning?"

"Sure, Dad. That sounds great."

"Then I'll tell him we can both go. Good night. I'm going to bed. I'll see you in the morning, Chase. Nice costume, by the way."

I sighed. "Thanks. Good night, Dad." I closed the door and hid the clothing and the boots in the back of my closet.

The next day I visited the thrift store. My costume needed some color. An extensive search through the bins of scarves and rows of miscellaneous clothing turned up a red sash.

The gray-haired lady behind the counter took the sash and asked, "Will that be all?"

"Yup, this should finish off my Halloween costume," I answered her.

"What are you going to be?"

"A pirate."

"A pirate? You look like too nice a boy to be a pirate," she said sweetly.

I took the bag and the receipt from her outstretched hands. "I guess I'll be a nice pirate, then. Thanks. Have a good night."

The next day after school I walked with Ellie to the library and lingered to visit. When I finally checked the time, I said, "Hey, I'll be late for soccer if I don't get going. See you later."

Coach had zero tolerance for lateness, and the whole team would be running Spartan laps on my account if I didn't hurry. I dressed in record time, shoving my feet into my cleats. I stuffed my school clothes in my locker and rummaged through my gym bag for my shin guards. "Shoot," I muttered, remembering I'd tossed them in the washing machine the night before. Grabbing my counter I made a beeline for an empty bathroom stall. I set the coordinates for home and pressed the Go button. No time for shuffling.

I smiled as I appeared in the laundry room. I lifted the lid to the washer and found the shin guards. A little damp, but they'd do. I slid them under my socks and pressed Return. Problem solved. Coach glanced at his watch as I slid into place for the warmups, but he spared us the dreaded Spartan laps.

On Friday night, I dreamed again. I ran through a forest that felt more like a swamp of molasses. Someone was stalking me. But more terrifying than being followed was the realization that I'd lost Ellie. I stopped to listen, but my pursuers rustled through the brush, getting closer. I tried to yell for her, but no sound came out. My enemies closed in from every direction. I reached for my sword. It was gone. A hand grasped my shoulder. I shoved my hand onto my attacker's throat and squeezed.

"What the—" my dad's voice yelled.

My eyes flew open. Light streamed in my room from the hallway, illuminating my dad's face in front of mine. His eyes blazed. He clutched at my hand, which had his throat in a choking grip. He let out a raspy cough.

I pulled away as if I'd touched a hot pan. "Oh crap! Sorry, Dad. I was having a bad dream. I don't know what I was thinking." Embarrassed, I sat up on the edge of my bed. I ran my fingers through my hair and looked up at my dad.

He stepped back, eyeing me cautiously and rubbing his throat. "Wow, maybe I need to start lifting weights. You've got an iron grip. I was trying to wake you up for fishing. We've got to leave in twenty minutes."

My dad turned to walk out of the room, and I called after him, "I'll be ready."

We spent the day in Uncle Steve's boat, trolling for salmon in Tillamook Bay. We diligently watched for the rods to throb with a bite. My dad got over being mad at me for attacking him. He told Uncle Steve the story twice while we were fishing. Adam and I each reeled in a Chinook salmon before we had to pack up and head for home.

Later that night, I stood in front of the mirror and adjusted the brim of the pirate's hat. I threaded the red sash through the belt loops and tied it securely in a knot. Picking up my sword from the bed, I fastened it around my waist. After drawing the blade, I stood in a fighting stance, eyeing my ensemble. Then I replaced the sword in its sheath. Luckily, the pirate pants had deep pockets, so I stored the counter in one of them.

TWENTY-ONE
Halloween Dance

"Wow, Chase, that's a great costume," my mom said as I walked into the kitchen to wait for the girls. "Where did you get it?"

I grabbed a handful of the cookies cooling on the counter and straddled one of the barstools. "Thanks, Mom. I—I borrowed it."

"What about the sword?"

I looked down at the chocolate-chip cookies in my hand and took a bite. I hated lying, and I couldn't look my mom in the eyes while I did so. "From my fencing instructor, Coach Bill. It's a practice sword. They're heavier than the competition fencing foils. He had an extra one and gave it to me, which I thought was really cool."

"That was nice of him. It looks awfully fancy."

I shrugged my shoulders. "Yeah, I guess."

"Do you still like the fencing class?"

"It's great."

Mom and I turned to look when we heard the girls' door open and the sound of footsteps on the stairs. My jaw dropped when I saw Ellie. She walked into the kitchen as if she'd stepped right out of the 1860s. Instantly, I knew what she had in the bag she brought back from the cabin.

I jumped to my feet, nearly knocking the stool over. I would have walked over to Ellie, but my mother's inquisitive stare sent me scurrying in the opposite direction. I deviated from my desired course and got a drink of milk out of the fridge instead, but it was impossible to keep my eyes off Ellie.

My mom smiled at her. "That is a beautiful dress. Wherever did you get it?" She studied the details of the dress.

While my mom was distracted, I stood behind the fridge door and examined Ellie's outfit at my leisure. Her dress went all the way to the floor. While the dress was modest by today's standards, the short sleeves and low-scooped neckline showed more skin than I would have expected from her. A white shawl hung over her elbows, and she had piled her hair on top of her head.

"My great-aunt in Boston made it for me. I helped with a reenactment of life in the 1860s last year when I visited her," Ellie explained. "This is a typical gown a girl would have worn to her debutante ball."

"It's so awesome, isn't it, Mom?" Jessica piped in.

My mom shook her head in awe. "Yes, and authentic-looking . . . even down to the handmade lace. You look beautiful, Ellie."

She smiled. "Thank you, Jennifer."

Mom turned to Jessica. "And Jessica, you look great in your poodle skirt. It really turned out nice. I'm so proud of you. You have quite the talent for sewing."

"Thanks," Jessica said. "I love it."

My sister had worked on the skirt for the past two weeks. It was her sewing project for the semester in her home economics class. She twirled around, showing it off. With her bobby socks, her white tennis shoes, and her hair up in two ponytails, she made the perfect 1950s girl.

Anxious to get out of the house—out from under my mother's scrutinizing gaze—I picked up the car keys. "Should we go?"

"You two go ahead. Ryan called, and he's picking me up in a minute," Jessica said.

I waited until I was safely out the front door before I turned to offer Ellie my hand as we walked down the steps.

"So, I take it this was in the bag you brought back from your cabin?"

"Yes. It's silly, really, but this is the finest dress I've ever owned, and I hated the thought of leaving it behind. Aunt Lydia, who I stayed with in Boston, gave it to me for Christmas. I wore it to the New Year's Eve ball. I couldn't bear to part with it when I left Boston. Then, when we got to the cabin, it was conveniently still packed—the bag was sitting by the door. I reckoned it wouldn't inconvenience us and collected it before we left."

I stopped next to the car, and Ellie turned to look at me, her brow furrowed over her green eyes. "I hope you won't get into trouble over it," she said.

"With the Master Keeper, you mean?"

"Yes, whoever it was that sent you back with that dreadful headache."

I stared intently into the depths of her eyes and inched closer. "He didn't say anything about dresses, so I'm sure we're fine." I still held her hand as I waited for her worried expression to soften. "But if I do get in trouble, it'll be worth it. I wouldn't miss seeing this dress on you for anything."

She relaxed and smiled back, then asked in her melodic voice, "Are we going to go to the dance, Mr. Harper, or do you intend on standing here all night?"

I dropped her hand and leaned forward, placing both of my hands on top of the car, trapping her. "Maybe we better stand here all night," I said seriously. "I'm afraid if I take you to the dance, I'll have to deal with Randy. You're much too pretty in this dress to take anywhere."

I didn't smile as I watched her face. I could tell she was wondering whether I was serious or not. Her brow furrowed again and she bit her lower lip, her soft eyes searching mine.

Abruptly, I lowered my arms and chuckled. With a grin, I opened the door. "Nah, I'm just kidding." I watched her breathe a sigh of relief and crack a smile before pulling the folds of her skirt into the car. "Not about the pretty part, though," I said.

I closed her door and walked around to the driver's side as headlights flashed in behind me. That would be Ryan. I got in the car with Ellie and waited. Soon, Jessica bounced down the steps of the front porch with her boyfriend, swinging his hand as she held it. I backed out of the driveway after Ryan and followed them to Hilhi.

Hordes of students in costume crowded the high school gym, dressed as everything from witches to football players. I held Ellie's hand as we meandered around the crowded dance floor. I scouted for Randy and Kim when we first walked in. Luckily, I saw no sign of either of them.

I leaned over to Ellie when the tempo of the music shifted to a slow song. "Do you want to dance?"

"Certainly," she said.

I steered her into the center of the dance floor. "I bet every guy in Boston fell in love with you the first time you wore this dress."

"No, only one."

I raised my eyebrows. Learning that only one guy had fallen for her actually bothered me more than imagining a flock of eligible bachelors after her. I'd never imagined the possibility of Ellie having a boyfriend in 1863. "Tell me about him. What was his name?"

"His name was Walt Griffith. He was studying to be a doctor and planned to join the Union army as a surgeon after he finished medical school."

"Hmm . . . a doctor, huh? Do you miss him?"

"Sometimes. But we had courted only a few months. There were no promises between us when I left for Utah."

I held her closer, swaying to the music, lost in thought. When the song ended, I was disappointed but loosened my hold.

"Hey, Harper, thanks for taking care of my girl," Randy interrupted loudly. He slapped me on the back and leaned in to give Ellie a hug. "Ells, wow, you look great. Let's go talk to the guys over here," he said, pulling her away from me.

I watched him lead her to the other side of the gym before I shoved my hands in my pockets and walked off the dance floor.

Adam tackled me from behind. "Chase, great costume!" He grabbed for the sword, and I twisted my body out of his reach, playfully pushing him back. "Is that sword for real?" he asked.

"Yeah, don't mess with it."

"Where'd you get it? Let me see."

"Later, dude. I don't want to get kicked out of here for having a real weapon." With Ellie on my arm, I'd made it through the door without anyone noticing the sword, but I didn't want to push my luck. I changed the subject. "Where's Rachel?"

"She's coming. How 'bout you? Where's Kim?"

"I don't know. I haven't seen her yet."

Adam pushed me toward the refreshment table. "Let's go see if they have anything to eat."

"Yeah, sure." I glanced over my shoulder at Ellie.

By the time we got there, Kim had joined us. She was dressed as a vampire in a stunning black dress, a long cape, pale makeup, and red lipstick. I listened as our group of friends compared costumes and planned the remainder of the night.

Suddenly, I felt the hair rise on the back of my neck. The same gripping panic I'd felt in my dreams coursed through me. I searched the crowds of students for any sign of danger, but everything appeared as it had before. I located Ellie on the dance floor with Randy; she looked fine. I tried to bury the feeling as unfounded, maybe a throwback to the nightmare I'd had that morning.

The back door to the gym opened, and three men stepped through. With the dim lighting and the random flashing of the mirrored dance ball, I strained to make out the details of their faces. But something about them struck me as familiar. The feeling of alarm escalated, and I turned to leave. "I'll be back in a minute," I said to Adam and Kim.

"Where—" Kim started to say, but I was gone, pushing my way through the crowds. I stood taller than most of the other students, so I easily watched the three men. They worked their way around the perimeter of the gym, obviously searching for something or someone. Two of the men were dressed as cowboys. The third, shrouded from head to toe in a long, dark cape, slinked after them. The shorter man moved into the light, turning his face slightly in my direction. My eyes widened—it was Miguel, the Mexican from Ellie's cabin. Instinctively, I put my hand on the hilt of my sword. The taller man pointed into the middle of the dance floor. Ortiz—Miguel's brother, whom I'd fought with by the river to rescue Ellie. I followed the direction he pointed: Ellie. My dread turned to rage.

I changed direction, plowing through the crowd to get to her before they did. Angry students swore at me as I shoved them aside. Ortiz battled the crowded mass of students as well. Judging the rate of our progress, I had a good chance of getting to Ellie first, but not by far. A slow song started to play. Most students paired up or moved to the edge of the dance floor, making it easier to maneuver. I met the fury in Ortiz's eyes as I beat him to Ellie. Obviously he recognized me, too. I grabbed her arm, pulling her away from Randy. "Ellie, we've got to go."

Randy held onto her and put his hand on my chest. "No, she doesn't. I'll take her home after the dance. You leave her alone, Chase."

In my panic, I had forcefully pulled at her. I let go and pointed at Ortiz. "Ellie, look who's here."

Her eyes flashed with recognition. "Oh no!" she gasped. "Yes, let's go. I'm so sorry, Randy. I've got to leave." I grabbed her hand and started to run, thinking that was the end of it.

But Randy pulled her back. "What's going on here?"

I didn't have time for this. Ortiz closed the distance, nearly knocking an unsuspecting couple to the floor. Weeks of pent-up jealousy and frustration reached the boiling point. Without thinking, I whirled around to face Randy and punched him in the stomach. He doubled over in pain, releasing Ellie.

I turned and ran for the exit, pulling her behind me. The other vaquero and the hooded man pushed through the crowd, attempting to cut us off.

"How did they get here?" Ellie frantically asked.

"I don't know!" I yelled. But even as I spoke, a random memory—one that had never been my own—flashed through my mind. A memory planted in my brain by Master Archidus. I recognized the hooded man for what he really was: a Sniffer. The words of the Master echoed in my mind: "Sniffers can follow your counter signatures through time, and some are able to pull humans through with them."

"The hooded one is Balcombe, a Sniffer," I told Ellie. "He must have brought the Mexicans here."

I reached the doorway first and rushed through, almost knocking over the vice principal as I exited. "Excuse me. Sorry, sir," I muttered, shoving my way past him.

I heard the vice principal try to stop and question the vaqueros, but they must have pushed him out of their way. Their spurs jangled as they ran behind us. I shoved the gym door open so hard it bounced back, almost hitting me in the face. Ellie and I raced down the concrete stairs toward the parking lot, but we would never outrun them with her in heels. The warning from Master Archidus echoed ominously through my mind, and I knew I eventually had to stop and fight.

I cut across the grass by the tennis courts, hoping to get out of sight of the gym entrance. The three men closed the distance between us. I contemplated using the counter to run, to find someplace or sometime to hide away. But the Sniffer would follow, so it would only prolong the inevitable. They had found us in 2011. I feared if I didn't take a stand now, it would only be a matter of time before they found my sister or my parents.

I took hold of the hilt of my sword. Pushing Ellie behind me, I spun around to face our attackers. They pulled out their pistols, and I rushed them. I changed directions so quickly I must've caught them off guard. Charging into them, I slit Ortiz's gun hand with my sword and then tackled Miguel to the ground. Miguel's gun skittered across the grass into the shadows. I rolled away and hopped to my feet. Looking stunned, Ortiz held his bleeding hand. I kicked his gun behind me and faced my enemies.

The rushing maneuver had removed their pistols from the equation, slightly evening up the odds. Both men drew their swords. Miguel, who was thicker set, was quicker on the draw, but I parried his attacks with more ease than before. Seconds later, with blood staining his sleeve, Ortiz yelled as he raised his sword and joined the attack. With two swords coming at me, I felt naked with nothing in my left hand. I wished I had something, even the rifle I'd had at the cabin, or another sword, or a baseball bat.

I managed to hold the two brothers at bay. Engaging one at a time, I alternated quick cuts between each of them. Ortiz's gaze darted to the side, and my eyes followed his. Ellie ran toward the abandoned pistol on the grass. Ortiz smiled and left me, racing toward her. Fearing for her, I tried to follow, but Miguel held me prisoner with his blade. I attacked with a ferociousness I didn't know I had, cutting his thigh and stabbing him in the left shoulder. Still, he kept attacking me.

A shot fired behind me, and Ellie screamed. I whipped my head around. She had the gun, but Ortiz restrained her hand, holding it above her head. He had stuck his sword in the ground. His right hand locked onto her throat, choking her, slowly squeezing the life out of her. I probably had only a minute to finish off Miguel if I was to get to Ellie in time. Ortiz's wicked laugh sickened me, and I realized that he delighted in slowly choking her. He could have slit her throat quickly and been done with it, but he clearly enjoyed watching her suffer. Hopefully, that would give me time to rescue her. The Sniffer slinked closer, a large knife protruding from the sleeve of his dark cloak.

In my next attack, Miguel missed deflecting my sword blade, and it glanced off his sword arm, drawing blood. He faltered briefly. Somehow I knew Ellie was out of time, so I turned my back on my opponent and raced across the grass toward Ortiz. He was so focused on watching Ellie die, he didn't see me coming. I drove my sword through his side. Grabbing him around the neck with my left arm, I angled the blade toward his heart and yanked him away from Ellie. He let go of her, clawing at my face before sputtering out his last breath.

What occurred next was a blur as three things happened all at once. Ellie collapsed to the ground, clutching at her throat and gasping for air. Miguel rushed behind me, and I felt his sword pierce the side of my back. And finally, a young man—dressed in work clothes from the 1800s and wearing a sword—appeared on the grass twenty yards in front of me. He raised an ancient rifle to his shoulder.

As the cold blade sliced my skin, I dropped Ortiz and jumped forward, pulling myself off Miguel's sword. Trying to get clear of Ortiz's body, I stumbled to the ground, using my free hand to catch myself. I regained my footing and turned to face my enemy. Searing pain radiated from the wound in my back, and I felt a warm sensation as blood soaked my shirt. I swung wildly at the vaquero.

The deafening blast of a rifle blew past my head, and blood began seeping out of a hole in Miguel's chest. His sword fell from his hand, and he glanced down before he crumpled in front of me. I turned to see the newcomer, with rifle in hand, smile and sharply salute me. In one fluid motion he pulled a gold counter from his pocket and flipped it open. He ran past me toward the Sniffer, who had turned tail and run the second the rifle fired. I watched the Sniffer disappear, followed immediately by the other Keeper.

Except for my breathing and Ellie's, the world fell silent. I bent to rest my sword hand on my knee and touched my back. My hand came away sticky with blood. I sheathed my sword and knelt down next to Ellie. Her wide eyes darted to the dead vaqueros.

I touched her cheek. "Ellie—" But before I could say more, she gasped. Their bodies began crumbling, like a sandcastle without enough moisture. Within seconds, they turned to dust. There were no bodies and no blood left. The only evidence of their existence was their clothes, boots, and weapons, lying where their owners died. An eerie gust of wind stirred the air, scattering their dust. Then all was still.

My heart thudded heavily in my chest. I'd killed a man, and then he'd disintegrated before my eyes.

Sobbing next to me, Ellie grabbed my wrist. "Chase, I'm so sorry. I was only trying to help. I didn't know what to do. It's my fault you're hurt."

Stunned, I shook my head. They were after the counter. After me. Not her. "Whoa, what are you talking about?"

"I tried to get the pistol from the grass. I planned to shoot one of them, but I only ended up getting in the way, being a distraction for you. Now you're hurt. Your back is covered with blood. You could have died. I'm so sorry, Chase." Ellie sounded nearly hysterical.

I wiped her cheek with my thumb, trying to caress away her tears. "Shush. Stop apologizing. It's not your fault at all. Hey, I appreciate you trying to help."

Jessica's voice interrupted me when she called from behind the gym, "Chase! Ellie!"

"Jess—behind the tennis courts!" I yelled back.

She found us a minute later. "Oh my gosh, Chase! Is that blood on your shirt? We heard gunfire after you two ran out. Who were those guys? The principal is calling the police, and they locked down the gym. Luckily, I got out the back door before they locked it. What happened? Did you get shot?" As usual, my sister rambled, firing off questions without ever leaving a gap for the answers.

Spurred into action at the mention of the police, I struggled to my feet and started to pick up the evidence. "We've got to hide all this stuff."

"Whose costumes are these?" Jessica asked. "Where are the people? Chase?"

I stooped to scoop up an armful of clothing, but the movement sent pain shooting through my back and drew a groan from my lips. "Later, Jess. Please, help me." I moaned involuntarily as more blood oozed from the wound each time I bent over.

Looking worried about me, Jessica and Ellie filled their arms with clothing, boots, and weapons.

"Where are your keys?" Jessica asked.

I dug the keys from my pocket and handed them to her.

Remembering Miguel's gun flying into the shadows when I tackled him, I asked, "Did you get the other gun, over by the fence?"

"I'll get it," Ellie said.

Jessica and I looked at each other as the sound of sirens grew louder.

"Hurry," I said. "Wait . . . take this too." I unbuckled my sword and placed it on top of the pile in her arms.

Knowing it was inevitable, I hobbled toward the parking lot to meet the police. Jessica and Ellie disappeared between the rows of parked vehicles to dump the strange evidence in our car. The trunk slammed shut, and the girls ran back toward me as the flashing red and blue lights came down the street. Jessica reached me first and protectively wrapped her arm around my waist, helping me walk the last few yards to the parking lot.

The police cruisers' spotlights nearly blinded us. More cars with their sirens blaring approached the high school as the first policeman stepped out of his car. The whole Hillsboro police squad must have been sent to Hilhi.

Standing behind his open door, the cop yelled, "Step away from each other, and put your hands where I can see them! On your head, on your head—put your hands on your head, now!"

Jessica stepped away from me and raised her hands. Ellie looked to be in shock at the mass of angry policeman converging on us. "Put your hands on your head," Jessica told her.

I felt lightheaded, and the cop cars seemed to sway in front of me. I blinked my eyes and tried to raise my hands. I got my right hand up, but the pain throbbing through the left side of my back made it impossible to raise my left hand.

He shouted at me again. "Son, put your hands on your head, now."

"I don't think I can," I mumbled to Jessica. I didn't feel well. But I tried again, forcing my left hand up to shoulder level. Then everything went perfectly dark.

TWENTY-TWO
Left

I woke to the sound of voices. The cold, gritty asphalt dug into my face. I opened my eyes, struggling to figure out where I was. My neck was twisted at an awkward angle.

"Listen to me, please. My brother's hurt," Jessica said, obviously trying not to cry. "He was leaving the dance when two guys attacked him. We need an ambulance. He's not armed. Please."

The next voice sounded close. "Move away from him, miss. Back up and keep your hands on your head."

I raised my head. A group of policeman in full SWAT gear— helmets, bulletproof vests, and rifles—surrounded us. One of them moved forward and patted me down for weapons. My arms were pulled into the classic "about to get arrested" position. A moan escaped my lips as the officer wrenched my left hand behind me and slammed a pair of handcuffs around my wrists.

Speaking loudly, the cop read me my rights. "You have the right to remain silent. Anything you say can and will be used against you in a court of law. You have the right to have an attorney present during questioning. If you can't afford an attorney, one will be appointed for you. Do you understand these rights, son?"

"Yeah," I said. "Am I under arrest?"

"Not yet, but you've got some explanining to do. We'll get medical to check you out, and then the detective will have some questions for you."

He hauled me to my feet and turned me over to the EMTs. Numerous policemen surrounded the gym, searching for the gunman. The EMTs placed me face down on the gurney, and I concocted a story as I lay there. The pirate shirt I'd intended to return was cut off my back.

"You're not going to try and run away, are you?" a different policeman asked as he removed the handcuffs for the EMT. He stood there waiting, pen and notebook in hand. I realized he must be the detective who wanted to question me.

"No, sir," I mumbled.

In dismay, I watched as Ellie and Jessica were each led away by a different cop. Undoubtedly, they would talk with each of us separately. What were the chances our stories would match up? Ellie cast a questioning glance in my direction, and I quickly mouthed, "Shh." She didn't need to say anything— the look on her face was heart-wrenching. I wished I were alone with her so I could do something to ease the anguish in her eyes.

Once the EMTs had taped a gauze pad over my wound and determined I wasn't in immediate danger of dying, the detective stepped forward. "You have the right to remain silent. Anything you say can and will be used against you in a court of law. You have the right to an attorney during questioning. If you cannot afford an attorney, one will be appointed for you. Do you understand these rights?"

"Yeah, the other guy already asked me that."

"Gunshots were reportedly fired on the school grounds. What can you tell me about that?"

"We were in the gym when my girlfriend started feeling sick, so I left the dance to take her home. Some crazy old Hispanic guys in cowboy costumes were snooping around, and they came out of the gym behind us. I don't know what they were doing, but they acted drunk. We watched those two get in their truck and drive away. But while we were distracted by them, two other guys got out of a car. They had a gun. They were parked in the handicapped spot near the sidewalk where we were standing. They yelled threats at us, demanding money. We ran across the grass, there by the tennis courts. I thought we could run around and reenter the gym from the back door. But they shot at us, or maybe they shot in the air. I don't know, because my back was turned to them.

"Anyway, we stopped running. I decided to give them my wallet like they asked. It wasn't worth risking my life for. But before I could do that, they started messing with my girlfriend. That's when I fought back. One of them pulled a knife and stabbed me in the back. I think they got scared off when my sister heard the gunshots and ran out after us. She yelled something about the vice principal calling the cops. After that, they ran to their car and drove away."

"Can you give me a description of the two men with the gun?" the detective asked.

I kept fabricating the story. "Not really. They had masks on—ugly, Halloween, monster-type masks, like an ogre or something."

Between questions, the EMT put an oxygen tube under my nose. The detective scratched notes on his paper. The rest of the policemen secured the school grounds, and K-9 units showed up to scour the area. The dogs showed extra interest in the location of the fight but apparently didn't find anything except traces of my blood.

After a complete sweep of the school grounds, the K-9 units and a few of the police cars started leaving. The principal unlocked the gym, and all the students filed out to gawk at what was happening. I didn't look forward to being the center attraction in the spectacle. I was ready to get out of there.

"Can you give me a description of the gunmen's car? Make, model, year, color, anything?" the detective prodded.

"Not really. It all happened so fast." I tried to think of a generic, extremely common type of car. "All I remember was it was a smaller-sized car like a Toyota or Honda. It might have even been a Mazda. I have no idea on the year, but the closest I could guess would be late 1990s. It wasn't white—it was a darker color, maybe blue, gray, black, or even dark green. I'm not sure."

Frowning at the vague information, the detective looked over my driver's license and wrote down my name and phone number. "Wait here," he ordered. "I'll be right back." After he left, several other cops kept me under close surveillance.

I watched the detective confer with the officers who'd talked with Ellie and Jessica. Ellie sobbed quietly, her face buried in her hands. Then he appeared to discuss the situation with the school principal and vice principal. When the detective returned to me, he said, "We'll get you on your way to the hospital now. If you think of anything else that might help us, call me. Let me get you my card."

"Okay."

He handed me his business card and turned to walk away. "Hope you're feeling better soon."

The EMTs lifted the stretcher into the ambulance. Truthfully, I thought the ambulance was a little much, since my stab wound wasn't that bad, but I was just happy I hadn't been arrested after all.

"We'll meet you at the hospital, Chase," Jessica called to me before an EMT slammed the door and the ambulance drove away.

I silently rehearsed the story I'd told the police, not wanting to mix up any details should I have to retell it again. I didn't think Ellie had said much, but I wasn't sure, and hopefully Jessica's story hadn't contradicted mine.

Four hours later, the doctor released me from the hospital with stitches in my back, my left arm in a sling, a big gauze bandage wrapped around my chest and back, and a prescription for Percocet. The doctor said I was lucky. The blade had cut through the muscle and glanced off my ribs. If it had slid between the ribs, my lung could have been punctured—a potentially fatal injury. Unfortunately, Ellie overheard all this as the hospital discharged me, and the anguish in her eyes only seemed to intensify. I wanted to talk with her alone, but there was no chance. My mom ushered me to her car, and she sent Ellie and Jessica home in the other car.

As soon as we were home, my mom hovered over me like a mother hen with her chicks. She got me something to eat and tucked me into bed. I planned to sneak down the hall to see if Ellie was all right, but the exhaustion of the long night, combined with the Percocet, knocked me out. Within seconds of closing my eyes, I was sleeping soundly.

I slept away half of Sunday, but Jessica was wise enough to set her alarm and get up early. She retrieved all the evidence hidden in the trunk of Dad's car and stowed it safely in my closet.

Mom made pancakes and eggs for breakfast. I think she felt bad about my injury and was trying to cheer us all up. Ellie seemed distant and lost in her own thoughts. I realized later she didn't play the piano that day. She avoided making eye contact or talking with me and hung out in her room.

I stayed home on Monday and rested, but by Tuesday I was stir-crazy and went back to school. Ellie was polite but increasingly distant. In Human Anatomy, I noticed she gave Randy the cold shoulder as well. I began to wonder if she was having some sort of post-traumatic stress syndrome. I decided to talk with her that afternoon and sort it all out.

I couldn't go to soccer practice because of my injury, so I walked with Ellie to the truck after the last bell rang. I opened the door for her and tried to offer her my hand, but she turned her back to me and climbed in on her own. I walked around and got into the truck.

"What's going on?" I asked, not even bothering to put the key in the ignition.

"I'll thank you to take me home now. I don't belong here. I'm a burden for you and your family. I simply can't suffer it any longer. When we get to your house, I'll be packing my things and leaving."

I shook my head. "You're not a burden. You're just upset about Saturday night. I don't want you to leave."

"You could have died that night, and I would have been partly to blame for it. I can't be around to put you in danger like that ever again."

The defiant set of her jaw and the firm tone of her voice told me her mind was made up. Still, I had to try. "Ellie, that's ridiculous." I was angry now. Angry at the Mexican vaqueros, angry at myself, and angry at her silly ideas about it being her fault. "It's nobody's fault. Things happen. Boys fight. It's all part of life. When things get tough, you don't walk away and give up."

She narrowed her eyes. "When I grabbed your arm and followed you here, that was when I walked away and gave up," she said, raising her voice. "I have an aged great-aunt in Boston who is sick and needs caring for, and a man named Walt who hopes I'll come back and marry him over Christmas. Chase, I'm done running away. It's time I faced the facts of *my* life, not yours. I expect you'll be complaisant in this matter and take me back once I gather my things."

My jaw went slack. Out of everything she'd said, all I heard was "come back and marry him." *Marriage,* I thought ominously. She'd said she wasn't all that close to the guy— had I been fooled or what? In a daze, I turned the key, staring intently at the diesel's wait-to-start light on the dash. My eyes burned from the hot tears I refused to let fall.

We drove home in painful silence. Ellie jumped out of the truck as soon as it was in park, abandoning her backpack on the seat next to me. Slowly, I followed her inside. I walked into the kitchen and stared at the scar on my hand—the fine, white line marking the cut she had tenderly stitched.

A few short minutes later, she walked downstairs, her hair pulled neatly in a bun, wearing her white blouse and long, navy blue skirt. She carried her worn satchel as she marched into the kitchen. "Maybe you should change," she said in a clipped tone, "in case someone sees us. It will make the explaining a little easier for me."

I numbly walked upstairs and put on the frontier outfit. As an afterthought, I picked up the pirate boots, hat, and pants. The shirt I had borrowed was a total loss, so I'd return one of the Mexican shirts instead. The one with the bullet hole had the least damage. I left the sling on my bed and walked downstairs, cradling my left arm next to my side.

"May I see the counter, please?" Ellie asked when I came back. I looked at her outstretched hand, tempted to say no, but I could never force her to stay if she didn't want to. I dug it out of my pocket and handed it over. She spun the globe to the northeastern part of the United States, situating the spot where the coastline dipped in to form a harbor, over where the pinpoint of light would be when I held it. "I don't know the numbers," she said, handing the counter back to me. "Set them for the fall of 1863, please."

I set the first four digits to 1863. "What month and day do you want?"

"I don't care. Just do today."

"Okay," I mumbled, "November 1, 1863."

Feeling utterly miserable, I took her hand and pushed the Shuffle and Go buttons. But when we appeared on the edge of a beautiful mountain meadow surrounded by a herd of bugling elk, I resolved to enjoy what precious time I had left with her. Was this what Archidus had seen—my returning Ellie to her own time? No wonder he'd been quick to forgive me. Sadly, this was it. I would never get the opportunity to share a time-travel experience with anyone again.

As soon as we walked into the meadow, the startled elk bolted for cover. The sound of their magnificent antlers crashing through the branches of the trees was the last thing I heard before Ellie and I shimmered away to China. We appeared on a hill above some rice fields. Hundreds of workers in pointed white hats walked below us on the valley floor, carrying baskets. We soon left China to appear on an island in the South Pacific. As we walked along the isolated beach, our feet sank in the fine white sand.

Next, we appeared in the Appalachian Mountains, surrounded by underbrush so thick it was impossible to move. I looked down at Ellie's face, hoping to see a glimmer of a chance she'd change her mind, but she stared straight ahead and refused to look at me. I smiled at the irony of our next shuffle zone—the southern Utah desert and the magnificent, orange rock formations of Arches National Park.

How odd that we had come full circle. In the scheme of things, we weren't really that far away from where we'd first met. I walked along, kicking at the orange dirt while I waited for the inevitable to occur. Ellie's curiosity got the best of her, because she finally motioned to the clothes and boots I had tied in a bundle and stuffed under my arm. "What are those for?"

"I thought I'd return the pirate clothes I borrowed, while I was out and about." I smiled at her, hoping to soften the grim look on her face. I wished I knew what she really thought. I had a feeling I wasn't getting the full story out of her.

A blast of cold wind off the Atlantic Ocean welcomed us to Boston Harbor. Ellie pulled her hand out of mine. "Thank you, Chase. I can find my way home from here."

I doggedly followed her up the dock. "I'll walk you home."

She turned her head and glanced at me. "It's not necessary. I'd rather you left."

I shrugged my shoulders. "Whether you like it or not, I'm going to see you safely through your front door before I'll leave."

She turned and walked briskly through the docks and into the main city. I followed close on her heels. We hadn't walked more than a mile before Ellie pointed to a white house on the corner. It wasn't a big house, but it appeared safe and sturdy, and the neighborhood looked nice.

She stopped and faced me. "Thank you, Chase, for everything. Please tell your parents and Jessica I appreciated their kindness. I'm sorry to make you explain this for me. But I didn't think I could say goodbye to them myself." She turned to leave.

I watched Ellie take one step away. Then I said, "Wait!" I reached out to grab her arm and turned her to face me again.

Dropping the clothes, I stepped closer. I tipped her chin up, forcing her to look at me. I looked into the depths of her eyes and tried to see why it was so important for her to be here, for her to leave me. But I found no answers in her pained expression.

Ignoring the pain in my back, I lifted my left arm and held her face softly in my hands. I gently traced the line of her cheekbone with my thumb. My fingers moved behind her neck, and I leaned forward to brush her lips with mine, gently at first, testing the waters.

"I've wanted to do that since the first night I saw you," I whispered.

I turned so my back sheltered her from the icy wind. Before she could tell me to stop, I kissed her again. She kissed me back at first, but the kiss held no promise of a future together. It felt more like a kiss goodbye.

Her body stiffened the moment before she looked down. She placed her hand on my chest and pushed me away, not looking me in the eyes. "It's cold. I should go. Goodbye, Chase."

She turned and hurried toward the white house. Stunned, I watched as she opened the gate, then walked up the porch steps and through the front door, never once looking back. I think deep down I expected her to change her mind. Slowly, I turned into the wind. And for the first time in more years than I could remember, I cried.

TWENTY-THREE
Alone

I wandered aimlessly through the darkening streets of Boston, unaware of my chattering teeth and shivering shoulders, until an older gentleman in a suit stuck his head out of a rolling carriage. "Son, do you have a place to stay the night?"

The driver of the carriage pulled the horses to a stop, and both men stared at me, waiting for a reply. I was tempted to climb in the carriage with this nice-looking man and see where it took me, but that wouldn't solve anything. It would only prolong the inevitable. "Yeah, I'm . . . I'm fine. Thank you anyway." I waved them off as I walked away.

I feared if I pushed the button on the counter and left, I would forever close the best chapter of my life, but I really had no choice. I turned down a shadowed alley, checking to see that I was alone before I set the counter for July 18, 1659, Tortuga. Pressing the Go button, I imagined the exact time and place I'd left. I jogged out of the trees toward the partition.

"Hey, where did you come from?" the nearly naked pirate yelled at me.

I tossed the clothes and boots at the man's chest. Then I threw the hat as if it were a Frisbee. "Are these yours?" I turned and ran back toward the cover of the trees. Two other pirates, waving swords and pistols, yelled as they followed me. I pressed Shuffle and turned the counter settings to November 1, 2011, Oregon, as I shimmered away. Thinking of my bedroom at 4:00 PM, I pushed Go.

There was little joy in arriving spot-on next to my bed at precisely 4:00 PM. I hid the frontier clothes, put on basketball shorts, and climbed into bed. I was tired, and I felt weak and chilled. I didn't have an ounce of energy for anything except lying in bed.

My phone vibrated next to me, and I shoved it away. One after another, the text messages from Kim piled up, then a couple from Adam and my soccer teammates. I had nothing to say to any of them, and no interest right then in what they had to say to me. I slept restlessly until my phone rang with Jessica's ringtone. I let it ring twice before I answered. I would have to tell her eventually, so I might as well get it over with.

"Hello," I answered.

"Chase, where are you and Ellie? Why aren't you answering my texts? It's almost dinnertime."

I glanced at the clock. It was 6:15 PM. "I'm in bed and I'm not hungry. Ellie's gone. She went back to Boston."

"What? I'll be right there," Jessica said, then disconnected the call.

She stormed into my room a moment later. "What do you mean she went back to Boston?"

I raised my voice, taking out my frustrations on my sister. "I mean, I just left her on November 1, 1863, in Boston, Massachusetts. She was upset, maybe even traumatized over what happened Saturday—I don't know. She wanted to go back and take care of her great-aunt. She's talking about marrying some guy named Walt. Did you know about that, Jess?"

That got her defensive. "No. She told me about him, but I never thought she loved him. I can't believe you let her go! Why didn't you stop her?"

"I tried. It's not like I could tie her up and hold her prisoner."

"You should have let me talk to her."

I sighed. "I know, Jess. I wanted to change her mind, but she was . . . very determined."

"I don't understand. She loved it here." Jessica slumped onto the bed next to me. "Why, Chase? What happened between you two that night? You must have done something. What did you do? You still haven't told me anything."

After a long pause, I began. "Do you remember the two Mexican vaqueros, the brothers I told you about? The ones who were after Ellie and the counter in 1863? Well, they were brought here by a Sniffer—a magical bad guy from the other world. I killed one of them with my sword when he was about to kill Ellie. I didn't have a choice. Then another Keeper—a guy with one of these counters—appeared and shot the other one. Maybe it was too much for Ellie—I don't know. What did she tell the police that night, anyway?"

Jessica shook her head. I didn't know if she shook her head in disbelief at what I'd said, because she didn't know the answer to my question, or in sadness over Ellie's leaving. "Ellie said she was so upset she couldn't say a thing to the officers. I pretty much told them the truth. I saw you leave and ran out to check on you when I heard the gunshots."

I nodded and Jessica continued. "At first I wasn't too excited about her being here, but after a while I actually loved it. I started to think of her as my sister. Seriously, where is she? And do you think she will ever come back?"

"I told you, Boston, 1863, and I don't see how she can come back. But it doesn't matter. She was dead set on leaving."

"What are we going to tell Mom and Dad?"

I turned on my side to face the wall. "I don't know. You take care of it. I don't feel good."

"Chase!"

My sister was clearly annoyed, but I didn't care. I closed my eyes and ignored her.

After a minute, she said, "Well, I guess I'll tell them she got a phone call at school today from her great-aunt in Boston. Her aunt Lydia bought Ellie a plane ticket and asked her to come stay with her while she recovers from an illness or surgery. We don't know exactly what is wrong, but Ellie said she will be gone indefinitely to care for her. You took her to the airport after school and are now exhausted. How does that sound?"

"Fine."

I stayed in bed the next day. When I didn't get up for school on Thursday, my mother came in my room and threatened to take me to the doctor. She assumed my injury wasn't healing right, or was infected or something.

Having no intention of going to the doctor, I got up and went to school. Each class period passed with agonizing slowness, but fifth-period Human Anatomy was pure torture. Randy glared at me across Ellie's empty seat. I should have apologized for hitting him at the dance, but that would undoubtedly bring up the subject of her absence, and I had no desire to discuss that topic with him.

I had a date with Kim on the weekend. I was absolutely miserable, and I realized I didn't have the energy or the motivation to act interested in her any longer. She looked as beautiful as ever, but her appearance no longer held sway over me. Halfway through dinner, I stopped eating and said, "Kim, I don't think we should keep dating each other. I don't want to be in a relationship right now. I'm sorry."

My abrupt decision must have felt like an atom bomb to her. "Why? Did I do something?" she asked, looking shocked. "Is there someone else?"

"It's not you, Kim, it's me. I'm just . . . I'm not going to be dating anyone right now. That's all. I want to focus on school and my sports."

We didn't eat much after that, and I took her home, actually relieved to close that chapter of my life. Then and there I made a resolution. From here on out, I'd go through life with no strings attached. I wouldn't put myself in a position to be hurt again like I'd been with Ellie.

Time passed at a slug's pace. Obsessively, I opened the picture of Ellie on my phone every chance I got. Finally, I set it as my permanent wallpaper picture. Now all I had to do was slide my phone open to look at her.

Not too long after she left, I started getting text messages from Uncle Roy. He wanted to meet me for dinner, and I knew he must have Ellie's ID ready. I ignored his messages. What good would the ID do now?

At night, dreams of stabbing people haunted me. I would wake up in a cold sweat. It bothered me that I'd killed a man and that I'd done it so easily, without a second thought. With Ellie's life in danger, I hadn't even hesitated. In fact, at the time I'd savored the feeling of ending his life to save hers. Unfortunately, it had made it so much more real, holding the man in my arms while I stole his life away. Thinking about it now sickened me. I didn't want to be a killer.

I eventually told Jessica the whole story of the fight, every detail made more painful now that Ellie was gone. Each detail of that night contributed to her leaving, and I hated them for it. Although I despised even thinking about that night, I couldn't get it out of my mind. Jessica tried to sooth my pained conscience, reminding me that if I hadn't killed Ortiz, he would have killed Ellie and me. It was self-defense.

I played pitiful soccer at the state championship. My coach assumed it was due to my unhealed injury, but in truth, my heart wasn't in the game. I simply didn't care. Luckily, my other teammates elevated their games, and we managed to win by one goal, bringing home the state soccer champions trophy for display outside the gym.

I walked around with a constant ache in the pit of my stomach. I tried to convince myself Ellie would be happier in the time she was familiar with. I told myself she would probably get married and have lots of babies and grandkids. Then it hit me—the devastating reality that whatever she chose to do with her life, it was done. She was gone by now. She was dead.

I nursed the anger I felt inside at losing the one girl I really cared about. To my dad's disappointment, I refused to play basketball, signing up for wrestling instead. I had no desire to play a team sport. I craved the physical confrontation of wrestling as an outlet for all my internal agitation. I pounded everyone who came within my grasp into the mat with a shocking fury. More than once, the ref disqualified me for illegal roughness. That infuriated my coach. But if I wasn't disqualified, I was winning.

My dad would study me with a disturbed look on his face, probably unsure how to handle a teenager with physically violent outbreaks. But it only happened on the wrestling mat. I didn't do anything violent at home, just sulked around. My mom worried about me also, but she believed the breakup with Kim was to blame. She assumed Kim had done the breaking up with me, and I didn't bother correcting her. It was easier that way.

On the night before Thanksgiving, something strange happened. That was the first time, but I would soon learn it wouldn't be the last. I was sleeping soundly when I found myself in the middle of a dream. Not a regular dream, though. This dream came on suddenly and with shocking clarity. I saw myself on a darkened dirt road during an older time. I heard faint laughing and other noises coming from a building down the street, maybe a bar. At the sound of shattering glass, I spun around and ran into the alley. Three guys restrained the same man who had come to my rescue at the Halloween dance—the other Keeper. A fourth man held a broken whiskey bottle, laughing as he prepared to slit the throat of the Keeper. Right then, a view of the counter flashed before me. The numbers and location on the globe seared themselves into my memory.

I shot awake. Adrenaline rushed through my body, like nothing I'd ever experienced before. I was possessed of an urgency that wasn't of my own making. Sitting on the bed, I tried to gather my thoughts, figure out what I'd dreamed, and why. But I couldn't sit still. I paced back and forth across my room. I saw the counter destination flash through my mind again and again: New York, August 14, 1817. I clearly remembered what the Master said about needing my services and sending a message. If this wasn't a message from Archidus, I didn't know what would be. Plus, considering the other Keeper had saved my life, I figured I owed him one. I picked up the counter and set the dials like I'd seen in my dream. Waves of anxiousness pushed me to go, to get it over with. I put on my frontier outfit and picked up one of the pistols I'd inherited from the vaqueros. With one last look at my room, I pushed the Shuffle and Go buttons.

TWENTY-FOUR
New York

I moved through my shuffle zones, hardly taking notice of where I was. The whole of my attention focused on the upcoming alleyway. As in my dream, I appeared in the darkened street. Across from me was a tavern. The faint laughter of a woman and the raucous banter of some men floated on a warm breeze. I turned toward the alley. Cocking the gun, I realized I'd never fired a pistol before. *Oh well, here goes nothing.* I ran into the alley as the whiskey bottle shattered against the wall of the building.

I aimed at the ground behind the attacker's legs and squeezed the trigger. Putting as much of Clint Eastwood's style into my threat as I could, I said, "Drop it or the next bullet goes in your back." I sized up the four men. They were a good deal older than me, and I really hoped this didn't turn into a gunfight. I had no desire to shoot anyone.

The man with the bottle stepped back but didn't seem convinced. "Who are you?" he asked.

Thinking fast, I improvised. "I'm his brother. Let him go, or I'll have to pull the trigger." I lifted my thumb and cocked the gun.

Dropping the bottle in the dirt, the attacker raised his hands. "Aw, shucks, kid, lower yer shootin' iron. We ain't fixin' to shanghai him or nothing. We're only cuttin' a few shines with yer brother, is all. Didn't mean no harm."

The Keeper shook off the three guys holding him and walked toward me.

I waved the gun at them. "Then get out of here!"

"Thanks, little brother," the Keeper said, slapping me on the shoulder. "Let's go."

After backing out of the alleyway, I turned and jogged down the street to catch the other Keeper. I followed a step behind his purposeful stride as he moved through the dark streets. He finally entered a building with a painted sign hanging above the door—"Rose's Boarding House." The Keeper swung the wood door open on squeaky hinges and held it for me. He seemed to want me to follow him, although neither one of us had spoken since we left the alley. Once in the boarding house, he tiptoed up the creaky steps. He walked down the hall and opened a door with a key he pulled out of his pocket.

Again he held the door, motioning me to enter. Once we were inside, he lit a candle. The room was sparsely furnished with two beds, and a small table with a couple of chairs against the wall. A cracked porcelain washbasin sat on the table. "Thanks again," he said, "I'm Garrick. How 'bout you?"

"My name's Chase, Chase Harper. By the way, thank you too, for the other night—with the rifle."

"Yeah, sure, anytime. Whatever happened to the pretty little lady you were with? She was sure a sharp looker."

Disgruntled that even here I couldn't escape the memory of Ellie, I said, "She left me."

Garrick dunked his hands in the washbasin, scrubbing them together. "Ahh. That's the pits. But they always do. Once the fighting starts and you disappear, only to come back bloodied and bruised, they always leave. A good woman wants a nice reliable man, not somebody like us. They want a man who goes to the office in a suit and tie, comes home at the same time each day with a fat paycheck, sits down to dinner at six, and gives 'em babies. That's what a woman wants. They don't want guys messed up in some crummy interdimensional warfare, like we are."

"When I talked with Master Archidus, it didn't sound all that bad."

Garrick scooped water from the basin and washed the blood off his face. "Kid, how long have you had your counter?"

"A couple of months."

"Well, no wonder. You're barely getting started. Just you wait. There's always another assignment—another mission from Archidus. That two-timing, no good, devil-of-a-brother of his causes more problems. I swear the guy never sleeps. He must lie awake at night dreaming of ways to steal our counters."

"You don't sound like you're from 1817."

Garrick shook the excess water from his hands. "I'm not. I'm from the sixties. I was born in 1944. When I was twenty-four—actually, I'm still technically twenty-four—I got a draft summons for the Vietnam War. That same week, I had an argument with my girlfriend. I wasn't too keen on the idea of going to war, so I've been dodging the draft and my girlfriend by wandering through time ever since. I think it's been close to six years since I've been home. I've lived here in Rome, New York, for almost a year. Right now I'm digging the Erie Canal, or Clinton's Big Ditch, as everybody around here calls it. Governor DeWitt Clinton came here to break ground on the canal on July 4. Half the men doubt it'll work, but that doesn't stop 'em from collecting their pay. The work is tough, but you get paid twice a month, and there are a lot of men, so it's easy to blend in."

"What did those guys in the alley want?" I asked.

"My poker winnings," he said, pulling a handful of coins from each pocket. "You could say those four are the town bullies. I should have known better than to stay at the tavern so late and then not watch my back. I got stuck in a poker game. This rich guy from Virginia wanted another chance to win back what he'd lost. We must have played for three hours straight. I'm dead tired. My roommate left for Ohio last week. If you want, you can take his bunk and come dig the canal with me tomorrow." Garrick blew out the candle and walked over to his bed.

I sat on the other bed. "Garrick, remember the night you came to help me? The guy in the dark cloak was a Sniffer, right?"

"Yeah. Name's Balcombe. He's a good tracker, but a coward. That's the fourth time I've chased him. He's a wily one."

"Did you catch him?"

"No. Sniffers must not get cold as fast as we do. He's learned he can run to the Arctic, and I can never last long enough to catch him there. The first time, I came back with frostbite on my face and hands. When I left him, he was still running across the snow-packed tundra."

"Do you think he'll be back?"

"Eventually, but he won't bother finding us again until he has some help."

I looked at the scrawny, lumpy mattress, then watched Garrick pull off his boots and collapse onto his bed, without an apparent care in the world. I contemplated my lonely, miserable life in 2011 and thought, *What the heck?* "Wake me up in the morning, and I'll go dig the canal with you."

"Sounds good. 'Night, Harper."

"One more thing. The man I killed that night—why did his body disintegrate when he died? It was like he turned to dust, or ash, or something."

"Whenever somebody dies outside of their proper time, they turn to dust. Probably has something to do with the Bible. I think it says something in there about 'dust thou art and unto dust thou shalt return.' I don't know for sure, but that's my guess."

"Oh . . . thanks. Good night, Garrick."

I pulled my boots off and shoved the pistol under the mattress. I lay down and was certain this was the most uncomfortable bed I'd ever been in. I looked at the dark ceiling and listened to the sound of silence—no heater vents blew air, no airplanes hummed overhead, and no cars drove down the road. I dreamed of Ellie that night, but it was a good dream. I stood in the doorway of our living room and listened as she played the piano. It was the sweetest melody I'd ever heard.

The next morning, I woke to the sound of a rooster crowing, but before I could move, Garrick shook my shoulder and said, "It's time to get up, little brother."

"Huh." I rubbed the sleep from my eyes and sat up on the edge of the bed. I looked around the small room as sunlight filtered through the dirty windowpane. "Last night wasn't a dream after all," I muttered.

Chuckling, Garrick pulled on his shirt and smoothed down his brown hair before settling a weather-beaten hat on his head. "Nope, and if you want breakfast, you'd better hurry. Food goes fast around here." This was the first chance I had to get a good look at the other Keeper. He was all muscle, with broad shoulders and a thick neck. He stood a little taller than me. The stubble of a growing beard shadowed his face. He had blue-grey eyes that transformed from a look as hard as steel to a cheerful twinkle when he cracked a smile.

While I pulled my pant legs over the top of my boots, I asked, "Did you play sports?"

"I played high school football, but I wasn't good enough for college. If I would've had the counter back then, I could've been a better player. I bulked up a lot after I got it. And I'm faster now. It's a nice little perk, if you don't mind living such a complicated existence otherwise. Come on, let's go."

"Yeah, sure."

I followed him down the narrow hallway and staircase to the crowded kitchen. Eight scruffy men mingled about, dishing up plates of food from platters piled high with scrambled eggs, hash browns, and biscuits. A pretty, brown-haired woman hurried around the room, cleaning up as the men finished.

"That's Rose," Garrick whispered, not taking his eyes off her while we ate.

After breakfast we walked along the streets of Rome, New York, to the canal site.

Garrick approached a serious-faced man who had the air of someone in charge. "Boss, you got a place for my kid brother to dig?"

The man looked me over and gave a curt answer. "He looks strong enough. Sign him in with the paymaster." Then he turned back to his maps.

We logged my name with the paymaster and picked up shovels. The men formed themselves into three-man teams. The canal was forty feet wide and four feet deep. We alternated the jobs of digging and hauling away the dirt.

The most challenging part of the process was clearing the stumps. Someone had invented a crude but effective stump-pulling system. It consisted of different-sized wheels for leverage. We hooked mules to the chains turning the wheels, and they ripped the stumps out of the ground. Garrick and I formed a team with an Irishman named Thomas Macaulay. We loaded the dirt into a wheelbarrow and transferred it to mule-drawn carts. I'd never worked so hard or so long in my life. Sweat poured down my back, and my hands bubbled with blisters before the end of the first day.

We literally worked from sunrise to sunset. We had an hour break for dinner, which consisted of some hardtack, jerky, and a handful of biscuits Garrick had saved from breakfast and brought with him in a cloth bag. After dinner, it was back to work. The boss rode his horse the length of the canal, looking for slackers. If he caught you not working, he docked your pay.

After work we ate chicken and dumplings at Rose's Boarding House. Rose agreed to let me rent the room with Garrick. Board was due the same day we got paid at the canal. Once back in our room, I flopped onto my bed. Absolutely exhausted, I didn't even have the energy to take my boots off.

Garrick washed his face and hands in the basin. "Harper, you want to go down to Tyke's Tavern with me?"

"Are you kidding? No, I'm too tired." Before Garrick left the room, I fell asleep. I hadn't slept so soundly in weeks. The rooster crowing in the morning was the next thing I heard.

We worked with men from all over the world. Irishmen were the most common nationality, but there were Germans, Britons, and Russians as well. Nearly every nationality was represented in the trenches of the Erie Canal. There were some indentured servants, brought over from Europe in trade for their commitment to work on the canal. Some of the plantation owners hired out their Negro slaves—a sobering thing to view firsthand. I knew about slavery from the history books, but to be there and see it with my own eyes was difficult.

On our first day off, I woke to find Garrick gone. I wandered through the boarding house looking for him. "Hey, Davy, have you seen Garrick?" I asked Rose's five-year-old son.

He looked proud to know the answer for me. "Yes, sir, he's splittin' wood out back for my ma."

"Thanks, Davy."

I took a handful of biscuits and spread them with butter and jam, then walked outside. It would be another hot and humid day. I found Garrick behind the house, splitting a pile of logs. He already had his shirt off, and a sheen of sweat was visible on his tanned skin. Split wood lay scattered at his feet.

I stopped far enough away to avoid being hit by a flying piece of wood. "What are you doing, Garrick?"

"Splittin' wood."

"I can see that. But why?"

He rested his hand on the ax handle. "Rose's husband died four years ago. I think she barely makes enough to keep this place going. She shouldn't have to pay someone to split wood, and I don't want her doing it. She works too hard as it is."

I wondered if Garrick had a soft spot for Rose or was simply a nice guy. "Hmm," I said, between mouthfuls of biscuit. "Do you want some help?"

"Sure. There's another ax hanging by the back door." I retrieved the ax and went to work.

It wasn't long before Garrick said, "Let's race. Line up ten logs. The first one to have them all split in half wins."

"Okay." I lined up ten logs, taking care not to choose any with big knots.

Garrick lined up his logs. "On your mark, get set, go!"

His ax was a blur. Split sections of wood flew in every direction. I was on log number six when he threw down his ax. Raising both hands in the air, he yelled, "Done!"

I laughed. "I want a rematch. I'm just getting warmed up."

We raced again and again, until Rose's pile of logs disintegrated into a mass of split wood. Garrick won every match, but his margin of victory steadily decreased. He won the last match ten to nine.

Little Davy clearly admired Garrick. The little boy followed him like a shadow and even helped us stack the wood in neat piles outside the back door.

The canal paymaster paid us every fortnight. After two weeks, Garrick and I waited in line to collect our coins. When the weather was bad we didn't work, but then we didn't get paid for the day, either. We were supposed to receive twelve dollars per month, but the paymaster deducted for the days not worked and for the tools we used. What I walked away with seemed a pitiful sum of money for the amount of physical exertion it took to earn it.

Eventually, the dig site would be too far away from the town of Rome to make it practical to stay at the boarding house. Many of the men already stayed in work camps on the outskirts of town. I paid Rose my board and hid the rest of the coins in our room. On our day off, I put on some of Garrick's clothes and washed mine. For my first washboard experience, I tried to imitate the woman I'd watched in Tortuga. I smiled at the memory of Ellie's fascination over the ease of the washing machine. After a few scrubs and rinses, I had water splashed down the front of me. Already sick of hand washing, I pulled my clothes from the water. "That's good enough," I said to myself. I wrung them out and hung them on the clothesline to dry.

The next two weeks flew by. The monotony of shoveling dirt was therapeutic for me. Immersing myself in the physical labor eased the pain and frustration of my broken heart while Garrick's happy-go-lucky attitude rubbed off on me. If he could do it, so could I.

One day while we were digging, I asked Garrick, "What's the name of your counter?"

"The Guardian."

"Do you know about the others?"

"I've talked with the Keepers who have Wisdom and Perception. The old Asian guy who has Illusion didn't stick around to talk after I rescued him a few years ago. Arbon has the other two counters, but I've never heard their names. Archidus told me the original sorcerers who had our counters—the Protector and the Guardian—were brothers. Supposedly, they were exceptional warriors, skilled in the arts of both physical and magical warfare. They were the guard detail for the other sorcerers. Knowing that, it intrigued me that you chose to call yourself my brother that night."

"Do you think that's our job now—protecting and guarding the other Keepers?" I asked.

"I never really thought of it like that before, but it does seem like that's all I've been doing since I got the counter." Garrick left me to ponder what he'd said while he dumped the wheelbarrow.

Halfway through the third week, the heel on one of my boots ripped off. The thrift-store pants weren't holding up to this heavy labor, either. I dug my extra money out of its hiding place. Garrick took me to the cobbler, who took one look at my boots and said they weren't worth repairing. He sent me to the dry-goods store, where I splurged for a pair of Wellington boots. According to the store clerk, they were "all the rage in fashion." I left Paddy's Dry Goods wearing my Wellingtons and carrying a bundle of fabric for the tailor. I left my measurements, the fabric, and sixty-two cents with David McCabe, the local tailor, thinking as I walked away what a bargain I was getting on a new shirt and a pair of custom-made pants.

TWENTY-FIVE
Paris

At the end of my third week in New York, it happened again. I was sound asleep, dreaming of driving home from school and listening to Ellie's melodic voice, when someone abruptly changed the channel on my dreams. Suddenly, I saw a narrow side street, slick with freshly fallen rain and lined with garbage cans. It was dark out, and there were no lights illuminating the short, narrow street. It looked more like an alley, although it was wide enough for a single car to travel down. The streetlights from the main crossroads cast their light only a short distance into the narrow space.

From somewhere in the middle, camouflaged by the shadows, came a woman's scream. It was quickly muffled, followed by the clang of a metal trash can rolling across the asphalt. Feet shuffled across the ground. The woman continued to scream hysterically, although it sounded like someone now held a hand over her mouth. Her screams soon turned to sobbing.

The sickening sound of human flesh being beaten to a pulp sounded in my eardrums. The gasping of breath, the spitting from a bloodied mouth—each sound was clear and distinct in the darkness. The whine of a siren and the occasional honking of horns made up the background noise.

Darkness masked the details of the men's features; only their shadowy silhouettes filled my vision. One restrained the sobbing woman, and one held the victim while another hit him repeatedly. As I walked forward, I saw a cloaked figure sulking in the shadows. He paced back and forth, apparently waiting for the perfect opportunity to join the skirmish. The counter coordinates flashed across my mind: France, September 4, 1989.

A feeling of overwhelming urgency flooded my system with adrenalin, and I woke instantly. Bolting upright, I looked around the room. Garrick sat on his bed, fastening his boots by the flickering light of a candle. He stood and started to button his shirt.

"Did you see it too?" he asked.

"Yeah," I mumbled, rubbing the sleep out of my eyes.

"Good. I was trying to decide if I should wake you."

"Who are they?" I asked.

"I don't know who the woman is, but I'm fairly certain the man is Raoul, Wisdom's Keeper. He's French, but he speaks English. I've met him twice. I'm guessing the woman is his girlfriend. Raoul is a real intellectual type, which is fitting, considering the name of his counter. Harper, what are you waiting for? Get ready!"

"Sorry." I threw on my shirt and shoved my feet into my boots.

"Harper, where's your blade? Didn't Archidus give you a sword?"

"Yeah, but it's back at my house."

"That's all right. You won't need it. Did you see the Sniffer in the shadows?"

"I noticed someone in a cloak. It looked like the Sniffer from the night you helped me."

"It was. The only way to kill a Sniffer is with a blade forged by magic. That's why Archidus gave you the sword. But I got dibs on this Sniffer. He's mine. I've waited a long time for an opportunity this good. Here's the plan. We'll go there together, with your counter. The Sniffer will sense your counter's signature when we arrive. You go in and break up the fight. Keep them busy for a while, and make it look like you're losing. The Sniffer will get drawn in, hoping to move in for the kill. That should distract him enough that I can sneak up and get my blade through his heart. You got it?"

I wasn't sure I liked the sound of Garrick's plan. "So, I'm the bait? I go in there and get my butt kicked until you kill the Sniffer?"

Garrick smiled. "Yeah, that sounds about right. Are you ready to go?" He slid a heavy sword with a gold hilt from under his mattress and fastened it to his waist.

"Don't I need some kind of weapon?"

"Nah, we don't want to scare him off. You've got to appear vulnerable."

"Great," I muttered. "What if they pull out a gun or something?"

"I don't think they had weapons. Looked like a bunch of thugs and pickpockets to me. But if they do, hit the Shuffle button and disappear. Then come back after you're armed."

I rolled my eyes, hoping he was right. I carefully set the counter to France, September 4, 1989.

"Harper, don't put us in the middle of the alley. I've got to be out of sight for this to work. Make sure you think about the cross street outside of the alley. You got that?"

"Yeah, I got it. You ready?"

Garrick put his left hand on my shoulder and nodded. I pressed Shuffle and then Go. We went through four uninhabited shuffle zones before coming up in a small western town. It was midday, and the street bustled with activity. Garrick and I hustled behind a building to disappear. We finally appeared in Paris on the main street, twenty yards from the narrow alley we'd seen in the dream.

The woman screamed, but the sound was quickly muffled by the attacker's hand. Garrick ran to the corner of the building and peered around. I followed him. He motioned for me to go, then shoved me into the dark alley. Not having formulated a detailed plan of action, I opted for speed and surprise. I took off at a run and threw myself directly into the fray.

I tackled the man doing the hitting, landing on top of him on the asphalt. His head made a sickening thud as we hit the ground. Before I could scramble to my feet, the other man yanked me off him. A heavy boot slammed into my side, and one of the men pulled me to my knees by my hair. Whoever had me by the hair slammed his fist into my face twice. With my ears ringing and my side aching, I fought to get my feet under me.

Two more times the heavy boot kicked my rib cage, knocking the air out of me. On the fourth kick, I grabbed his boot with both hands. I twisted the man's leg until I pulled him off balance, throwing him on the ground. Once he fell down, I turned and slammed my fist repeatedly into the stomach of the man holding me by the hair. The one holding the girl joined the fight and hit me in the back. Surrounded and gasping for breath, I tried to stagger out of their reach. I never made it.

The Sniffer circled like a vulture around a dead animal. Someone always had a hold of me, pounding me with his fists, while I pounded someone else with mine. I'd throw one off me, but there was always another guy in line. The French Keeper lay moaning on the ground, his face covered in blood. His sobbing girlfriend tried to help him up. He looked at me, and I sensed he was trying to get himself into the fight, but a cut above his eye bloodied his vision. He frantically wiped at it, trying to watch the Sniffer. The Keeper struggled to his feet and engaged one of my attackers. As I felt the fatigue of the fight begin to overwhelm me, the Sniffer pulled out a dagger. He came directly toward me, close enough now that I could hear him. His voice escaped his lips in a hiss. "Two for one—fortune is indeed smiling on me this day."

Frantic now, I threw punches in every direction, desperate to escape, desperate to reach my counter. Where was Garrick? Obviously I had no difficulty making it look like I was losing. A sharp pain shot through my side as two heavy-handed hits landed on the back of my rib cage, in the same spot as the sword wound—the same ribs the guy's boot had kicked. The searing pain threatened to drive me to the ground. But I resisted, knowing if I went down, I'd most likely never get up again.

A high-pitched scream pierced the night air. The unearthly shriek caused every one of us to cover our ears and abandon all attempts to hit each other. Garrick had suddenly appeared behind the Sniffer, driving his sword through the Sniffer's back and piercing his heart. The Sniffer's blood-curdling scream continued as he weakly swung his dagger behind him. Garrick dodged the blade. He was too fast, and the Sniffer never stood a chance. Collapsing onto the wet pavement in an eerie silence, the Sniffer died.

All three attackers stood frozen in place, watching as the Sniffer's body crumbled to dust and blew away in an unexplainable gust of wind.

A mischievous grin spread across Garrick's face. Swinging his sword in front of him, he tossed it from hand to hand. Steadily, he advanced toward us and eyed our attackers. "Who's next?" he taunted.

The French Keeper yanked open one of the men's jackets and retrieved his gold counter and a wallet from the inside pocket. "Allez-vous en!" he yelled, shoving the man away from him. "Get going." The men raced down the narrow street and disappeared around the corner.

Garrick slid his sword into its sheath as the three of us stared at all that remained of the Sniffer—his clothing and dagger. "That'll make Arbon mad." Garrick reached out to clasp wrists with the French Keeper. "Wise Wolf, good to see you, my friend."

Raoul spit out a mouthful of blood and then smiled. "Arbon may be mad, but I'm quite pleased. Nice work disposing of our Sniffer, though maybe next time you could get here before his minions take their fists to my face." Smiling, the French Keeper looked at me. "Who's your friend?"

"This is the Protector's Keeper. Harper is his name. Harper, this is Raoul Devereux. His name, Raoul, means wise wolf."

I weakly offered my hand. "It's good to meet you. I'm Chase Harper."

Raul shook my hand. "Nice to meet you too. Where and when are you from?"

I wiped the trickle of blood from my nose and wrapped my arms protectively around my aching rib cage. "I'm originally from Oregon, in the United States, 2011, but most recently from New York, 1817."

"It's a privilege to make your acquaintance. And thank you for the assistance. You took the counter from the cave, didn't you?"

"Yeah, that was me. Where are you from?"

"Right here—good old Paris, France, 1989," Raoul said proudly. With a tall, lean build, he looked to be in his early forties.

I had forgotten about the woman, who cowered in the shadows near the trash cans. She quietly moved next to Raoul and spoke a few rapid sentences in French. He answered her in French before turning to us.

"I'd better get her home. I'll see you around. Thank you, Garrick. Thank you, Harper." Raoul shook our hands again before he turned to leave. He leaned on his girlfriend as he hobbled down the street.

A huge smile spread across Garrick's face. "Did you see that Sniffer, little brother? That played out perfectly. He thought he was taking both of you down. He never even suspected I was here until it was too late. Nice work, Harper. Very authentic. You made it look like you were losing while giving the impression you were fighting your hardest. I'm impressed."

"I *was* fighting my hardest," I mumbled.

He jovially slapped me on the back. "Oh well, good work anyway."

I cringed away from him, breathing shallowly. Anything more than that sent shooting pain through my side. "Ouch! I think they cracked my rib."

Garrick took a closer look at me. "Wow, they really pounded you good. Cracked rib, huh? Those are painful. Give it a few weeks, though, and you'll be fighting with the best of them. You should heal fast because of your counter—at least I seem to. Hey, you want to see the Eiffel Tower before we leave?"

Exasperated, I said, "Garrick, would you look at us? We're not exactly dressed for sightseeing in 1989. Plus, I'm tired and I'm in pain. Let's go home." I winced as I pulled out my counter. My thumb hovered over the Shuffle button. "Are you coming with me or not?"

"Sure," he said. "I can't believe we got that Sniffer. But I am sorry you took such a beating."

"That's okay. Did you see the thugs' faces when he disintegrated? They took one look at you swinging your sword and started running like a bunch of babies. It was priceless."

I started to chuckle, but the pain drove me to clamp my mouth shut. With Garrick's hand on my shoulder, I pressed Shuffle and then Return. I hobbled through the shuffle zones, listening to Garrick's play-by-play account of what had transpired with the Sniffer, how Garrick had used his counter to appear behind him at the perfect moment. My friend's elation was infectious.

By the time we arrived in our room, we both felt like heroes. Groaning with pain, I collapsed onto my bed. Once I found a relatively comfortable position, Garrick lulled me to sleep with his retelling of the victory.

TWENTY-SIX
Healing

The next morning I didn't hear the rooster until Garrick shook my shoulder. "Little brother, wake up. Time to go."

I pushed him away. "Leave me alone. I can't move."

"Come on, or the boss will dock your pay. We've already missed too many days this week because of the thunderstorms."

I tried to roll over, but gave up as pain shot like a skewer through my lung and made my breath catch in my throat "Garrick, I don't think I could dig an irrigation ditch, let alone the Erie Canal. Maybe I should go home."

"That's probably not such a good idea. You haven't seen your face."

"What?" I struggled to open my eyes.

Garrick stood over me with his arms folded. "How are you going to explain to your parents, waking up in the morning looking like you just walked out of a bar fight?"

"Is it that bad?"

"Swollen eye, split lip, bruises, blood-smeared face—I'd call that bad."

"If I go to work, the boss is going to think I'm loafing, and I won't get paid anyway."

"No, he won't. I'll cover for you. I can dig enough for both of us. The boss will never know. Give me a chance. All you have to do is get there and act like you're digging. I'll tell Thomas you got beat up by the bullies last night—he'll help cover for you too."

"Okay." I gritted my teeth as Garrick pulled me into a sitting position.

He picked up the empty washbasin. "Don't move. I'll get you some water to wash your face." He hurried out of the room.

"Don't worry, I'll be right here. I promise I won't go running off anywhere," I muttered to the empty room. Shaking my head at my pitiful state, I studied my battered knuckles and felt the tender swelling around my right eye.

Soon, Garrick burst into the room carrying the washbasin, along with a plate of flapjacks and bacon. "Eat. You'll feel better once we get some food in you."

Obediently, I shoveled in mouthfuls of food. Garrick set the washbasin on the table and slid it next to the bed. He pulled a small white towel from inside his shirt.

"That looks like one of Rose's kitchen towels," I said.

"It is. I lifted it off her bread. Don't worry—the boys will eat the bread before she notices it's gone." Garrick dipped the towel in the water and wrung it out. "Sorry this is cold. No hot water, you know, unless we heat it over the fire, which we don't have time for."

"That's all right," I mumbled between bites of food. I took the towel from Garrick and cleaned the dried blood from my beat-up face.

When I finished and looked up at him, he pointed. "You missed a spot on your chin. No, a little lower. Yeah, right there. Good, that'll do. You want a hand up?"

He pulled me to my feet. I still had my boots on from the night before.

"Well, let's get this over with," I said as I gingerly walked out the door.

I pulled my hat down on my head and lowered my gaze while I followed Garrick to the job site, shoving my battered hands deep in my pockets. He picked up two shovels, threw them in the wheelbarrow, and found Thomas.

"What in Sam Hill happened to ya, lad?" Thomas asked with a frown.

I let Garrick tell the story, and I nodded at the appropriate times. Thomas cursed the bullies and threatened to give them a piece of his Irish mind. Garrick assured him it was in the past, and we wanted it left there.

"Harper, I'll keep a pile of loose dirt in front of you," Garrick said. "If the boss walks by, scoop some of that in your shovel, and he'll think you're digging. You got it?"

I attempted to smile until my lip threatened to split open again. I nodded. "Yeah, thanks, Garrick."

"Don't ya worry any, lad. We'll cover for ya," Thomas added.

"Thanks, Thomas. You're the best."

Garrick and Thomas shoveled harder and faster than I'd ever seen anyone shovel. I felt guilty watching their sweat-stained backs strain under the heavy labor. As the day wore on, the pain and stiffness in my rib cage lessened slightly, and I put a few token shovelfuls of dirt into the wheelbarrow. That night both Garrick and I hit the sack after supper. For the first time, he was too tired to visit the tavern.

The next few days were tolerable, each day passing much like the one before, with exhaustion overtaking us by nightfall. Gradually, the pain in my rib cage lessened, and I could breathe normally with only minor irritation. I began shoveling again, slowly at first, since any sudden movement sent shooting pain through my side. It seemed like I was healing quickly, and I wondered if Garrick was right—that the magic counter had healing properties, as well.

As we walked to work Tuesday morning, I saw a wagon stopped on the side of the road. A blonde girl in a bonnet was unsuccessfully trying to get her horse to move. She had a load of produce piled in the bed of the wagon.

I pointed at the girl. "I'm going to go see what's wrong," I told Garrick.

"You'll be late for work," he replied.

"I'll hurry."

I jogged across the street, careful not to jar my ribs. "What's the problem?" I asked her.

She looked ready to cry. "I don't know," she said with a heavy Dutch accent. She pointed to the horse. "He started limping a little, but now he is refusing to move. I'm already late getting this load to the market."

"Let's see." I looked over the animal's legs for any sign of swelling, then began picking up each foot.

"My ma's expecting a baby any time now. My pa's sick today—ate something bad yesterday, he thinks. I'm certain you were wondering why I'm driving this wagon to town alone."

"Hmm. Actually, I hadn't given it a second thought." I checked another hoof.

"Mister, were you in a fight, if you don't mind me asking? Because you look like you were. However, you don't seem much like the fighting type."

"I'm not." I leaned over to pick up the third foot.

"But you were . . . fighting, I mean?"

"I'm finding sometimes it's necessary."

"So, this was necessary fighting?"

"Absolutely. I think I found your problem. Your horse has a rock stuck in his foot. Do you have a hoof pick?"

"A what?"

"We need something to pry this rock out with. Maybe a stick." I looked beneath the trees along the road and found a sturdy branch, then broke off a piece. Moments later I dislodged the rock, sending it flying off the road.

I dropped the horse's hoof. "There, that should help him feel better. Why don't you try again?"

She slapped the reins down on the horse's back, urging him forward. I pulled him from the front, but he still refused to take a step.

"He doesn't know his foot won't hurt him now. Keep pushing him. Once he takes a couple of steps, I think he'll realize he's fine."

She urged him onward, but without success. I picked up a longer stick and climbed in the wagon next to her. "Do you want me to try?"

Obviously still upset, the girl passed me the reins. "Yes, please."

"Yah," I yelled, imitating the teamsters I'd seen driving around the canal site. I slapped the reins down on the horse's back and brought the stick down on his rump. With the increased pressure, the big horse must've decided it was better to move forward than stay within the reach of my stick. He limped the first three or four steps, but in no time at all, he trotted along smoothly. I pulled the wagon to a stop.

"I've got to get to work," I said, climbing down.

"Thank you. I'm Anna. What's your name?" she said as I started across the street.

"Chase Harper, and you're welcome," I called back, hustling toward the canal.

"You're late, Harper," the paymaster said when I checked in.

"Sorry, sir."

"I'll let it slide this once, but don't let it happen again."

"Yes, sir," I answered. I picked up my shovel a little too quickly, wincing at the pain in my side.

The paymaster's gruff voice stopped me. "Are you hurt, Harper?"

"No, sir, just a little stiff this morning," I lied.

He waved me on. "All right, get to work then."

When I found Garrick, the first thing out of his mouth was, "So you met Miss Anna Van Dousen, did you? You know she's about your age."

"Yeah," I mumbled. "So what."

Garrick pushed me for information. "Well, did you help her? What did you talk about? She's cute, isn't she?"

"Yeah, I helped her. Her horse had a rock stuck in its foot, and I got it out. But Garrick, I'm not getting involved with another girl from a different time zone. Last time I did that it caused me nothing but grief." I attacked the dirt in front of me with more zeal than I should have, and my rib cage soon complained with a dull throb.

On our next day off, Garrick and I again chopped wood for Rose. Midmorning, little Davy ran behind the house and said, "Mr. Harper, a man's here to see you."

I looked at Garrick and shrugged my shoulders. I buried my ax in the chopping block and walked to the front door.

"Chase Harper?" the man said in a heavy accent similar to Anna's.

"Yes, sir, that's me."

I had to listen carefully to understand him. Every "W" came out sounding like a "V," and every "Th" sounded more like a "D."

"I want to thank you for helping my daughter last week," he said. "Can you be at my house on Sunday at six for dinner?"

I smiled and waved him off. "That's not necessary—it was nothing."

"Ya, it was something. I had a contract to fill. Without the money from that load of produce, it would have been difficult for my family. We're much obliged. I insist you come to dinner. My wife will cook a feast."

I didn't want to offend him by refusing. "Can I bring my brother?"

"Ya, that would be good. We will see you then?"

I nodded. "Sure. Where do you live?" I asked as he started to leave.

"The white farmhouse by the new canal, between the two oak trees."

"Okay," I said, wondering when people would start using addresses.

On Sunday morning, Garrick and I washed our clothes, not wanting to show up at the family dinner covered in a week's worth of dirt and grime. That evening, we walked to the canal and located the two large oak trees towering above a small, white farmhouse in the distance. Garrick teased me about Anna until I finally told him to shut up and shoved him away from me.

"All right, all right! Heck, Harper, you don't need to get so bent out of shape. I'm just having a little fun."

After that we walked in silence. Within minutes of arriving, Garrick had the three youngest Van Dousen children, all boys, wrestling with him on the floor. Anna's unabashed staring, and her father's unending questions, left me feeling like a piece of meat at a cattle auction. I made up lies as fast as I could. Where we grew up, what happened with our parents, the names of our siblings, our plans for the future, and so on. I hoped Garrick listened so we wouldn't get caught in our lies by him saying something contradictory.

Mrs. Van Dousen, who looked exhausted from the burden of pregnancy, dished up apple pie while Mr. Van Dousen continued talking. "Mr. Harper, I'm expanding my farm next spring and will be needing to hire someone. I'm friends with Benjamin Sealy, the canal contractor, and he speaks highly of ya. I'd like that someone to be you, if ya're willing."

Caught completely off guard, I glanced between Mr. Van Dousen's hopeful expression and his daughter's blushing cheeks. "Thank you, sir, for the offer, but I don't know that I'll be here next spring. I'm . . . heading out west soon."

"West! What's out west? Everything a man needs is right here. Out west ya'll find nothing but a slow death at the hand of savage Indians."

I had to bite my tongue to keep from saying, "I'm not going out *vest,* I'm going out west." Wishing the dinner would end, I gave a firm answer. "That may be true, but my mind is made up, sir."

"Well, son, give it some thought. If ya change your mind, ya let me know."

I took another bite of the best apple pie I'd ever tasted. "Yes, sir. This is really good pie, Mrs. Van Dousen."

As we walked home later that evening, Garrick said, "I'd say Mr. Van Dousen was playing matchmaker tonight."

"Yeah, and I want no part in it," I muttered. We walked for a while before I told Garrick my plan. "My bruises are almost healed. After the next payday, I'm going home."

"I'll be sad to see you go. I haven't had this much fun in years."

I smiled at him. "It has been fun, hasn't it?"

Hands in our pockets, we walked through the last of the fading light and arrived at the boarding house after dark.

The day before I planned to leave, Garrick and I again split wood for Rose. Little Davy judged our races.

Garrick poised his ax for action. "Okay, Davy, we're ready."

"On your mark, get set, go!" yelled Davy.

Whack, smack! Split sections of logs flew in every direction. I had a good rhythm going. It would be a close race.

I threw down my ax a split second before Garrick. "Done! Wahoo!" I did a victory dance until Garrick tackled me onto the parched grass. We stopped wrestling each other when Davy, squealing with delight, jumped on top of us.

Garrick turned all his attention to Davy, letting himself get pinned. "Hey, little man, you got me. Are you some kind of tough guy?"

While they wrestled, I rolled onto my back, watching the first stars twinkle in the darkening sky. I listened to the playful conversation between Garrick and the boy. Davy never tired of playing with Garrick, and it was clear that Garrick never grew tired of Davy. They played until Rose called her son in for bed. The longing look Garrick exchanged with Rose was unmistakable.

TWENTY-SEVEN
Searching

After six weeks in 1817, I thought I was ready to face life in 2011. I gave my notice to Rose and paid her what I owed, plus a little extra. I found Garrick and told him goodbye.

With a knowing wink, he said, "Sounds good, little brother. Don't be a stranger, though. You can come back anytime."

"Okay, I'll keep that in mind." He had become the brother I'd never had, and I did want to come back someday. "Garrick, if you ever need anything, you can find me in 2011. But just don't look for me before Thanksgiving, or I won't know who you are yet. Here's my phone number so you can call me. Thanks, brother, for everything."

We shook hands, and I set my counter, imagining the quiet dark of my bedroom. A few shuffles through time later, I stood in my room. Home felt strange and foreign. I'd never been gone so long before, but to my family and friends, it would be as if I'd never left. The thought boggled my mind.

With my Erie Canal clothes hidden in my closet, I visited the bathroom. I locked the door and turned on the light, marveling for a moment at the white ceramic sink and shiny faucet. I stuck my mouth under the stream of cold, clear water, drinking until

I couldn't hold any more. Then I looked in the mirror. Newly expanded muscles from six weeks of hard physical labor rippled underneath my sun-bronzed skin. More than once Garrick and I had shed our shirts, trying to get relief from the humid heat of late summer in New York.

I rubbed my hand over my chin, assessing the fullness of my youthful beard. Not bad, I thought. A fine layer of dust fell from my head as I ran my fingers through my sun-bleached hair. I needed a haircut. I turned on the shower and got in. Never had a shower felt better, and I didn't get out until the water ran cold.

I shaved and was about to go to bed when I realized how obvious my change in appearance looked. Something had to be done about this hair before I saw anyone. I pulled out the scissors and started cutting. It wasn't my best haircut, but it would have to do. It was early morning by the time I finished and climbed into bed.

Nobody woke me that morning, so I slept until noon. I remembered being a grump before I'd left, so it's no wonder they didn't want to wake me. The aroma of roasting turkey greeted my senses when I opened my door. Not thinking anything of it, I nearly walked downstairs in my basketball shorts and no shirt. I heard my mom and Jessica talking in the kitchen and beat a hasty retreat to my bedroom. A tan and a crappy haircut would be hard to explain on Thanksgiving morning. I pulled on a hooded sweatshirt and my baseball cap before I ventured downstairs. My mom had left the kitchen by the time I walked in.

Jessica stared at me, then pulled the sweatshirt away from my neck.

"Knock it off," I said, shrugging away from her.

She propped her hands on her hips. "Have you been to the tanning salon, Chase?"

I couldn't put anything past my sister. I adjusted my ball cap. Seeing my dad coming down the hall, I knew I didn't have time to explain. I raised my finger to my lips. "Shh. Don't tell anybody, Jess, or you're going to be in trouble with me."

She raised her eyebrows and shook her head. "Okay, I just didn't take you for a tanning salon kind of guy."

My dad walked through the kitchen on his way to the garage. "Happy Thanksgiving, kids." My mom came in the kitchen carrying two cans of green beans. "Good morning, Chase. Don't eat too much because we're having our big meal in a couple of hours."

When I reached to take the cereal bowl she offered, she grabbed my hand. "What's this? How'd you get all these blisters?" She tried to grab my other hand, but I yanked it away.

"It's nothing," I said. "It's . . . they're just calluses . . . from weightlifting."

My mom rolled her eyes, but let it go at that. "After you eat some cereal, will you peel the potatoes?"

"Sure, Mom."

After being gone for so long, I'd gained a new appreciation for my family, and I thoroughly enjoyed Thanksgiving. My phone had another message from Uncle Roy, which I ignored. I didn't want to deal with him today. During the weeks in 1817, I'd spent countless nights dreaming of Ellie—committing to memory every moment we'd shared together. I didn't want to forget anything. I determined I could face living alone if I knew she'd been happy. Now all I had to do was confirm that.

The Monday after Thanksgiving, I found a genealogical library. Nervously, I entered. Computers sat on desks around the room, and filing cabinets lined the wall.

A gray-haired woman pulled her glasses off her nose and smiled at me. "I'm Gail. Can I help you find something?"

"Could you help me research someone who lived in 1863?" I asked.

"Yes, I can do that. What information do you have on them already?"

"Her name is . . . was Ellie Williams, well, Ellen Elizabeth Williams. She was eighteen in 1863." I remembered back to the conversation I'd had with Ellie before slipping the paper with her personal information and her passport photos into the backpack with the money. "Her birthday was May 28."

Pulling out a calculator, Gail spoke quietly to herself, "Let's see, 1863 minus 18 gives us 1845." She typed Ellie's name and birth date into the computer. "Here we go. I found the birth record for Ellen Elizabeth Williams. Born in New York to George Amyot Williams and—"

"Great. What else? Was she married? Kids, grandkids? When did she die?"

"I can't see anything cross-referenced with this name. Do you know what her married name was?"

Thinking of the med student she'd been dating, I said, "Can you try Griffith, Ellen Elizabeth Griffith, or Ellie Griffith? She probably got married in Boston, Massachusetts. She goes by Ellie."

Gail looked at me strangely. "Don't you mean she *went* by Ellie?"

"Yeah, sorry. That's what I meant."

Gail searched everywhere, finally letting out a sigh. "I'm sorry I can't find anything more. There are no records of a marriage, children, or her death."

I frowned. "What does that mean?"

"The records may not be available online. In that case, you would have to go to the archives in Boston and look the old-fashioned way. You may find the marriage and death records there. Or it could mean those events were never recorded. Sometimes in those days, people married or died and no public record of the event was ever made. It's also possible the records were accidentally destroyed or damaged at some point in time. I'm sorry I can't be of more help. Is there anything else?"

Disappointment threatened to sink me like a lead ball. "No, that's okay. Thanks for your help anyway," I said, then walked out the door.

During the next week, the overpowering frustration I'd felt before staying with Garrick returned with a vengeance. I stewed over the dilemma of what had become of Ellie and why I'd been unable to find more information on her, until it nearly drove me insane.

I was sitting on the bleachers, lost in thought, when my wrestling coach yelled, "Chase, what are you doing? Get warmed up. Your match is next."

I shed my sweatshirt and sweatpants. "Sorry, Coach." I tossed them on my gym bag and stepped onto the warm-up mat with the other wrestlers.

Travis DeMarco, the top wrestler in the school district, bumped shoulders with me when he walked past. "Harper, I'm going to clean your clock," he taunted. "You haven't got a chance against me, and you know it. I've been whipping your butt ever since we were kids. Maybe you should forfeit before you embarrass yourself."

This would be the first time I'd met him on the mat since freshman year. It was true—I had never won a match against him. We'd competed together in youth wrestling, and he'd always been a bully. I gave him a dirty look and walked away. I'd settle up with him on the mat.

Five minutes later, we shook hands, took our positions, and waited for the whistle. Considering the incredible quickness I'd acquired, courtesy of the counter's magic, I decided to try a new strategy: takedown artist. I'd try to repeatedly force Travis to the mat, under my control, only to allow him to get back up again. The takedown would be worth two points, and Travis's escape would be worth only one. I could quickly outpace him in the scoring if I secured a takedown every fifteen to twenty seconds. A sly smile crept across my face. He would be humiliated if I pulled it off.

The ref signaled the opening of the first period. Travis and I stood as the whistle blew, and then we circled each other like predators. I saw an opening and dived for his legs, quickly securing the back of his left ankle with my right hand. Using his captured leg as leverage, I threw him to the mat. After keeping him down long enough to get my two points, I let him escape.

Smiling at the look of shock in his eyes, I circled him. Then I shot under his outstretched hands and grabbed both of his legs. I lifted them to my chest, forcing him to the mat again. I alternated between the ankle pick and either a single- or double-leg takedown, as I relentlessly forced him to the mat three more times. The look of shock on his face turned to blind rage.

On my fifth attempted takedown, he anticipated my move and stretched his legs behind him, slowing me down. I eventually secured his legs and tried to pull them out from under him. But he threw his legs backward and brought all his weight crashing down on top of me. It was a lot of weight, and it surprised Travis, who swore under his breath, that I didn't collapse beneath his pancake attack. We were positioned in such a way that when he threw a punch into my rib cage, right where the Frenchmen had cracked my rib, the ref didn't notice.

Gasping for air and surprised the whistle hadn't blown for my opponent's foul, I went down on my knees and elbows. Travis and I grappled with each other, each of us struggling to gain control. After the prematch taunting and the punch in my rib cage, his elbow driving into the back of my neck was the last straw. I exploded. Wildly throwing punches into his stomach, I drove him off me. The whistle blared, and the referee ran toward us. He put his hands between us, trying to stop the match.

Travis threw a punch into my face. I retaliated with a power-packed slug to the side of his head. He staggered from the blow, falling backward onto the mat. The referee grabbed me by the shoulders and shoved me away. "You're disqualified!" he yelled.

Travis's words followed me off the mat. "I'll get you for this, Harper."

"You're disqualified too!" the ref yelled at him.

Coach glared at me as I got my things and left the gym. I followed my dad across the parking lot in silence. We got in the car, and my dad leaned his head back against the seat. He closed his eyes and sighed. "What's going on, Chase? Are you on steroids or something? Because this isn't normal behavior for you."

Shocked by the accusation, I leaned forward, staring at him. "What—? No! Dad, how could you think that?"

"Just look at yourself. You've bulked up overnight. You're significantly faster. You played soccer better than anyone on Hilhi's team, and yet half the time, it looked like you were loafing. It's the same with wrestling—you're clearly stronger and quicker than anyone I've seen yet, but you can't keep your emotions in check. It's like rampant testosterone or something. I can't figure you out." He paused, probably to let me digest what he'd said. "I want you to come clean with me. Is it the fencing coach? Has he got you involved in something? Because this all started about that time."

"No, Dad. Coach Bill is great. He wouldn't do anything like that. I'm definitely not on steroids, I can promise you that. I'll even take a drug test if you don't believe me. I've been lifting. Plus, I've had a lot on my mind lately. I'm having a hard time dealing with some stuff." We sat in silence, each of us staring forward, watching the rain drum on the windshield.

"Can we talk about it?" Dad asked.

"No, not really. I'll take care of it. I promise. Can we go now?"

Clearly unhappy, my dad looked at me for another minute and then started the car. We drove home without talking. I knew I should be more careful, but right then it was hard to care. Frankly, I didn't give a rip what anybody thought. That night I tossed and turned, dreaming again that I'd lost Ellie. I woke the next morning as discontented as ever, and not at all rested.

Two days later, Jessica came into my room with a large manila envelope and tossed it on my bed. "Uncle Roy called me yesterday. He said you wouldn't return his messages. He wasn't happy about it, either. I had to miss swimming to go pick that up for you in downtown Portland. I'll be mad if Coach cuts me from the relay for missing practice."

I ripped open the envelope and dumped out a driver's license, a blue Social Security card, and a perfect birth certificate, complete with the State of Oregon seal and watermark. Lettered neatly across the top were the words "Certification of Vital Record, Oregon Health Division," and Ellie's beautiful name.

Seeing her name made me sick inside, and the loneliness of my existence left my heart feeling crushed. It was tangible and painful. I hated feeling this way. Hated not knowing what had happened to Ellie. Hated that she was dead whenever I was home. At least when I was with Garrick in 1817, she hadn't even been born yet. I could deal with it there.

I sank down on the edge of my bed. In a flash of anger, I started to tear the birth certificate. But something stopped me an inch into it. After throwing the paper on the floor, I punched the wall. My fist buried itself in the Sheetrock, dusting everything with white powder. Astounded at the ruin I'd made of my wall, I extracted my hand from the wreckage.

Jessica stormed back into my room. "What was that? Oh my gosh! Mom is going to kill you."

Dejected, I lowered my head into my hands.

My sister stood in front of me. "What's wrong with you, Chase? I've heard Mom and Dad talking. They're really worried. You seem different—something has changed. You even look different. The tan, the muscles. Is this some early midlife crisis? Or is it all about Ellie? I want answers, now."

Without raising my eyes, I answered her questions. "The tan and some of the muscle came from digging the Erie Canal for six weeks with another Keeper. I went back to August of 1817 to help him with something the night before Thanksgiving, and I didn't come home. I got a job working on the canal in New York. It was a lot of long, hot days, full of hard physical labor."

"Well, that's not what I expected to hear. Did you know Dad asked Mom if you could be on steroids? You aren't, are you?"

"No, of course I'm not."

"Well, you can't blame him for being suspicious. Look at yourself," Jessica said. "But the Erie Canal? Chase, you ask me to believe the most bizarre things."

"Well, they're true." I raised my head to look at her. "Honestly, Jessica, I'm sick about Ellie leaving. I've never felt this way about anyone before. It's not like breaking up with a normal girl, where you have another chance at getting back together next semester. I can't get over the fact she's dead right now. I left her in 1863. It's 2011. She's gone.

"I tried to find out what happened to her, see if she got married, had kids, stuff like that. But there was nothing, no record of anything except her birth in 1845. I thought if I could find some way to prove she'd been happy, I'd be able to move on—to live without her. But her life is already over, and I don't think I can make it through mine like this. I'm miserable without her." I absentmindedly slid my phone open to look at her picture again, like I'd done a thousand times before.

Jessica reached for my phone. "Stop looking at that picture." But I was too quick for her and put the phone behind my back. "You're only making it worse for yourself," my sister said, then shook her head and gave me a condescending look. "Chase, sometimes you can be a real idiot. Aren't you a time-traveling man? Or are you finally admitting it was all a big lie?"

I glared up at her. "I already told you it's true."

"Then for you, Ellie's never dead. If you can't live without her, go back where you left her and tell her that!"

"But she didn't want anything to do with me. She left. I can't go crying back to her, like a big baby. And I don't want to show up there if she's already started a new life. It was always more of a one-sided relationship anyway."

"You're being prideful. Go do a reconnaissance mission, then."

"What, like spy on her?"

"Of course. Feel out the situation without her knowing you're there," Jessica said. "See if she looks happy, and then decide what to do after that."

I nodded, slowly at first. Then a smile spread across my face, probably the first one in weeks. "Okay, I can do that. I'll go see if she's all right, then I'll come back."

"Good. I'm glad we got that worked out. Now, try to act a little more normal, will you? You're freaking Mom and Dad out." Jessica put extra emphasis on the word "normal." She folded her arms and leaned against the doorframe. "By the way,

I think I'll watch this time-travel miracle for myself, if you don't mind."

"I don't mind, but I've got to get ready first." I dug through my closet until I found an old poster of a yellow Corvette, which I strategically hung over the glaring hole in my wall. I brushed the Sheetrock dust under the bed and was satisfied I'd adequately hidden the evidence of another one of my rampant testosterone episodes.

Jessica watched me from my open doorway. I checked the clock: an hour until my parents would be home from work—plenty of time for a little reconnaissance. I pulled my Erie Canal clothes and my Wellingtons out of the closet and chuckled.

"What's so funny?" Jessica demanded.

"I bought these clothes in 1817. I might look old-fashioned when I show up in 1863."

Jessica didn't look convinced or even slightly amused. "Humph."

"Do you mind closing the door for a minute while I change?" I asked.

"You're not going to tell me you time-traveled but forgot to open the door and show me, are you?" she asked.

"I promise I won't go anywhere without opening the door."

Without saying another word, Jessica closed my door. *It's a good thing I didn't try to tell anyone else,* I thought. She obviously thought there was still a chance I was plain crazy.

"All right, come in!" I called. I sat on my bed and shoved my feet into my boots.

Jessica opened the door and folded her arms. "Now what?"

I smiled at her. "Watch."

TWENTY-EIGHT
Reconnaissance

I set my counter for the same date as the day as I was leaving 2011—December 2—only in the year 1863. I carefully positioned the globe near Boston Harbor. I imagined the street by the corner house where I'd left Ellie. "See you later, Sis." Anxious to be gone, I pushed Shuffle and Go before she could reply. In my excitement to get to Boston, I didn't bother looking around in my shuffle zones—I simply jogged through them.

Hoping no one would see my magical appearance, I focused on the predawn hour of the night. Fortunately, I appeared at my scheduled time. The street was quiet except for one wagonload of milk containers pulled by a fat draft horse. I watched as the old man driving the wagon stopped at each house and placed a bottle of milk on the porch. I found a tall hedge across the street from which I could easily watch Ellie's front door and waited.

The frigid temperature soon had me shivering. Why hadn't I thought to dress warmer? I rubbed my hands together, blowing into them. I wiggled my toes in my boots and then jogged in place, trying to generate body heat.

As the darkness gave way to the gray of early morning, a kind-looking black woman emerged from Ellie's house. She retrieved the milk, then quickly shut the door against the cold. Half an hour later, I was about to abandon my watch and shuffle to someplace warmer when Ellie stepped through the doorway. The sight of her warmed my insides quicker than a cup of hot cocoa. She walked through the gate and headed down the street. I waited until she turned the corner and then ran after her, my numb feet feeling like stumps. I followed her for a mile before she stopped. I quickly stepped behind a tree and watched her unlock the door to a small building—a one-room schoolhouse. I moved closer, only to immediately seek cover again when she reemerged. Still bundled in her coat, hat, and gloves, she carried two buckets. She walked around the side of the building and filled them with kindling.

After she went back inside, I hurried to the side of the building and peered through the frosty windowpane. She bent over an ancient cast-iron stove at the front of the room. There were twenty desks, neatly arranged in rows. Ellie started a fire and set the buckets against the wall. She hung her coat and hat on a hook before she sat at her desk and looked through a stack of papers.

I longed to walk boldly into the schoolhouse and warm my frozen fingers by her fire. It would have started to put off heat by now. But Ellie looked busy and content, and I worried she wouldn't welcome such an obtrusive interruption in her peaceful morning. It satisfied me, thinking of her teaching school each day, and I stepped away from the window.

My frozen fingers clumsily retrieved the counter from my pocket. I pressed Shuffle and Return. When I reappeared in front of Jessica, I said, "Dang, it's cold there." I kicked off my boots and rubbed my numb feet to get the circulation going. Shivering, I watched Jessica, standing like a statue in my doorway. Her jaw hung slack, and her eyes were wide as saucers.

I chuckled and waved. "Jessica, hello? Do you believe me now?"

She pulled herself out of the stunned stupor and stepped forward to touch my icy hand. "Yeah, I guess I do. That was really weird, Chase. You vanished into thin air. I walked through where you had been standing, and there was nothing. You were gone for, like, a full minute. Tell me what happened."

"Close my door. Let me get out of these clothes, and then I'll tell you what I saw." After returning my clothes to their hiding place, I opened the door and motioned for Jessica to follow me. "I'm freezing. Let's talk by the fireplace," I said. My sister watched me in awe as I started a fire in the fireplace and curled up on the couch with a blanket.

"I appeared in Boston at first light," I began. "There was an old milkman making deliveries. I waited behind a hedge across the street from Ellie's house for her to come out. When she finally left, I followed her to a one-room schoolhouse. She's the teacher. She built a fire in the woodstove and sat at her desk to grade papers. That's when I came back."

"Wow . . . I . . . I don't know what to say," Jessica muttered.

"Just say you believe me."

"I believe you, Chase. Sorry I ever doubted you."

"That's okay. If the tables were turned, I don't know that I'd be any better."

Jessica left to do her homework, and before long I dozed off, lost in the depths of a dreamless sleep.

Despite my grogginess, the temperature soon woke me. Severely overheated, I threw off the blanket. I was dying of thirst and pouring sweat. I made a beeline for the kitchen and drained two glasses of water.

My mom put her hand on my face. "Are you feeling okay? You're burning up. Do you have a fever?"

"No, I fell asleep by the fire. I've got to go outside and cool down."

"Feed the horses while you're out there, please."

"Sure." I slipped on my boots and walked into a misty evening. I went through the motion of bringing the horses in and feeding them. I contented myself with replaying in my mind what I'd seen in Boston. With a satisfied smile, I decided to give it a few days and check on Ellie again.

Five days later, I prepared to return to Boston. I had made a greater effort to act normal at home, as Jessica suggested. After seeing Ellie, it became easier. I reconciled myself to my situation, knowing that looking in on her from time to time would help. I repressed my frustration over my personal disappointment, expecting that soon no one would suspect anything was amiss.

Not wanting to freeze this time, I layered my Under Armour beneath my clothing. With a knitted hat and gloves that didn't look too modern, I left. After shuffling, I appeared across from Ellie's house in the late afternoon, hidden behind the hedge. The sun was out and the snow glistened brightly, like little diamonds from heaven. I watched the horse-drawn sleighs and the people who walked past carrying their packages. I knew the direction Ellie would come home from and watched it intently.

Finally, I received the reward for my wait. She walked briskly down the street, carrying a small bag. After she entered the house, I started to move out from behind the hedge, intent on sneaking a peek at what was happening inside. No sooner had I stepped into full view than Ellie walked out the back door of the house. I dodged behind the hedge again. She went to a small shed and reemerged carrying an ax. A large pile of unsplit logs lay next to the street. They hadn't been there last time. She proceeded to chop wood, a painfully slow process. Twice I almost left my hiding place to take the ax from her. Finally, looking exhausted, she dropped the ax on the pile and carried an armful of wood to the house. She must have split enough for the night, because she didn't come back.

I shook my head. Splitting the entire stack of logs would take her a ridiculous amount of time. There was no way I would put up with that. I pulled out the counter and turned the dial, marking the day a half turn forward. I pressed the Go button, and everything began to shimmer. When the air cleared, the darkness of predawn surrounded me. I waited while the milkman made his rounds. A few minutes after that, the same black woman as before retrieved the milk bottle from the porch. Moments later, Ellie left for school, looking forlornly in the direction of the large pile of wood.

As soon as she rounded the corner, I jogged over to her woodpile. A fresh dusting of snow covered everything. I uncovered the ax and began splitting wood, soon finding an easy rhythm. Where it had taken Ellie six or seven strikes with the ax to split a log, I easily split one with each swing. I sent the wood flying upwards of ten feet away. Within a short time, I had so many split logs underfoot, I had to stop and stack it. I loaded my arms with wood and turned toward the house. I stopped mid-stride when I noticed the black woman staring intently at me from the back window.

I smiled and nodded to her, then continued walking toward the house. She opened the door and stepped onto the porch. "Mister, I hope you's not expectin' to get paid fer that. We ain't got no money to pay fer wood splittin'."

"Where do you want me to stack this?" I asked.

With a grunt, she pointed.

"I'm not doing it for money. But I could sure use a glass of water, if you have any to spare."

She smiled. "Well, now, that I do have, and I reckon some brown bread and cider in a bit, if you'd like."

"I'd appreciate that."

She nodded and went inside while I continued stacking the wood. She left a tin cup and a pitcher of water on the porch for me. Imagining myself racing Garrick, I raced the sun. My goal: finish the job before the sun set—before Ellie returned. I figured she'd appreciate having her wood split, but I doubted she would welcome the sight of me doing it.

"Here's yo' dinner, mister," the woman called.

After dropping the ax, I walked to the porch and took the plate from her outstretched hand. I was famished. There were two thick slices of brown bread layered with ham, cheese, and butter. I stuffed a huge bite of the sandwich into my mouth.

She narrowed her eyes and watched me. "What's yo' name?"

Thinking while I chewed, I finally answered, "Joseph."

"Joseph who?"

"Just Joseph," I said.

"Well, Mr. Jus' Joseph, I'm Mary, and I reckon we're much obliged to you. I s'pose if you've a mind to, you could stay on fer supper tonight. Miss Ellie would most def'nitely want to meet you."

"No, I'll need to be gone by then, but thank you for the offer. It's nice to meet you, Mary." I extended my hand to shake hers.

Her eyes opened wide. She gave my hand a strange look, but she reached hers toward it. I gave it a quick shake and then went back to eating my sandwich.

She shrugged her shoulders, then quietly turned and went inside. I finished off the sandwich and the cup of hot cider she'd left on the porch, and then I retrieved the ax. Although my arms ached, I attacked the pile again, not intending to leave even one log for Ellie to struggle with. As the sun traveled the western half of the sky, I worried she'd catch me in the act. Finally, I finished.

With the ax stowed in the shed, I hastily piled up the last of the wood and hurried down the street in the opposite direction from which I expected Ellie to return. I pulled out my counter, but the urge to see her reaction to what I'd done tipped the scales. I retraced my steps, returning to my hiding place behind the hedge.

Almost immediately, she appeared from around the corner, walking toward her house. The hedge offered me a perfect side view of the home, encompassing both the front and back doors. She entered the front door and moments later burst out the back door.

"Mary, who did you say split all this wood?" Ellie called over her shoulder.

Mary followed right on her heels. "He said his name was Joseph."

"Joseph," Ellie said thoughtfully. "I don't know any Joseph. What was his last name?"

"Wouldn't give no last name, Miss Ellie. Jus' Joseph was all he said."

"Did he want money?"

"No, just wanted to split the wood, and he was in an awful hurry from the looks of it. He was a handsome one, too. I tried to get him to stay on fer supper. I think you might've taken a cotton to him if you coulda met him."

Ellie let out a deep breath and turned to go inside. She spoke so quietly I almost missed hearing her words. "Yes, I would have liked to thank him myself."

I would have liked that too, I thought. Satisfied with my good deed, I got out the counter and returned to my bedroom. Although physically exhausted from hours of wood splitting, I hadn't felt this good in weeks.

No sooner was I home than I remembered the evening wrestling match at Liberty High School, across town. My arms felt like lead. I glanced at the clock. My dad would be home from work in an hour to take me. I dressed for the match and went downstairs, falling asleep the second I lay on the couch.

My dad shook my shoulder to wake me. "Son, we better be going if we're going to make it on time."

I opened my eyes. He stood at least an arm's length away from me. Fighting extreme exhaustion, I sat up. "Thanks, Dad."

When it was my turn, I wrestled a clean match—no fouls. Being as tired as I was, I wrestled my hardest, barely winning. Although to me it felt like I'd done poorly, both my dad and my coach were ecstatic. The obvious effort I'd put in, the clean performance, and the resulting win must have pleased them.

On the drive home, my dad asked me again how I was doing. With a smile, I answered him more confidently this time. "I'm fine—actually, I'm feeling a little better these days, Dad."

Three days later, I went back again. I chose to watch Ellie come home from school. It surprised me when she didn't walk down the street like I expected. I contemplated changing the counter and trying an earlier time, but then a fancy black carriage rolled to a stop in front of her house. A dark-haired young man got out of the carriage and walked toward Ellie's door. My mouth dropped into a frown. Being raised with Jessica's constant chatter, I could hear it already. At the sight of him she would have said, "Isn't he gorgeous? That guy's to die for."

He knocked on the door, and a moment later, Mary let him in. I watched the doorway intently now. Soon, the man exited the house with Ellie, her hand draped over his arm. She looked up into his face and smiled. With care, he led her over the slippery, snow-covered walkway. He offered her his hand in a flourish of gentlemanly charm, and she stepped into the enclosed carriage. He walked around the back and climbed in the other side, then signaled the driver to be off.

I struggled to douse the jealousy that flamed inside me when I watched Ellie and the young man leave together. I told myself over and over that this was what I wanted. I wanted her to find happiness. I wanted her to get married, have a family, and live a long, happy life.

But in spite of the pep talk, unbidden loneliness washed over me as I stood rooted in place behind the hedge. I didn't move until the chill of the approaching night drove me to action. Using the counter, I returned home. I went straight to Jessica's room and told her everything I'd seen and done.

Her eyes were sympathetic but her voice matter-of-fact. "Well, it appears she found her happily ever after. Are you going to be able to let it go now?"

"I don't know," I said.

"Didn't you get what you wanted?"

"Yeah, but it's still hard to see Ellie with another guy."

"I know, but if you really care for her, you'll be happy that she's happy."

"You're right, but . . ."

I sat on the edge of my sister's bed, thinking it all sounded good in theory. But I felt rotten.

TWENTY-NINE
Life or Death

During Christmas vacation, an overpowering curiosity—born partly out of boredom—got the best of me. Jessica had gone skiing with Ryan on Mount Hood. My parents were shopping together, and I was left home alone. I'd completed my mother's famous chore list, and there was nothing on TV.

I sat in my room, looking at the counter in the palm of my hand. I thought about visiting Garrick—spend a few days in the trenches, so to speak, and enjoy the early October sunshine. And maybe I would, but first, I'd satisfy my curiosity about Ellie. What if she had more wood that needed splitting? I didn't know how long a woodpile lasted when it was the sole source of energy.

I layered my clothing and set the counter: December 21, 1863. I pressed Shuffle and Go. I smiled, grateful to be on the move again and out of the monotony of my regular life. I appeared behind the hedge, immediately sinking into a foot of snow. I realized too late school was probably out for Christmas. I watched the house for a while. All appeared quiet. I clicked the counter forward half a notch, jumping to the early-morning hours. The faithful milkman made his regular delivery. Mary hustled out to get the milk and hurried back inside. Something about the way she carried herself seemed strained.

When Ellie didn't leave the house awhile later, I jumped forward another half notch to that evening. There was a carriage parked outside the house. I watched the door intently, expecting any second to see Ellie with her beau.

I waited a good while before a gray-bearded gentleman, carrying a small black bag, exited the house. He paused on the porch to speak to Mary. His shoulders were stooped, and he shook his head from side to side. I barely made out Mary's words through the distress in her voice. "Thank you, Doctor. I'll do me best."

Baffled, I watched him get into his carriage and drive away. Perhaps Ellie's great-aunt was sick, but I hadn't seen or heard of her the day I'd split their wood. What if Ellie was sick? Either way, I needed to know. I walked to the back of the house and peered into the window of the kitchen. Mary stood at the cast-iron stove, stirring something in a pan. Then she poured it—it looked like broth—into a cup. Carrying the steaming cup, she hurried up the stairs.

After making sure no one in the neighboring houses could see me, I moved the counter forward and backward, catching glimpses of what happened in the kitchen at random times that week. Not once did I see Ellie. Unable to contain my worry any longer, I set the counter and pressed Go, arriving December 22, 1863. I decisively walked to the front door as the doctor's carriage rolled down the street, away from the house. I knocked.

Mary opened it a crack. "Mr. Joseph, it ain't a good time. Come back another day."

As she started to shut the door, I slid the toe of my boot between the door and the frame. "Mary, I need to see Ellie."

"No, Mr. Joseph. Miss Ellie done got real sick. She ain't up to visitin' right now."

I forced my way through the door and closed it behind me. "What's wrong with her? What did the doctor say?"

When I didn't get an answer right away, I ran up the stairs, taking them two at a time. Mary yelled at me. "Mr. Joseph, get out this instant! I'm tellin' you, she's too sick for visitors."

I ignored her, leaving her no choice but to follow me. I opened the first door I came to. Nothing except a neatly made bed. I burst through the next door, and a mixture of both relief and horror hit me at once. Ellie lay on the bed, ashen-faced and covered with quilts. Even with all the blankets, she shivered. I crossed the room quickly and touched her forehead. She was burning with fever and moist with sweat. My voice nearly choked out her name. "Ellie?"

There was no response. I swallowed, trying to hold my rising panic at bay. She muttered incoherently, slowly moving her head from side to side.

I turned to face Mary, who had silently entered the room. "What's wrong with her?"

"You's the boy from out west, aren't you? You's the one Miss Ellie's been pinin' over."

"What's wrong with her?" I asked again, almost yelling now. "What did the doctor say?"

Mary broke into tears and slumped into the chair next to the door. "Miss Ellie's dyin', Mr. Joseph. I'm sorry. She's got pneumonia real bad. Ain't nothin' the doctor can do 'bout it."

I looked back at Ellie and noticed an envelope propped on the nightstand addressed to Chase Harper, complete with my address and a small notation at the bottom that said, "Please mail in November 2011."

"What's this?" I picked up the letter and turned back to Mary.

She shook her head, clearly fighting to control her sobbing. "I don't know, but I think she done lost her mind. Miss Ellie keeps mumbling 'Chase.' She pulled this letter out two days ago and made me promise, 'fore I died, to find someone who'd make sure it got mailed in 2011. Sounds like a fool's errand, if you ask me. Who's Chase Harper? I've never heard of such a name."

I folded the envelope and stuffed it in my pocket. "I'm Chase Harper. Joseph Chase Harper is my name." I watched Mary as she registered what I'd said. I looked back at Ellie, knowing what had to be done. "She needs to go to the hospital," I said. Discreetly, I pulled out the counter, quickly setting the coordinates. Then I pulled off all but one quilt, scooped Ellie into my arms, and started for the door.

"Doc said ain't nothin' at a hospital can help her. He said keepin' her home was best. You hear me, Mr. Joseph? Where you think you's takin' her? She can't go out in this cold. She'll die for sure." Mary sobbed as I pushed past her and left Ellie's room.

I went down the stairs and stood by the front door. "Please open the door for me, Mary. Trust me. I can help her. Open the door, and close it behind me."

She looked from me to Ellie, touched Ellie's face once, and then opened the door. Ellie burrowed her head into my chest as a blast of cold air hit us. The door slowly closed behind me. I crossed the street and stepped behind the hedge. The instant we were hidden, I pushed Shuffle and Go. I held her close. Her entire body trembled with the chills. Never had the shuffle zones felt so long.

She opened her eyes and seemed to see me for the briefest of seconds before closing them once again. She let out a weak moan and muttered, "Finally, a good dream."

"Ellie, Ellie?" I tried to get her attention again, but she didn't respond. I was racing time. I didn't know much about pneumonia, but it couldn't be a good sign that she was unconscious.

Once in my room, I set her carefully on my bed. I put the counter in my pocket and picked up my wallet, cell phone, and keys. I ran downstairs and propped open the back door. Then, taking the stairs two at a time, I raced up and got Ellie. The quiet drizzle of a Northwest winter day followed us to the truck. I managed to get the truck door open while holding her shivering frame. She looked so thin and frail. In fact, it worried me that I could carry her so easily. I laid her across the backseat of the truck, closed the door, and ran to the driver's side.

I turned the key and growled when the wait-to-start light glared back at me. I waited for a second but refused to give the engine its full warm-up time before I turned over the key. The diesel roared to life, and I sped to the hospital. With the heat on high, I was pouring sweat within minutes. Ellie moaned occasionally, but her shivering seemed to have lessened. After carelessly hitting the curb, I parked directly in front of the emergency-room entrance and carried her inside.

It wasn't until people started to stare at me that I realized I was still dressed for the 1800s. I walked directly to the nurse's station over which hung a huge "Check in Here" sign. I lucked out, because the waiting room wasn't as crowded as usual. Upon seeing us, the receptionist jumped into action, immediately calling for a nurse to come up front.

The nurse opened the huge door to the emergency section of the hospital. "What happened?" she asked as she pulled a rolling bed away from the wall. "Lay her right here."

"She's unconscious. She has pneumonia, we think. Fever, chills," I said. I ran my fingers through my hair, anxiously watching the nurse check Ellie's vital signs.

The nurse looked at her thermometer. "High fever—104 degrees. What's her name?"

"Ellie, Ellie Williams," I answered.

"Is she taking any medications?"

"No, she hasn't had any medicine. Will she be all right?"

The nurse shot me a disbelieving look. "Not even Tylenol? Or Advil? Are you certain?"

"Yeah, I'm sure."

She shrugged her shoulders and made a note on her clipboard. "Some Tylenol would have made her more comfortable, and it's safe for most people—"

I interrupted the nurse. "I know, I know. But is she going to be all right?"

The nurse looked up at me. "We'll do everything we can for her, but you'll need to talk with the doctor after he looks at her." She set her clipboard on the bed and pushed it down the hall. "Follow me. We'll put her in room 4."

The nurse situated the bed in the center of the curtained-off area and set the brake. "Someone will be right back with some forms for you to fill out."

The room soon bustled with nurses coming in and out to attend to Ellie. I paced back and forth in the small area, unintentionally listening in on the sprained-ankle story from the kid on the other side of the curtain.

Ten minutes went by before the registration person appeared. She handed me a clipboard with papers. While I started on the medical history, the nurse inserted an IV in the top of Ellie's hand and hooked it up to a bag of fluids.

"I'm giving her intravenous pain medicine and fever reducer, along with some fluids," she explained.

"Thank you," I said.

I finished the papers, at least what I could of them. I took my best guess on the questions related to her medical history and then signed my name as the person responsible for medical expenses. They would probably want an adult's signature, but I'd worry about that later. The empty boxes for insurance information stared back at me. We didn't have any insurance for her. That problem would have to be solved another day. All I could think about now was Ellie. I sat next to her bed and held her hand. I was so deep in thought I didn't notice the doctor walk in until he spoke to me.

"Hello, I'm Doctor West. It looks like you've got one sick girl here."

My head shot up. "Yeah. Is she going to be okay?"

He placed his stethoscope on her chest. "Well, let's take a look and see. Why did you wait so long to bring her in? We should have seen her days ago. I don't like to see cases get this bad before we start treatment. She's extremely dehydrated."

Sickened by what he said, I weakly mumbled a response. "I didn't know she was so sick. I would have brought her in sooner if I'd only known."

"I want to have a chest X-ray taken and then start her on oxygen and intravenous antibiotics. We'll need to check her into the hospital."

"Okay," I said.

The doctor wrote some notes on the clipboard and left.

One of the nurses poked her head between the curtains. "Is that your truck in front of the emergency entrance?"

"Oh yeah, I forgot about it," I said.

"They need you to move it or they'll have it towed."

Nervous to leave Ellie, I asked, "Will you watch her?"

The nurse smiled at me. "Don't worry. We'll keep an eye on her, and the radiologist should be here in a minute to take her for X-rays."

"Thanks." I hurried out to move my truck. It took longer than I wanted to find a parking space big enough to fit the truck. Ellie was gone when I got back to curtain number 4.

"She's down in radiology," the nurse called from her desk.

I nodded in her direction and slumped into the chair to wait.

Within the hour, Ellie returned from radiology and received her first dose of IV antibiotics. She still wasn't awake. A thin tube under her nose supplied her with additional oxygen. Again I pulled my chair next to her bed and held her hand. She labored to breathe, and occasionally a fit of coughing shook her frame. I closed my eyes and prayed for her recovery.

Another hour passed before the doctor came in with his report. "Ellie has a serious case of pneumonia—one of the worst I've seen this year. Overall, her heart looks good, although there is some mild inflammation in the outer lining. It's not serious yet. If we get the pneumonia cleared up quickly, the inflammation shouldn't have any lasting effects. If this is a bacterial pneumonia and it's not a resistant strain, she has a good chance for a full recovery. If it is a resistant strain of bacteria, or if it's viral, then I'll worry about potential heart damage, or worse. We're running a culture and should have preliminary results by tomorrow. Do you have any questions for me?"

Without thinking, I said, "It can't be a resistant strain."

The doctor looked up from his notes. "You'd be surprised how many strains of bacteria are resistant to antibiotics these days."

I nodded and thought to myself that surely good old penicillin would be sufficient, if in fact it was bacterial. There couldn't have been resistant strains of bacteria in 1863. In my history class, we'd just learned about the invention of penicillin during World War II. Bacteria in 1863 wouldn't have had the opportunity to develop resistance to any antibiotics. But of course, I couldn't mention that to the doctor.

He tucked his pen in his pocket and hooked Ellie's chart onto the bed. "A nurse will be in to move her upstairs in a few minutes."

"Thanks, doc," I called as he stepped through the partition.

Within the hour, they moved Ellie upstairs to the critical care unit. She still hadn't awakened, but her fever had come down, and she seemed to be sleeping peacefully. A decent reclining chair sat in the corner of the room, so I pulled it next to the bed. My stomach ached in a twisted sort of way that left me wondering if I was hungry or just sick with worry. I couldn't sort it out, but regardless of what my stomach thought, my heart had no desire to leave Ellie to search for food. I leaned forward and closed my eyes. The quiet room was dimly lit. I gently intertwined my fingers with hers and rested my head on the side of her bed.

When my cell phone rang in my pocket, I nearly jumped to my feet. The adrenalin surging through my veins shocked my system to life. I felt the folded letter I'd taken from Ellie's nightstand as I dug through my pocket to find my phone. I slid the phone open and said, "Hello."

"Chase, Ryan and I just got home," Jessica said, obviously upset. "The back door is wide open, and the house is freezing. Where are you? What's going on? Where are Mom and Dad?"

"I'm at the hospital. I don't know where Mom and Dad are."

My sister snapped back a response. "What happened now? Are you hurt?"

I sighed. "It's Ellie. I brought her back. She's got pneumonia. Jessica, it's pretty serious. She's unconscious."

"Oh my gosh! I'm sorry, Chase. Do you need anything? What can I do to help?"

"I could use a change of clothes. I'm sitting here in my Erie Canal outfit. The nurses keep giving me strange looks, but luckily no one has said anything."

"Okay. I'll be there in a little while."

"Thanks, Jessica. Bye." I slid my phone closed, still fingering the folded envelope in my pocket. I watched the steady rise and fall of the blankets covering Ellie. Her breathing didn't seem as labored now.

I leaned back and looked at the envelope. She'd clearly addressed it to me, but it hadn't technically been sent to me yet. I looked at the note across the bottom of the sealed letter. Curiosity soon overcame any propriety I felt at not having officially received the letter yet, and I broke the seal.

THIRTY
Confessions

I opened the envelope and pulled out several pages filled with Ellie's neat script.

December 15, 1863

Dearest Chase,

I have contemplated writing this letter for some time now. Yesterday, I felt a sickness coming on, and today I've chosen to remain in bed, hopeful of a quick recovery. Nevertheless, since I'm resting, I thought it a good excuse to put into writing what transpired since I left you that cold and bleak November afternoon.

I arrived in Boston to find my great-aunt Lydia quite ill. It seemed as if she had aged years instead of months while I was gone. Considering her drastic decline, I went so far as to verify the date, wondering at first if you had left me in the wrong year. The first few weeks were busy as Mary and I cared for her. Thankfully, bearing in mind the condition of Aunt Lydia's suffering and inability to care for herself, she passed away peacefully during the night of November 19. Funeral arrangements were taken care of, and life for me continued.

I secured a teaching position at the schoolhouse not far from my home. I love teaching the children, watching them grow and interact with each other. I find they are the only source of joy available to me amidst the drudgery of daily life. You may be amused to know I frequently find myself missing many of the modern conveniences you introduced me to, but I try not to think about that too much, as they will never come about in my lifetime.

I confess you were right. I was running away. It seemed as if every time we were together, something went awry and you got hurt. The night you saved me by the river, that day in the cabin, and finally the night of the Halloween dance outside of the school—each time I feared I was apt to be the cause of great injury to you or even death. I tried to hide it, but it bothered me greatly. I knew it would only be a matter of time before my worst fears became a reality and I caused you to lose the counter or your life. I thought, perchance, if I removed myself from your life, it would be better for you. You would be free to take care of yourself, and the counter, without having to worry about and protect me. I knew I would only slow you down and get in your way in the future, as I had in the past.

I apologize for what I said about Walt, but I felt the situation necessitated it. I knew saying that was the quickest way to get you to comply with my wishes. It is true he seeks my hand in marriage, but I don't return his affections. Upon arriving here and realizing I would never see you again, I put genuine effort into the relationship when he came to call. I had hoped to find some measure of happiness. However, last week I confessed to him that I did not feel I could, with clear conscience, continue seeing him when my heart belonged to another. He hounded me for details, but what could I say? "I am in love with someone who hasn't been born yet"? Oh, wretched me! I've got myself in an awful fix. All I told him was I met someone out west. He wasn't pleased with me, I'm sure, but I was happy to hear yesterday that he's begun courting Amanda Berkshire. He deserves to have someone who will love him in return, without reservation.

Perchance I've said too much. I feel as if my words wander aimlessly across the page. Most certainly I have made a terrible mistake in coming back here. At length I'm left to cogitate the miserable consequences of my decision. In my distress, I acted rashly. Other than the comfort I offered my great-aunt Lydia in her last days, there is no purpose in my existence here. Perhaps you will return my sentiments. But I would not blame you if you never wanted to see me again after how dreadfully I treated you. Oh, my soul is harrowed up in despair over walking out of your arms. I've regretted it every day since. I would that I could turn back time and do it all over. But although I can't, you can.

That brings me to the purpose of this letter, in which I am placing the biggest gamble of my life. Can you forgive me? Will you come back for me? For aught I know, you may be relieved to be free of the burden I was. However, I long to see you again more than anything else. The longing is so terrible that at times I feel it will overwhelm me. If you choose not to come back, you must know I will never hold it against you. I wish only for your safety and happiness, above all else, and for you to continue where my grandfather left off. His legacy is yours to carry on now.

December 20, 1863

I fear my health is failing. What began as a mild illness has grown worse. The doctor thinks I've developed pneumonia. I'm certain he's right. I can feel it in my chest, and the gripping ache of it is slowly overtaking me. I'm weakening. Considering this is the same illness my mother died of, I'm not holding out much hope of recovering, although, truth be told, I'm not sure I want to get well. All my hopes for a happy future are tied in this letter. I have not yet decided whom I can trust with such a grave responsibility. What if the letter is lost or burned, or opened and discarded at whim? But I can't think about that now; it will drive me insane with worry. I must trust that all will work out for my good in the end.

It will be so many years before you can possibly get this that I long to have the time pass quickly. I find myself thinking fondly of sleeping off the years in my grave, of waking suddenly to find you have come back for me and spared me the awful loneliness and impending death that now imprison me. Unfortunately, all this depends on your feelings for me. Are they mutual? Are you willing to forgive my rash behavior? I do hope you are, because I love you, Chase Harper. I've loved you since the first night I saw you in your funny clothes, during the summer of 1863, rescuing me from danger. You will forever be my knight in shining armor.

With love, always and forever,
Ellie

With moist eyes, I leaned back and folded the letter, then placed it in the envelope and returned it to my pocket. A calming peace filled the room. I smiled as I digested the meaning of Ellie's letter. At times I had suspected she liked me, but I'd chalked it up to wishful thinking. It was nice to know for sure. I only hoped I hadn't found her just in time to lose her.

As fear and dread gained entrance into my thoughts, I removed the gold counter and fondly caressed its engraved cover. If I were too late, I stubbornly told myself, I'd go back earlier and try again. I would have her back if it was the last thing I did.

The door opened, and I quickly returned the counter to the safety of my pocket. Jessica walked in, carrying a grocery sack full of clothes and a brown paper lunch bag.

She glanced at Ellie and then smiled at me. "Hey, Chase, here are your clothes. I brought you a sack lunch, too, in case you get hungry."

"Thanks, Jess." I took the clothes from her. "Will you sit with her while I change?"

"Sure."

After feeling self-conscious in my old-fashioned clothing, it was a relief to be back in jeans and a sweatshirt. I closed the door to the bathroom behind me and pulled up a chair next to Jessica.

"What now?" she asked.

"We wait. It sounds like after twenty-four hours, they'll have a better idea of how she's doing. If they culture any bacteria, the preliminary results should be available then. If it's viral, then I don't know. The doctor said that could be a lot more serious."

"Okay. We'll hope for bacterial, then. Mom and Dad should be home soon. There was a message on the answering machine. They went to a movie after their Christmas shopping. It sounds like they have something big to show us. Have you decided what you're going to tell them?"

"I've got some ideas, but I'm not sure yet. Ellie's great-aunt passed away in November. I guess I could say she decided to come back once her great-aunt's affairs were in order. But right now I can't get past just hoping she lives."

"How long did the doctor say she'd be in here?"

"A few days, at least. It depends on how she responds to the treatment."

"I'll work on softening Mom and Dad up to the idea of her coming back home with us. When will you be home?"

"I'll come home when she does."

"Dad's not going to like that."

I shrugged and stared intently at Ellie's peaceful expression as she slept. Did she even realize she wasn't in Boston anymore? Maybe to her this all seemed like a dream.

Jessica gave Ellie's hand a squeeze before she walked to the door. "I guess I'll go back home. It'll only worry them more if we're both gone. I'll see what I can do to buy you some time."

"Thanks, Jess. I appreciate it."

She smiled at me. "Don't worry, Chase. She'll get better."

"I hope so."

I watched my sister close the door behind her. I got the letter out and read it again, savoring each word. My phone had vibrated off and on over the past few hours. The next time it vibrated, I pulled it out—six new messages. I read each one. Adam wanted me to meet him at the gym for a pick-up game of basketball. I replied, telling him about Ellie's pneumonia. Kim wanted to know what I was doing the day after Christmas; she was planning a big party for a bunch of friends. *I don't think so.* I sent a short reply that I'd be busy this week. Jessica had also sent a message. No need to reply to that, since I just talked to her.

There was a text from Mom informing me of her and my dad's dinner and movie plans. She hoped I'd be able to find something to eat on my own. I took a deep breath. I figured I should get this over with. I hit reply. "Ha ha, very funny. I can find food on my own. Ellie returned from Boston a few days ago, but she has pneumonia. Her friends picked her up from the airport, but they left 2 go out of town 4 the holidays. She asked me 2 take her 2 the hospital. I'm still here. It looks serious, so I'm going 2 stay @ the hospital w/ her tonite. Don't worry, Mom. I'll call u in the morning." I pushed "Send" and slid my phone shut.

I held Ellie's hand again and leaned forward to rest my head on the side of the bed. I must have dozed off, because the next thing I knew the door was opening. I expected a nurse to walk in, but it was my dad, followed closely by my mom. I stared at them across the dimly lit room and then shifted my gaze back to Ellie's sleeping form.

"Hi, Dad, Mom," I said.

"We talked to Doctor West," my mom said.

Dad moved over to stand behind me with his hand on my shoulder. My mom affectionately brushed the hair back from

Ellie's forehead before surveying the IV bag and glancing over her chart. "How is she doing?"

"A little better, I think, but she's been out ever since we got here."

"The meds are probably making her drowsy," my mom said.

My dad squeezed my shoulder and spoke firmly. "I think you should come home, Chase. There's nothing more you can do here. The doctors and nurses will take good care of her. You should be home where you can get some rest. You can come back in the morning."

I looked from my mom to my dad, trying to settle on what I would say to them. Nothing came to me at first. In discouragement, I lowered my head and closed my eyes.

"Chase, you look exhausted, and it's late. Let's go get you to bed," my mom said. "Everything always looks better after a good night's sleep. I'll be here at seven in the morning to start my shift, and I can check on Ellie then."

"You shouldn't ask me to leave," I said firmly, looking at both my parents. "I've already decided I need to stay. I don't want her waking up alone."

The three of us stared at each other, and it was clear that neither side wanted to concede. Eventually my dad looked from me to the unconscious Ellie and then shrugged his shoulders. "If it's that important to you, I guess it's okay. Call us if you need anything."

I sighed with relief. I didn't have the energy to fight with them, but I refused to leave her side. "Thanks, Dad."

"I'll see you in the morning, then," my mom said. "Good night, Chase."

I offered a weak smile in return and watched them leave the room. I rested my head on the bed again and surrendered to an uneasy sleep. Like clockwork, every four hours a nurse checked Ellie's vital signs. I watched eagerly as her blood pressure was taken, hoping the sensation of the cuff squeezing her arm would help bring her out of her deep slumber. But each time there was no response.

Before the first light of dawn crept through the blinds, Ellie jarred me awake by pulling her hand out of mine. I jerked my head up. Her fingers grasped at the oxygen tube, pulling it away from her nose. Her eyes were still closed.

I jumped to my feet. "Ellie, wake up," I said softly. She must have felt the IV tubing on her arm, because she reached to pull at that next. I shot my hand out and grabbed hers, restraining her so she wouldn't dislodge the IV.

I held her wrists while she struggled futilely against the strength of my grip. "Ellie, can you hear me? Wake up, please."

Surrendering to me at last, she relaxed her arms and tried to open her eyelids. They fluttered open, and she whispered, "Chase?"

I chuckled. "Yes, Ellie, it's me. If I let go of you, will you promise me you won't touch anything until I can explain? Promise me you'll hold still?"

She nodded weakly. "Yes." Resting her head on the pillow, she closed her eyes again. I loosened my grip on her wrists, gently lowering her hands.

"Ellie, you're in the hospital. The tube in your hand is an IV. It's putting life-sustaining fluids and medicines into your bloodstream. You have to leave it in there for now, okay?"

She smiled. "Like I'm eating and drinking, but I'm really not?"

I laughed, thankful she felt good enough to joke around with me. "Yeah, something like that."

"Good, because I haven't felt like eating in days. It's much too difficult. You're certain I'm not dreaming?" Her eyes remained closed, and her hands rested quietly next to her on the bed.

I leaned closer, hovering over her. Then I rested one hand on the bed next to her shoulder and gently caressed her face as I smiled down at her. "Open your eyes, Ellie. You're not dreaming."

Right then it seemed as if she shot awake. "Chase, how did you know? Did you get my letter?"

"Yes, I got the letter."

"I can't believe it. I thought it would be lost before it could get mailed. I'm so pleasantly surprised."

Something clouded her expression, and she furrowed her eyebrows. "Can you ever forgive me, Chase? You're kind enough that I could see you returning for me even if you didn't share my feelings. Did I die? Did you come back and change it?"

I realized now what she was getting at. My voice cracked with emotion as I explained. "No! Ellie, I got the letter, but I picked it up from your nightstand in 1863. It never had the chance to get mailed. You never died. On December 22, I brought you back to 2011 with me. I was already looking for you, long before you wrote the letter. I tried to convince myself I could live without you. I thought if I knew you were happy, I could move on. I saw you with your boyfriend, and it nearly killed me. But I kept going back to Boston to check on you. I couldn't help myself."

"I wish I would have known you were there. But what about Kim?"

"I dumped her, right after you left."

Ellie looked confused. "What did you do to her?"

"I dumped her—I broke up with her. I told her I didn't want to be in a relationship with her. Ellie, she means nothing to me. I only pretended to like her so my parents wouldn't see how I really felt about you."

"What about your parents now?"

"I don't know, but I'm not giving you up again. The last two months were torture."

Ellie attempted to laugh, but it triggered a coughing fit instead. I held a glass of water to her lips and helped her drink. "They weren't much to set store by for me, either," she said.

The gratitude I felt at hearing her voice filled me with relief. Yet, the tiniest of exertions—even speaking—clearly exhausted her. "Ellie, you need to rest. I'll be right here, waiting."

She sighed. "I agree. I am tuckered out."

We sat in a perfectly comfortable silence, and I never took my eyes off her. She slept off and on throughout the early morning. My mom stopped by to check on us after she started her shift. Ellie woke up and visited with her.

"Chase, can I talk with you outside for a minute?" my mom asked after a while.

"Sure, Mom." I followed her into the hallway of the critical care unit.

"Chase, the billing department talked to me this morning. Because of the privacy policies, they wouldn't tell me anything except that I should talk with you. Can you explain that?"

I glanced down the hall and then at my feet. "Yeah . . . well, maybe that's because Ellie doesn't have any insurance, so I signed as the person financially responsible."

My mom shook her head. "I don't think a minor can sign as financially responsible. Why doesn't she have insurance? Someone should have talked to me about this before now. I can't believe it. There are student health insurance plans available through the schools, state-provided insurance—anything would have been better than this. It could be tens of thousands of dollars before she's done here. How is she going to pay for this?"

"Mom, we didn't know about insurance. I'm sure Ellie never even thought about it. But don't worry. We can . . . she can pay for it. She has money that her grandfather left her."

"I expect someone from the billing department will be up to talk with her about this later today."

"Mom, can't you sign as legal guardian or something so it won't be a problem? I guarantee you won't have to pay a dime."

My mom thought about it for a minute. "I'll see what I can find out from billing if you make Ellie promise she'll look into health insurance as soon as she's well. And you better be right about her having the money to pay these medical bills, because I sure don't—not after your dad's Christmas present."

"What Christmas present?" I asked curiously.

She smiled. "Oh, you'll see. I'm not going to spoil the surprise. You'll have to get your dad to show you."

"All right. Thanks, Mom. I love you."

My mom shook her head at me, but cracked a smile anyway. "You're welcome, and I love you too, Chase."

After she left, I returned to Ellie's bedside. She smiled and said, "There is something I've been wondering about. Was it you that split the wood for us?"

I laughed. "Yeah. At the rate you were going, it would have taken you forever."

"I could have managed, but thank you. So why did you tell Mary your name was Joseph?"

I smiled. "Because it is. Joseph Chase Harper—that's my full name."

"I didn't know that."

"I didn't think you did. That's why I used the name. I

worried you wouldn't be happy if you knew it was me. Ever since you've known me, it's been constant chaos for you. I'm sorry I've put you through so much."

"No, Chase, I'm sorry. I feel guilty you're always having to protect me from something or someone. My grandfather kept the counter safe for years, and here I almost caused you to lose it. I feared I would be the ruin of the counter and the death of you someday. It scared me."

My heart longed for her to know how I really felt. "Ellie, you need to know two things. First, if there is one thing I've learned in the last two months, it's that I would rather die a hundred painful deaths than live another day without you. And second, I *have* to protect the counter, but I *want* to protect you. Please don't ever take that away from me again."

Ellie smiled and reached up to push my hair out of my eyes. I leaned down to kiss her, but she blocked me with her hand. "Don't kiss me yet. I don't want you to get ill."

Pulling her hand away from my mouth, I smiled. "I won't wait long, so you'd better hurry and get well."

THIRTY-ONE
Christmas

The doctor read and signed the papers the nurse had prepared. "Merry Christmas, Miss Williams. You're free to go home as soon as the nurse arrives with a wheelchair to take you down—hospital policy. Here are your discharge papers and instructions. Continue taking the antibiotics for the next ten days. Use Tylenol or Advil as needed for any pain or discomfort. I've included a prescription for cough medicine, if you need it. You've made quite a miraculous recovery. Surprisingly, you had a unique and easily treatable strain of pneumonia. I think we could have given you plain old penicillin and you would have recovered."

The doctor, busy with the paperwork, missed the knowing glance I exchanged with Ellie.

She took and signed the discharge papers. "Thank you, Doctor, for everything," Ellie said just before he walked out the door.

I handed her a large box. "It's time for you to open your Christmas present."

"Chase, you shouldn't have. I don't have anything for you."

"All I need is you. That's present enough for me. Now open it before the nurse comes."

Ellie removed the red bow and wrapping paper, then opened the box and pulled out a blue Columbia Sportswear coat with matching hat, scarf, and gloves. She looked up at me, and I smiled at her.

"Let's try it on," I said, walking over to her bed and holding the coat for her. She slid her arms into the sleeves, and I zipped it. She stood there patiently while I wrapped the scarf around her neck and carefully put the hat on her head, tucking in her curls. "There. I don't want you to get sick on me again."

She smiled. "Thank you, Chase. It's a beautiful coat."

"It's not as beautiful as you are." I stepped closer. "And I'm not waiting any longer." I pulled the hat off her head while I leaned in to press my lips against hers, wrapping my fingers in the curls at the nape of her neck. She kissed me back, wholeheartedly this time. Her arms wrapped around my shoulders, and I felt her fingertips slide down my arm.

"Are you bigger?"

With an invitation like that, I flexed my muscles for her. "Do you think so?" I asked with a grin.

She giggled and nodded her head. "My! Aren't you a tease. Yes, I know so."

I wrapped my arms around her waist and pulled her close. "Six weeks of hard labor digging the Erie Canal, and a little magic, can change a guy."

Ellie rested her head against my chest. "The Erie Canal. Really? I've got to hear that story sometime."

"Excuse me," the nurse said. "Sorry for interrupting, but they want to see you in the billing department before you leave. I can walk you down there on our way out."

"Okay." I moved away from Ellie. "I thought my mom got that all straightened out."

"It will only take a minute," the nurse assured me as she seated Ellie in the wheelchair, then began pushing her down the hall toward the elevator.

I followed behind, quite content with the direction my life was headed. Whatever Master Archidus wanted and whoever hunted me and the counter next, I could handle it as long as I had Ellie to come home to. I simply needed to keep her out of the line of fire.

"You're sure you don't have any insurance, Miss Williams?" the lady in the billing department asked Ellie.

I answered for her. "No. Just send us the bill and we'll pay it. There won't be any problem, trust me."

The lady smiled and handed me her business card. "All right, but if you need to schedule a payment plan, call me and we can work with you on that, too."

"Thanks. I'll let you know if that's necessary." Visions of the silver dollars and gold half eagles I'd seen in 1817 danced through my mind. They'd be worth a fortune in 2011. I smiled confidently, convinced that with an endless supply of time I wouldn't have any trouble with the bill. It might take a year on the Erie Canal, but I'd get it done, and no one would even notice my absence.

About the Author

Kelly Nelson was raised in Orem, Utah, and now resides in Cornelius, Oregon, in the heart of the beautiful Pacific Northwest. She enjoys life on a ten-acre horse property with her husband, four children, and, of course, lots of horses. Kelly has a bachelor's degree from Brigham Young University. She worked as a certified public accountant for several years before opting to stay home and raise a family. As a young girl, she was an avid reader and had a passion for creative writing. Her travels to England, France, Egypt, Israel, West Indies, Mexico, and across the United States sparked a love of history, adventure, and exotic places. This led to the inspiration behind her debut novel, *The Keeper's Calling,* the first book in The Keeper's Saga. Learn more about Kelly and the upcoming sequels at kellynelsonauthor.com.